I0595154

Asa Maxon Fritz Randolph

The Trial of Sir John Falstaff

The Trial of Sir John Falstaff

Asa Maxon Fritz Randolph

The Trial of Sir John Falstaff

ISBN/EAN: 9783741186424

Manufactured in Europe, USA, Canada, Australia, Japa

Cover: Foto ©Andreas Hilbeck / pixelio.de

Manufactured and distributed by brebook publishing software
(www.brebook.com)

Asa Maxon Fritz Randolph

The Trial of Sir John Falstaff

The Trial
of
Sir John Falstaff

WHEREIN THE FAT KNIGHT IS PERMITTED TO ANSWER FOR
HIMSELF CONCERNING THE CHARGES LAID AGAINST
HIM; AND TO ATTORNEY HIS OWN CASE

BY

A. M. F. RANDOLPH

---

*"Go thy ways, old Jack; die when thou will, if manhood, good
manhood, be not forgot upon the face of the earth, then am I a shotten
herring. There live not three good men unhanged in England; and
one of them is fat and grows old: God help the while! a bad world,
I say. I would I were a weaver; I could sing psalms or any thing.
A plague of all cowards, I say still. . . . Play out the play:
I have much to say in the behalf of that Falstaff."*
KING HENRY IV., Part I., Act II., Sc. 4.

G. P. PUTNAM'S SONS

NEW YORK
27 WEST TWENTY-THIRD STREET

LONDON
24 BEDFORD STREET, STRAND

The Knickerbocker Press

1893

COPYRIGHT, 1893
BY
A. M. F. RANDOLPH
Entered at Stationers' Hall, London
BY G. P. PUTNAM'S SONS

Electrotyped, Printed, and Bound by
The Knickerbocker Press, New York
G. P. PUTNAM'S SONS

TO

HON. DANIEL W. WILDER,

FROM HIS YOUTH UP, A TRUE SHAKESPEARE-LOVER,
WHO SUGGESTED TO ME THAT I PUT FALSTAFF
BETWEEN BOOK-COVERS, AND WHO HAS
AIDED AND ABETTED ME IN SO DOING,
THESE PAGES ARE DEDICATED.

THE AUTHOR.

PREFACE.

Falstaff has been so thoroughly bewritten that whoever attempts to say anything new of Sir John will soon find that he can do little more than borrow the thoughts of Shakespearian scholars, criss-cross what they have written about the fat knight, scribble at random in the narrow margins of their ample pages, and make a cento of quotations therefrom.* This book is the result of an endeavor, not simply to repeat what critics have said of Sir John, but rather to put him in such a predicament that he must speak for himself and serve as his own commentator, and, in so speaking, interweave into his discourse, as far as it is possible, the very words which he uses, here and there, in the dramas wherein

---

* " Opinions," says Augustine Birrell, " no doubt, differ as to how many quotations a writer is entitled to, but, for my part, I like to see an author leap-frog into his subject over the back of a brother."—*Obiter Dicta* (second series), Am. ed., p. 224.

" If that severe doom of Synesius be true—'it is a greater offence to steal dead men's labours [lucubrations], than their clothes'—what shall become of most writers?"—Burton's *Anatomy of Melancholy.*

he plays his part; and, further, to give his companions, Bardolph, Nym, Poins, Peto, Pistol, Mrs. Quickly, Justice Shallow, and the rest—each and all—a chance to do the like. Royal Hal must, of course, be counted out of this group, for it is to be presumed that the order which he made on his coronation-day, banishing Falstaff, on pain of death, " Not to come near our person by ten mile," remained in full force and effect ever after. Moreover, King Hal, having rid himself of his unyoked humors, and thrown off his loose behavior, and being no longer " engraffed to Falstaff," was preparing to invade France and win a glorious victory at Agincourt.

To enable Falstaff to realize his own words during the scene wherein Sir John and Hal act, interchangeably, the part of the King and the Prince, to wit, " Play out the play : I have much to say in the behalf of that Falstaff," he is supposed to have been " had up " before Shallow and Silence, two of the King's justices of the peace in the county of Gloucester, to answer an information wherein many and grievous public offences were formulated against him. It may be objected that the two Gloucestershire justices had no jurisdiction of Falstaff in Eastcheap, London ; that Justice Shallow was plainly prejudiced against Sir John ; that many of the so-called crimes charged against him were not crimes at all, and frivolous ; that the justices could not have examined him in the unique manner stated; and that the account of the trial is full of anachronisms of thought and language, and so forth. It may

be answered that the supposed trial is hardly more
irregular in many respects than Falstaff's first examination before Chief Justice Sir William Gascoigne. Granting that this great magistrate had the
right to intercept Sir John on a London street, and
tax him with having refused to obey the summons
served upon him to attend at his Lordship's chambers, that he might answer the information laid
against him on account of the robbery at Gadshill,
still it plainly appears in the report of the examination that the legal altercation between the Chief
Justice and Sir John was not conducted according to
any known code of criminal procedure. In this very
amusing interview, the questions and answers are,
in the main, impertinent to the felony charged
against Sir John ; and, as soon as he has made a
sufficient answer to the threat of the Chief Justice
to " lay him by the heels," that magistrate partly
pulls off his judicial robe and thenceforth acts the
part of *Præfectus Morum*, or " superintendent of
manners," in dealing with the defendant. Granting,
also, that when Falstaff was brawling with Officers
Fang and Snare, who were trying to arrest him for
debt at the suit of Dame Quickly, the Chief
Justice had the right to intervene and command
the belligerents to keep the peace, still the main
controversy between Sir William and Sir John on
that occasion is more personal than judicial in its
character.

In the report of Falstaff's examination before
Justices Shallow and Silence, the truth of his declaration to Prince Hal that he was " no coward,"

seems not to have been seriously brought in question. But whoever has read Maurice Morgann's *Essay on the Dramatic Character of Sir John Falstaff**—written specially to vindicate the fat knight's courage—will probably think that, on this particular issue, judgment ought to go in favor of Falstaff.

The critic, if he looks into this book, may pronounce the circumstantial story of the discovery of the manuscript notes of Falstaff's examination before Shallow and Silence, JJ., as well as the trial itself, as all "too thin," † and render judgment accordingly.

---

* Croker, in a note to his edition of *Boswell's Life of Johnson*, says that Johnson, being asked his opinion of this essay, answered : " Why, sir, we shall have the man come forth again ; and, as he has proved Falstaff to be no coward, he may prove Iago to be a very good character."

† English writers have frequently referred to the phrase " too thin " as " a notable Americanism " ; but, as a matter of fact, it has a most reputable English paternity. The Rev. Dr. William Cave, who was born in 1637, in his *Life of St. Athanasius*, used the expression in the following connection : " For procuring a synod to be called at Antioch, Eustathius is charged as heterodox in the faith, though they knew that to be too thin to hold water." And many years later, Lord Chancellor Eldon used this phrase in his opinion delivered in the case of *Peacock v. Peacock*, 16 Vesey's Chancery Rep. 49. The point under discussion was whether " partnership, without any provision as to its duration, may be determined without previous notice." The eminent jurist decided that the question was one for the court and jury to act upon, summing up his opinion in these words : " I cannot agree that reasonable notice is a subject too thin for a jury to act upon ; as in many cases juries

It may be so as to the entire book—except the excerpted parts thereof ; but I will only say, as lawyers sometimes say when they proffer evidence which they surmise that the court will regard as unimportant, " I offer it for what it is worth."

A. M. F. R.

and courts do determine what is reasonable notice." Here the expression was applied in what we term its slang sense.

In Shakespeare's *King Henry VIII.*, Act V., sc. ii ., the King says :

> " You were ever good at sudden commendations,
>   Bishop of Winchester.   But know, I come not
>   To hear such flattery now ; and in my presence,
>   They are too thin and bare to hide offences."

CONTENTS.

Contents.

V.

VI.

VII.

VIII.

IX.

X.

XI.

XII.

Contents.

SIR JOHN FALSTAFF.

I.

The Fat Knight.—His Character.—What Critics have Said of Him.

IN comic power Shakespeare culminates in Falstaff. Sir John is perhaps the most substantial and original, the most witty and humorous, all-around rogue that ever was portrayed. He presents a most portly presence in the mind's eye, and his figure is drawn so definitely and individually, that even to the mere reader it conveys the clear impression of personal acquaintance. This *Miles Gloriosus* seems to have as veritable a place in history as Alexander the Great, Julius Cæsar, Richard of the Lion Heart, or even Shakespeare himself; and he so comes home to our apprehension and credulity that the historic persons in *King Henry IV.*, compared with him, appear to be idealized characters, and created to set him off to better advantage. His jokes come upon us with double force and relish because of his ponderous person, as he shakes his fat sides with laughter, or "lards the lean earth as he walks along," or goes before his page bearing his sword and buckler, " like a sow that hath overwhelmed all her litter but one." Sir John Paunch is himself " a tun of man," for whom " the grave doth gape thrice wider than for other men." He is not "such stuff as dreams are made on "; and if we approach and touch him, he does not burst like a bubble, and is not " melted into air, into thin air." Hath not Sir John " hands, organs, dimensions, senses, affections, passions ? " Is he not " fed with the same food, hurt with the same weapons, subject to the same diseases, healed by the same means, warmed and cooled by the same winter and summer, as a Christian is? " This enormous wallet of flesh, this " sweet creature of bombast," habitually enriches his discourse with allusions to eating and drinking ; takes his ease in his inn ; lugs his own larder about with him ; and yet this " huge bombard of sack " is not made of a " clay that gets muddy with drink " ; his sensuality does not sodden and brutify his faculties, but it quickens their temper and edge, gives wings to his imagination, and fills it with " nimble, fiery, and delectable shapes." Sir John Fustilugs, though corpulent beyond measure, and always intent upon cherishing his body with eating, drinking, and sleeping, is not fat-witted ;* nor have his brains

---

* It is frequently averred that fat is deadening to the brain, and consequently a foe to intellectual activity. But is this so? Some of the greatest men the world has ever known were plump even to obesity. Napoleon was decidedly *embonpoint*. Dr. Johnson was fleshy even to flabbiness. So was his biographical shadow, Boswell. Balzac, the great French novelist,

and bowels exchanged places. There is a natural activity about this "fat-kidneyed rascal"—"the veriest varlet that ever chewed with a tooth"— which for lack of proper employment, shows itself in a sort of swell or bustle, that seems to correspond with his bulk, as if his mind had inflated his body, and demanded a habitation of no less circumference. Thus conditioned, he puffs and blows and rolls like a whale, scattering the smaller fishes, but affording, in his turn, noble contention to Poins and Prince Hal, who may, in the part they play with this deboshed sea-monster, be compared to the thresher and the sword-fish.

Sir John Sack-and-Sugar would not be in character if he were not so fat as he is. The very pinguidity and ponderosity of his person are the most felicitous correspondents to the unlimited opulence of his imagination ; and but for this conjunction the character would be inharmonious, incomplete, and disjointed, if not inherently impossible. Imagine, if you can, either that "very

---

was so stout that it was a day's exercise to walk around him, and he was encircled with handages as if he were a hogshead. Rossini, the composer, was a regular Jumbo, since for six years he never saw his knees. Jules Janin, the prince of critics, broke every sofa he ever sat down upon. Lablache, the Italian singer, was charged three fares when he travelled. Dumas *père* was stout, and Sainte-Beuve was cursed with the stomach of a Falstaff, as Renan was. Eugene Sue had such an aversion to his growing corpulency that he drank vinegar to keep it down, and yet he wrote *The Wandering Jew*. A man is not necessarily fat-witted because he has a boundless stomach.—*The Churchman*, New York.

genius of famine," Justice Shallow, or that *iota subscript* in the great alphabet of humanity, his cousin Silence, in the character of Falstaff. With such a physical structure as theirs, even Shakespeare could not make them "not only witty in themselves, but the cause that wit is in other men." The oily old rogue lives in conformity with the Epicurean maxim, "Take thine ease, eat, drink, and be merry." He does not distress himself with the question, "Is life worth living?" nor ask whether marriage is a failure, nor declare what he would do if he were a woman, nor inquire, like Pontius Pilate, "What is Truth?" He is never at a loss ; he devises a shift for every difficulty. To furnish evidence that he had borne himself bravely in the Gadshill exploit, he hacked his sword with his dagger, and said to his companions that "he would swear truth out of England" but he would make Prince Hal believe it was done in fight with the travellers having fat purses. Lies sprout out of him, fructify, increase, and beget one another. In the affair on Gadshill, he declares that he fought alone against two rogues in buckram suits. The next moment he is at half-sword with four men. Presently in his narrative we have seven, then eleven buckram men, reinforced by "three misbegotten knaves in Kendal green," all at once upon poor old Jack. The incomprehensible lies that this same fat rogue tells : "how thirty, at least, he fought with ; what wards, what blows, what extremities he endured "—" these lies are like their father that begets them ; gross as a mountain, open, palpable." When cross-examined and unmasked, he does not lose his temper, and is the first to laugh at his boastings. To Hal he says : "By the Lord, I knew ye as well as he that made ye. Why, hear ye, my masters : Was it for me to kill the heir apparent ? Should I turn upon the true prince ? Why, thou knowest, I am as valiant as Hercules : but beware instinct ; the lion will not touch the true prince. Instinct is a great matter ; I was a coward on instinct. I shall think the better of myself, and thee, during my life ; I, for a valiant lion, and thou, for a true prince. But, by the Lord, lads, I am glad you have the money. Hostess, clap to the doors ; watch to-night, pray to-morrow. Gallants ! lads ! boys ! hearts of gold ! All the titles of good fellowship come to you ! What, shall we be merry ? Shall we have a play extempore ?"

When Hostess Quickly tells Prince Hal that Falstaff said the other day that Hal owed him a thousand pound, "Sirrah," said the prince to him, "do I owe you a thousand pound ?" Sir John answers : "A thousand pound, Hal ! a million : thy love is worth a million ; thou owest me thy love." The dialogue continues :

Hostess. Nay, my lord, he called you Jack, and said he would cudgel you.

Fal. Did I, Bardolph ?

Bard. Indeed, Sir John, you said so.

Fal. Yea, if he said my ring was copper.

Prince. I say 't is copper ; darest thou be as good as thy word now ?

Fal. Why, Hal, thou knowest, as thou art but man, I dare ; but as thou art prince, I fear thee as I fear the roaring of the lion's whelp.

Prince. And why not as the lion ?

Fal. The king himself is to be feared as the lion ; dost thou think I 'll fear thee as I fear thy father ? Nay, an I do, I pray God my girdle break.

" Falstaff," says Dr. Johnson, " unimitated, unimitable Falstaff, how shall I describe thee ? thou compound of sense and vice ; of sense which may be admired, but not esteemed ; of vice which may be despised, but hardly detested. Falstaff is a character loaded with faults, and with those faults which naturally produce contempt. He is a thief and a glutton, a coward and a boaster ; always ready to cheat the weak, and prey upon the poor— to terrify the timorous, and insult the defenseless. At once obsequious and malignant, he satirizes in their absence those on whom he lives by flattering. He is familiar with the prince only as an agent of vice ; but of this familiarity he is so proud as not only to be supercilious and haughty with common men, but to think his interest of importance to the Duke of Lancaster. Yet the man thus corrupt, thus despicable, makes himself necessary to the prince that despises him by the most pleasing of all qualities, perpetual gayety—by an unfailing power of exciting laughter, which is the more freely indulged, as his wit is not of the splendid or ambitious kind, but consists in easy scapes and sallies of levity which make sport, but raise no envy. It must be observed, that he is stained with no enormous or sanguinary crimes, so that his licentiousness is not so offensive but that it may be borne for his mirth.

" The moral to be drawn from this representation

is, that no man is more dangerous than he that, with a will to corrupt, hath the power to please ; and that neither wit nor honesty ought to think themselves safe with such a companion when they see Henry seduced by Falstaff."

Maurice Morgann thus comments on Falstaff's character :   " It cannot escape the reader's notice that he is a character made up by Shakespeare wholly of incongruities :   A man at once young and old, enterprising and fat, a dupe and a wit, harmless and wicked, weak in principle and resolute by constitution, cowardly in appearance and brave in reality, a knave without malice, a liar without deceit, and a knight, a gentleman, and a soldier, without either dignity, decency, or honour.   This is a character which, though it may be decompounded, could not, I believe, have been formed, nor the ingredients of it duly mingled, upon any receipt whatever ; it required the hand of Shakespeare himself to give to every particular part a relish of the whole, and of the whole to every particular part ; alike the same incongruous, identical Falstaff, whether to the grave Chief Justice he vainly talks of his youth and offers to caper for a thousand, or cries to Mrs. Doll, ' I am old ! I am old ! ' although she is seated on his lap, and he is courting her for busses. How Shakespeare could furnish out sentiment of so extraordinary a composition, and supply it with such appropriate and characteristic language, humour, and wit, I cannot tell ; but I may, however, venture to infer, and that confidently, that he who so well understood the uses of incongruity, and that

laughter was to be raised by the opposition of qualities in the same man, and not by their agreement
or conformity, would never have attempted to raise
mirth by showing us cowardice in a coward unat-
tended by pretense, and softened by every excuse
of age, corpulence, and infirmity. And of this we
cannot have a more striking proof than his furnish-
ing this very character, on one instance of real terror, however excusable, with boast, braggadocio,
and pretense, exceeding that of all other stage cowards the whole length of his superior wit, humour,
and invention."*

Schlegel, in his *Lectures on Dramatic Art and
Literature*, remarks : "Under a helpless exterior,
Falstaff conceals an extremely acute mind ; he has
always at command some dexterous turn whenever
any of his free jokes begin to give displeasure ; he
is shrewd in his distinctions, between those whose
favour he has to win and those over whom he may
assume a familiar authority. He is so convinced
that the part which he plays can only pass under
the cloak of wit, that even when alone he is never
altogether serious, but gives the drollest colouring
to his love-intrigues, his intercourse with others,
and to his own sensual philosophy. Witness his inimitable soliloquies on honour, on the influence of
wine on bravery, his descriptions of the beggarly
vagabonds whom he enlisted, of Justice Shallow,

---

* *An Essay on the Dramatic Character of Sir John Falstaff.*
pp. 146, 147, (London ed. 1777). "No piece of eighteenth-
century criticism of Shakspere is more intelligently and warmly
appreciative than is this delightful essay."—DOWDEN.

etc. Falstaff has about him a whole court of amusing caricatures, who by turns make their appearance, without ever throwing him into the shade. The adventure, in which the prince, under the disguise of a robber, compels him to give up the spoil which he had just taken ; the scene where the two act the part of the king and the prince ; Falstaff's behaviour in the field, his mode of raising recruits, his patronage of Justice Shallow, which afterwards takes such an unfortunate turn :—all this forms a series of characteristic scenes of the most original description, full of pleasantry, and replete with nice and ingenious observation, such as could only find a place in a historical play like the present."

Verplanck says : " In his peculiar originality, Falstaff is to be classed only with the poet's own Hamlet and the Spanish Don Quixote, as all of them personages utterly unlike any of those whom we have known or heard of in actual life, who, at the same time, so impress us with their truth that we inquire into and argue about their actions, motives, and qualities as we do in respect to living persons whose anomalies of conduct perplex observers. Thus Falstaff's cowardice or courage, as well as other points of his character, have been as fruitful subjects for discussion as the degree and nature of Hamlet's or Don Quixote's mental aberration."

Richard Grant White, in his *Studies in Shakespeare*, pp. 29–31, writes : " In *Henry IV.* we have the highest manifestation of Shakespeare's humor ; but not in Falstaff only, whose vast unctuosity of mind as well as body has, to the general eye, unjustly cast his companions into eclipse. Prince Hal himself is no less humorous than Falstaff, while his wit has a dignity and a sarcastic edge not observable in the fat knight's random and reckless sallies. Falstaff, however, is peerless in a great measure because he is reckless, and because Shakespeare, fully knowing the moral vileness of his creature, had yet, as a dramatist, a perfect intellectual indifference to the character of the personage by whom he effected his dramatic purpose. But besides these principals, the attendants upon their persons and the satellites of their blazing intellects, Poins, Bardolph, Nym, Pistol, Mrs. Quickly, Justice Shallow, Silence, and the rest, form a group which for its presentation of the humorous side of life has never been equalled in literature. It surpasses even the best of *Don Quixote*, as intellectual surpasses practical joking. This history, take it all in all, is the completest, although far from being the highest, exhibition of Shakespeare's varied powers as poet and dramatist. No other play shows his various faculties at the same time in such number and at such a height. The greatest Falstaff is that of the Second Part. He is in every trait the same as he of Part First ; but his wit becomes brighter, his humor more delicate, richer in allusion, and more highly charged with fun ; his impudence attains proportions truly heroic. As the Falstaff of Part Second of *Henry IV.* is the best, that of *The Merry Wives* is the least admirable of all the three. In this comedy the

Falstaff is comparatively feeble, and the laughter provoked by the scenes in which he appears is in a great measure due to practical joking. This deterioration in the fat knight's quality, and in that of the pleasure that he gives, agrees with and supports the tradition that the comedy was written in compliance with the request of Queen Elizabeth, that Falstaff should be shown in love. It is not reasonable to suppose that the man who conceived Falstaff would, without external and superior suggestion, present him as a lover, or had conceived him as capable of the amorous passion ; and his part of this comedy, charming in other respects, has all the air of being produced under constraint."

Hazlitt, in his *Characters of Shakespear's Plays*, says : " Sir John is old as well as fat, which gives a melancholy retrospective tinge to his character ; and by the disparity between his inclinations and his capacity for enjoyment, makes it still more ludicrous and fantastical. The secret of Falstaff's wit is for the most part a masterly presence of mind, an absolute self-possession, which nothing can disturb. His repartees are involuntary suggestions of his self-love ; instinctive evasions of everything that threatens to interrupt the career of his triumphant jollity and self-complacency. His very size floats him out of all his difficulties in a sea of rich conceits ; and he turns round on the pivot of his convenience, with every occasion and at a moment's warning. His natural repugnance to every unpleasant thought or circumstance, of itself makes light of objections, and provokes the most extravagant and licentious answers in his own justification. His indifference to truth puts no check upon his invention, and the more improbable and unexpected his contrivances are, the more happily does he seem to be delivered of them, the anticipation of their effect acting as a stimulus to the gayety of his fancy. The success of one adventurous sally gives him spirits to undertake another; he deals always in round numbers, and his exaggerations and excuses are 'open, palpable, monstrous as the father that begets them.' "

Furnivall says : " Of Falstaff, who can say enough ? He is the incarnation of humour and lies, of wit and self-indulgence, of shrewdness and immorality, of self-possession and vice, without a spark of conscience or reverence, without self-respect, an adventurer preying upon the weaknesses of other men. Yet all men enjoy him—so did Shakspere, and he carried his delight in successful rogues to the end of his life. See how in *Winter's Tale* he bubbles and chirps with the fun of that rascal Autolycus, and lets him sail off successful and unharmed."

Dowden in his *Shakspere: A Critical Study of His Mind and Art*, * comments : " Sir John, although, as he truly declares, 'not only witty in himself, but the cause that wit is in other men,' is by no means a purely comic character. Were he no more than this, the stern words of Henry to his old companion would be unendurable. The central principle of Falstaff's method of living is that

---

*Am. ed., pp. 325, 326.

the facts and laws of the world may be evaded or
set at defiance, if only the resources of inexhaustible wit be called upon to supply, by brilliant ingenuity, whatever deficiencies may be found in
character and conduct. Therefore, Shakspere
condemned Falstaff inexorably. Falstaff, the in-
vulnerable, endeavours to coruscate away the
realities of life. But the fact presses in upon Falstaff at the last relentlessly. Shakspere's earnestness here is at one with his mirth ; there is a certain
sternness underlying his laughter. Mere detection
of his stupendous unveracities leaves Sir John just
where he was before ; the success of his lie is of
less importance to him than is the glory of its
invention. 'There is no such thing as totally de-
molishing Falstaff ; he has so much of the invul-
nerable in his frame that no ridicule can destroy
him ; he is safe even in defeat, and seems to rise,
like another Antæus, with recruited vigour from
every fall.' (Morgann.) It is not ridicule, but
some stern invasion of fact—not to be escaped
from—which can subdue Falstaff. Perhaps Nym
and Pistol got at the truth of the matter when
they discoursed of Sir John's unexpected collapse:

> *Nym.* The king hath run bad humours on the knight;
>   that 's the even of it.
> *Pistol.* Nym, thou has spoke the right ;
>   His heart is fracted and corroborate." *

Charles Cowden Clarke, in his *Shakespeare-
Characters*, says : " With the genial spirit in which

---

* " Strange to say, no critic has attempted to make sense of
corroborate."—ROLFE.

his sweet nature was conceived, Shakespeare contrives to throw in some dash of feeling—a motion of our common humanity—some extenuation, even in his worst characters; for, whatever they were besides, they were also men, and unmitigated evil belongs only to the origin of all evil—not to human nature. With the accurate perception, however, of true morality, he has not imparted to the character of Falstaff—attractive as it is for its sociality, wit, humour, and imagination—any of those intrinsic qualities which would set him up as an object of imitation—of course in his convivialities, his roystering, and other laxities; but he has associated them with the meaner vices of profligacy, turning these to the fullest account in completing the character. Gross as the knight is, and wonderfully as the poet has relieved that grossness by the most brilliant flashes of wit and drollery, no mortal, it is to be presumed, ever arose from reading the plays in which he shines with a less firm appreciation of the wealth of virtue in all its senses; still less could any one desire to mimic his propensities. This cannot be said of some modern creations that might be instanced, which, from their sneers at sympathy and mutual confidence—their constant depreciation of the most generous feelings of our nature, inducing suspicion and distrust of all human profession, would go to sap the foundations of what alone can support the social fabric."

From John Payne Collier's Diary, it appears that Coleridge gave the following character of Falstaff:

"He was no coward, but pretended to be one merely for the sake of trying experiments on the credulity of mankind: he was a liar with the same object, and not because he loved falsehood for itself. He was a man of such pre-eminent abilities, as to give him a profound contempt for all those by whom he was usually surrounded, and to lead to a determination on his part, in spite of their fancied superiority, to make them his tools and dupes. He knew, however low he descended, that his own talents would raise him, and extricate him from any difficulty. While he was thought to be the greatest rogue, thief, and liar, he still had that about him which could render him not only respectable, but absolutely necessary to his companions. It was in characters of complete moral depravity, but of first-rate wit and talents, that Shakspere delighted ; and Coleridge instanced Richard the Third, Falstaff, and Iago."

By the way, Ignatius Donnelly has ciphered out and completely demonstrated—to his own satisfaction, at least,—not only that Francis Bacon was the real author of the plays which William Shakespeare, in his lifetime, claimed as his own ; which all his personal friends, as well as his personal enemies, believed to be his ; and which have been accepted as his for nearly three hundred years ; but also that the fat Shakespeare was gross and coarse in his nature and life, a glutton in his diet, and fond of the bottle ; that he was not devoid, however, of a certain ready wit ; that he was the original Falstaff ; that, before sickness broke him down, he acted on the stage his own shameful character in the disguise of Falstaff—a farce inside of a comedy ; that sweet Anne Hathaway was the model from which Bacon drew Mistress Quickly ; and that the statesman-philosopher shared with the player-poet the theatrical profits realized from Shakespeare's Plays. (*The Great Cryptogram*, Book II., Part II., Chapters xvii., xviii.)

Professor Corson, in his *Introduction to the Study of Shakespeare*, says of the Shakespeare-Bacon controversy : " If Shakespeare did not write the Plays attributed to him, certainly Lord Bacon did not write them. That Bacon was one of the most august of human intellects is freely conceded. But vast as is the range of powers exhibited in his works, there is no evidence in them that he possessed the *kind* of powers required for the composition of the Shakespeare Plays. The evidence is of the strongest kind that he was strangely deficient in such powers. His spirituality appears to have been in inverse proportion to his intellectual power. And his intellectual power was not of the creative order. In fact, intellectual power, however great, cannot be, of itself, creative. It must be united with spiritual power. Bacon's mind was signally analytic, inductive, deductive, judicial ; the mind which produced the Shakespeare Plays was as signally intuitive (by reason of its spiritual temperament), and as signally synthetic (taking in everything which was presented to it, in its completeness, and in all its relations). . . .

" The works of Francis Bacon bear an emphatic

testimony to his having been the coldest of mankind. No one, certainly, of the great Elizabethan men, who has left a sufficient record of himself, by which he may be judged, was so deficient in sympathetic warmth as Lord Bacon. And yet this man wrote *Romeo and Juliet!* (See his essay *Of Love.*) This man was the creator of a Cordelia, a Desdemona, a Miranda, a Perdita, a Hermione, and, more surprising still, of a Cleopatra! This man, we are asked to believe, wrote dramatic blank verse which has never been equalled on this earth as a manifestation of feeling and of perfect dramatic identification—verse which no mere metrical skill nor metrical sensibility, even, could have produced. But see *The Translation of Certain Psalms into English Verse: by the Right Honourable Francis, Lord Verulam, Viscount St. Alban*, and dedicated 'To his very good friend, Mr. George Herbert,' who translated part of the *Advancement of Learning*, into Latin. (The Psalms are I, XII, XC, CIV, CXXV, CXXXVII, CXLIX.) The translation was published in 1625, in Quarto, two years after the publication of the First Folio edition of the great Plays. This doggerel, Lord Bacon thought it worth while to publish, in his 65th year, though he ignored the authorship of what are regarded as the greatest productions of human genius!"

The first stanza of Lord Bacon's translation of Psalm I is as follows :

> Who never gave to wicked reed
> A yielding and attentive ear ;
> Who never sinners' paths did tread,

> Nor sat him down in scorner's chair ;
> But maketh it his whole delight
> On law of God to meditate ;
> And therein spendeth day and night :
> That man is in a happy state.

Bacon versified a part of the CIVth Psalm, thus:

> The higher grounds, where waters cannot rise,
> By rain and dews are water'd from the skies ;
> Causing the earth put forth the grass for beasts,
> And garden herbs, served at the greatest feasts ;
> And bread, that is all viands firmament,
> And gives a firm and solid nourishment ;
> And wine, man's spirits for to recreate ;
> And oil, his face for to exhilarate.
> The sappy cedars, tall like stately towers,
> High-flying birds do harbour in their bowers ;
> The holy storks, that are the travellers,
> Choose for to dwell and build within the firs ;
> The climbing goats hang on steep mountains' side ;
> The digging coneys in the rocks do bide.
> The moon, so constant in inconstancy,
> Doth rule the monthly seasons orderly ;
> The sun, eye of the world, doth know his race,
> And when to show, and when to hide his face.

Bacon, as a versifier of the Psalms, is a worthy rival of Sternhold and Hopkins ; but not every versifier is a poet.

II.

The Gadshill Robbery.—Falstaff before Chief Justice Sir William Gascoigne.—Pleadings.—To " Lay by the Heels." —Sir William as *Censor Morum*.—Sir John Exhorted to be Honest.—Arrested for Debt at Suit of Mrs. Quickly. —Reprimanded and Discharged by the Chief Justice.— Prince Hal Becomes King.—" Woe unto My Lord Chief Justice !"

IT has been objected to the very amusing inter-view, in Act I., Scene 2, of the Second Part of *King Henry IV.*, between Falstaff and the Lord Chief Justice, that if Shakespeare had been much of a lawyer, he would have known that this great magistrate could not examine offenders in the manner supposed, and could only take notice of offenses when they were regularly prosecuted before him in the Court of King's Bench, or at the assizes. On this point Lord Campbell, in his *Shakespeare's Legal Acquirements*, says :

" Although such is the practice in our days, so recently as the beginning of the eighteenth century that illustrious judge, Lord Chief Justice Holt, acted as a police magistrate, quelling riots, taking depositions against parties accused, and, where a *prima facie* case was made out against them, committing them for trial. Lord Chief Justice Coke actually assisted in taking the Earl and Countess of Somerset into custody when charged with the murder of Sir Thomas Overbury, and examined not less than three hundred witnesses against them, writing the depositions with his own hand. It was quite in course that those charged with the robbery at Gadshill should be had up before Lord Chief Justice Gascoigne, and that he should take notice of any of them who, having disobeyed a summons to appear before him, happened to come casually into his presence."

Falstaff, while walking in Eastcheap, asks his page what the water-doctor says concerning his case. The boy answers: "He said, sir, the water was a good healthy water ; but, for the party that owed [owned] it, he might have more diseases than he knew for." Sir John, being highly displeased with this diagnosis, remarks : "Men of all sorts take a pride to gird at me ; the brain of this foolish-compounded clay, man, is not able to invent anything that tends to laughter, more than I invent, or is invented on me : I am not only witty in myself, but the cause that wit is in other men." And thereupon he vents his spleen on his page, and also upon Master Dombledon, who would not furnish the satin for his short cloak and loose breeches, unless he procured better security than Bardolph. Presently the page espies the Chief Justice, and tells his master of his Lordship's approach ; and Sir John, knowing himself to be in question for the Gadshill robbery, says to the boy : "Wait close ; I will not see him." The Chief Justice sends his servant, or tipstaff, who follows him like

his shadow, wherever he officially appears, to call
the fat knight back again, and notify him that the
Chief Justice must speak with him. Sir John pre-
tends to be deaf ; and when his Lordship's servant
plucks him by the elbow, he turns and says :
"What ! a young knave, and begging ! Is there
not wars ? is there not employment ? doth not the
king lack subjects ? do not the rebels need soldiers ?
Though it be a shame to be on any side but one, it
is worse shame to beg than to be on the worst side,
were it worse than the name of rebellion can tell
how to make it." During this dialogue, and just
as Sir John is huffing the servant out of his way,
Chief Justice Gascoigne intervenes and speaks
peremptorily : "Sir John Falstaff, a word with
you." Though cornered at last, the slippery old
rogue does not lose his presence of mind, nor are
his wits belated. He professes to treat the Chief
Justice with profound reverence, and interlards
his salutatory sentences plentifully with "your
Lordship," thus : "My good Lord ! God give
your Lordship good time of day. I am glad to see
your Lordship abroad ; I heard say your Lordship
was sick : I hope your Lordship goes abroad by
advice. Your Lordship, though not clean past
your youth, hath yet some smack of age in you,
some relish of the saltness of time ; and I most
humbly beseech your Lordship to have a reverent
care of your health."

Looking at the legal altercation between the
parties as a proceeding at common law, it may be
reported as follows : The Chief Justice thus de-

clares : "Sir John, I sent for you before your expedition to Shrewsbury."

To this *declaration*, Falstaff files the impertinent *plea :* "An 't please your lordship, I hear his Majesty is returned with some discomfort from Wales."

The Chief Justice, by way of *replication*, says : "I talk not of his Majesty ; you would not come when I sent for you."

Falstaff files *instanter* this irrelevant *rejoinder ·* "And I hear, moreover, his Highness is fallen into this same whoreson apoplexy."

And thereupon the Chief Justice gently interposes, not a *surrejoinder*, but precatory words : "Well, God mend him ! I pray you, let me speak with you."

Falstaff, continuing his rejoinder, says : "This apoplexy is, as I take it, a kind of lethargy, an 't please your lordship ; a kind of sleeping in the blood ; a whoreson tingling."

Then the Chief Justice interrupts with an *obiter dictum :* "What tell you me of it ? be it as it is."

Falstaff continues his rejoinder : "It hath its original from much grief, from study and perturbation of the brain : I have read the cause of his effects in Galen ; it is a kind of deafness."

The Chief Justice lets loose an opinion, and makes his *surrejoinder :* "I think you are fallen into the disease, for you hear not what I say to you."

And thereupon Sir John makes his *rebutter :* "Very well, my lord, very well ; rather, an 't please you, it is the disease of not listening, the malady of not marking, that I am troubled withal."

The Chief Justice, as a minatory *surrebutter*, remarks : "To punish you by the heels would amend the attention of your ears ; and I care not if I do become your physician."

And then Sir John, by way of confession and avoidance, meekly says : "I am as poor as Job, my lord, but not so patient : your lordship may minister the potion of imprisonment to me in respect of poverty ; but how I should be your patient to follow your prescriptions, the wise may make some dram of a scruple, or indeed a scruple itself."

Sir William says : "I sent for you, when there were matters against you for your life, to come speak with me ;" and Sir John answers : "As I was then advised by my learned counsel in the laws of this land-service, I did not come."

It has also been objected that a Chief Justice could not be supposed, by any person acquainted with his station and functions, to use such vulgar language as that put into the mouth of Sir William Gascoigne when Falstaff will not listen to him ; and that this rather smacks of the butcher's shop in which it is alleged that young Shakespeare employed himself in killing calves. But to "lay by the heels" was the technical expression for committing to prison. The case of the *Mayor of Hereford* is thus reported in 1 Salkeld, 396 : " Per Holt, C. J.: The Mayor of Hereford was *laid by the heels*, for sitting in judgment in a cause where he himself was lessor of the plaintiff in ejectment, though he by charter was sole judge of the court." In *Henry VIII.* the Lord Chamberlain says :

> As I live,
> If the king blame me for 't, I 'll *lay ye all*
> *By the heels*, and suddenly ; and on your heads
> Clap round fines for neglect.   —*Act V., Sc. 3.*

A petition being heard in the Court of Chancery, before Lord Chancellor Jeffreys, against a great city attorney, who had given him many briefs at the bar, an affidavit was read, swearing that when the attorney was threatened with being brought before my Lord Chancellor, he exclaimed : "My Lord Chancellor! I made him!" Lord Chancellor Jeffreys replied : "Then will I lay *my maker by the heels*." A warrant of commitment was instantly signed and sealed by the Lord Chancellor, and the poor attorney was sent off to the Fleet.

Lord Chief Justice Holt once committed a blasphemous impostor by the name of Atkins, who belonged to a sect, half cheats, half gulls, called "The Prophets." One of the brotherhood immediately waited on him and said authoritatively, "I come to thee, a prophet from the Lord God, and sent by the Holy Ghost, who would have thee grant a *nolle prosequi* to John Atkins, his servant whom thou hast sent to prison." Such a demand might have puzzled some judges, but Lord Holt's grim humor and English sagacity darted at once to the point which betrayed the falsity of the fanatic's claim. " Thou art a false prophet and lying knave," he answered. "If the Holy Ghost had sent thee, it would have been to the Attorney-General, for He knows that it belongeth not to the Chief Justice to grant a *nolle prosequi.* But there is one thing which I, as Chief Justice, can do. I can lay a lying knave by the heels"; and thereupon he committed the false prophet to prison.

The Chief Justice, seemingly satisfied with Sir John's excuse for not coming before him, partly pulls off his judicial gown, and thenceforth during the interview, assumes the office of *Censor Morum*, and at once applies himself to the discharge of its duties ; not, however, with the characteristic vigor and acrimony of hard, stern, coarse, and crabbed Cato the Censor. The imparlance continues :

Ch. J. Well, the truth is, Sir John, you live in great infamy.

Fal. He that buckles him in my belt cannot live in less.

Ch. J. Your means are very slender, and your waste is great.

Fal. I would it were otherwise ; I would my means were greater, and my waist slenderer.

Ch. J. You have misled the youthful prince.

Fal. The young prince hath misled me ; I am the fellow with the great belly, and he my dog.

Ch. J. Well, I am loath to gall a new-healed wound : your day's service at Shrewsbury hath a little gilded over your night's exploit on Gadshill ; you may thank the unquiet time for your quiet o'er-posting that action. . . . You follow the young prince up and down, like his ill angel.

Fal. Not so, my lord ; your ill angel is light ; but I hope he that looks upon me will take me without weighing : and yet, in some respects, I grant, I cannot go, I cannot tell. Virtue is of so little regard in these costermonger times that true valour is turned bear-herd ; pregnancy is made a tapster, and hath his quick wit wasted in giving reckonings ; all the other gifts appertinent to man, as the malice of this age shapes them, are not worth a gooseberry. You that are old consider not the capacities of us that are young ; you measure the heat of our livers with the bitterness of your galls : and we that are in the vaward of our youth, I must confess, are wags too.

Ch. J. Do you set down your name in the scroll of youth, that are written down old with all the characters of age? Have you not a moist eye? a dry hand? a yellow cheek? a white beard? a decreasing leg? an increasing helly? is not your voice broken? your wind short? your chin double? your wit single?* and every part about you blasted with antiquity? and will you yet call yourself young? Fie, fie, fie, Sir John !

Fal. My lord, I was born about three of the clock in the afternoon, with a white head and something of a round belly. For my voice, I have lost it with hallooing and singing of anthems. To approve my youth further, I will not : the truth is, I am only old in judgment and understanding ; and he that will caper with me for a thousand marks, let him lend me the money, and have at him ! For the box of the ear that the prince gave you, he gave it like a rude prince, and you took it like a sensible lord. I have checked him for it, and the young lion repents ; marry, not in ashes and sackcloth, but in new silk and old sack.

Ch. J. Well, God send the prince a better companion.

Fal. God send the companion a better prince ! I cannot rid my hands of him.

Ch. J. Well, the king hath severed you and Prince Harry : I hear you are going with Lord John of Lancaster against the Archbishop and the Earl of Northumberland.

---

* Clarke remarks here : "That the Chief Justice should use the epithet *single* here to express *simple* affords a notable instance of Falstaff's being ' the cause that wit is in other men ' ; and that his lordship should apply the epithet *single* to Falstaff's *wit* is as notable a token of how thoroughly the knight's imperturbable humour has power to put him out of humour, just as, later in the play, he loses his temper so utterly as to. call Falstaff ' a great *fool !* ' "

Fal. Yea ; I thank your pretty sweet wit for it. But look you pray, all you that kiss my lady Peace at home, that our armies join not in a hot day ; for, by the Lord, I take but two shirts out with me, and I mean not to sweat extraordinarily : if it be a hot day, and I brandish any thing but a bottle, I would I might never spit white again. There is not a dangerous action can peep out his head but I am thrust upon it : well, I cannot last ever ; but it was alway yet the trick of our English nation, if they have a good thing, to make it too common. If ye will needs say I am an old man, you should give me rest. I would to God my name were not so terrible to the enemy as it is ; I were better to be eaten to death with a rust, than to be scoured to nothing with perpetual motion.

The Chief Justice, instead of committing Sir John to Newgate to answer for the robbery at Gadshill, says to him : " Well, be honest, be honest ; and God bless your expedition ! " Thereupon the fat knight is emboldened to ask : " Will your lordship lend me a thousand pound to furnish me forth ? " To lower the law still further, my Lord Chief Justice is made to break off the conversation, in which Falstaff's wit is so sparkling, with a very bad pun.

Ch. J. Not a penny, not a penny ; you are too impatient to bear crosses.* Fare you well ; commend me to my cousin Westmoreland.

The second meeting of the Chief Justice and Falstaff was, like the first, a casual one, and in a London street. It happened thus: When Sir John had, as Widow Quickly said, "eaten her out of house and home, and put all her substance into

---

* The *penny* and all the royal coins then had impressed upon them the sign of the *cross.*

that fat belly of his," that poor lone, lorn landlady brought her action against that organized appetite and omnivorous boarder, to recover "a hundred mark" long overdue on his board bill at the Boar's Head tavern. In regard to this debt she says: "I have borne, and borne, and borne, and have been fubbed off, and fubbed off, and fubbed off, from this day to that day, that it is a shame to be thought on. There is no honesty in such dealing; unless a woman should be made an ass and a beast, to bear every knave's wrong."

When the two officers, Fang and Snare, reinforced by this irate hostess, were about to arrest Falstaff at her suit, Snare, who seems to have been of a cautious, retiring nature, and, in cases of danger, rather reluctant to "stand to 't," says: "It may chance to cost some of us our lives, for he will stab." And Fang, who appears, according to his own estimate of himself, to have had plenty of grip and grit in reserve, and ready for use in an emergency, replies : "If I can close with him, I care not for his thrust. . . . An I but fist him once; an a' come but within my vice,—" While these three Furies were at Pie-corner, and lying in wait for the delinquent debtor who was about to be on his way to York, the plaintiff widow of Eastcheap exclaims : "Yonder he comes : and that arrant malmsey-nose knave, Bardolph, with him. Master Fang and Master Snare, do me, do me, do me your offices." When Hostess Quickly and the officers begin to close in on him, Falstaff says : "How now! whose mare 's dead ? what 's the matter?" At once Sheriff Fang bristles up himself and shouts: "Sir John, I arrest you at the suit of Mistress Quickly"; and thereupon he tries to arrest the knight by installments. But Sir John resists arrest, orders the varlets away, directs Bardolph to draw his sword and cut off Mr. Fang's head, and throw Mrs. Quickly into the gutter. Whereupon she screams: "Throw me in the channel! wilt thou? wilt thou? thou bastardly rogue! Murther! murther! Ah, thou honey-suckle [homicidal] villain! wilt thou kill God's officers and the king's? Ah, thou honey-seed rogue! thou art a honey-seed, a man-queller, and a woman-queller." And so the war of words worsens until the Chief Justice appears on the scene, commands the beligerents to keep the peace, asks Sir John why he is brawling here, and tells him that he should have been well on his way to York. The poor plaintiff interpleads, and states her case with a "tempest of exclamation"; and then his lordship says to the defendant debtor: "Are you not ashamed to enforce a poor widow to so rough a course to come by her own?" Falstaff answers: "My lord, this is a poor mad soul; and she says up and down the town that her eldest son is like you: she hath been in good case, and the truth is, poverty hath distracted her. But for these foolish officers, I beseech you I may have redress against them." The Chief Justice replies: "Sir John, Sir John, I am well acquainted with your manner of wrenching the true cause the false way. It is not a confident brow, nor the throng of words that come with such more than impudent sauciness from you, can thrust me from a level consideration; you have, as it appears to me, practised upon the easy-yielding spirit of this woman, and made her serve your uses both in purse and in person. . . . Pay her the debt you owe her, and unpay the villainy you have done her; the one you may do with sterling money, and the other with current repentance." Falstaff rejoins: "My lord, I will not undergo this sneap without reply. You call honourable boldness impudent sauciness; if a man will make courtesy and say nothing, he is virtuous. No, my lord, my humble duty remembered, I will not be your suitor. I say to you, I do desire deliverance from these officers, being upon hasty employment in the king's affairs."* And the Chief Justice says: "You speak as having power to do wrong; but answer in the effect of your reputation, and satisfy the poor woman."

Falstaff takes Hostess Quickly aside, glozes and pacifies her, tells her not to pawn her plate and the "fly-bitten tapestries" of her dining-chambers as she proposes to do to raise money, persuades her to withdraw her action against him, accepts her invitation to supper where he is to meet that "honest, virtuous, civil gentlewoman," Doll Tearsheet, and sends the plaintiff widow away under the escort of red-nose Bardolph, whom he directs to "hook on, hook on." In the meanwhile Chief

---

* "Falstaff claimed the protection legally called *quia profecturus* (see *Coke upon Littleton*, 130 a). This is one of the many examples of Shakespeare's somewhat intimate acquaintance with legal forms and phrases."—KNIGHT.

Justice Gascoigne is talking with Master Gower, who has brought news of the King, Prince Hal, and the war in Wales and the north of England. Having rid himself of Dame Quickly, and forgetting his double declaration just made to her, "As I am a gentleman," the fat knight, with great impropriety of manners, forthwith intrudes himself into the dialogue between his Lordship and Master Gower.

Fal. My lord !

Ch. J. What 's the matter ?

Fal. Master Gower, shall I entreat you with me to dinner ?

Gow. I must wait upon my good lord here ; I thank you, good Sir John.

Ch. J. Sir John, you loiter here too long, being you are to take soldiers up in counties as you go.

Fal. Will you sup with me, Master Gower ?

Ch. J. What foolish master taught you these manners, Sir John ?

Fal. Master Gower, if they become me not, he was a fool that taught them me.—This is the right fencing grace, my lord ; tap for tap, and so part fair.

Against this attack, the Chief Justice, losing his temper, parries and riposts with the home-thrust: "Now the Lord lighten thee ! thou art a great fool."

In this scene, Falstaff is less distinguished for wit than for effrontery. His whole behavior to Chief Justice Gascoigne, whom he despairs of winning by flattery, is singularly insolent, and shows the taint of the vulgar society of the Boar's Head tavern.

Prince Hal is, as Sir John supposes, "so much

engraffed to Falstaff," that, when the latter hears the old king is as dead as " nail in door," and that " Harry the Fifth 's the man," he throws out threats and promises, and issues commands as follows:

Away, Bardolph ! Saddle my horse. Master Robert Shallow, choose what office thou wilt in the land, t' is thine. Pistol, I will double-charge thee with dignities.   .   .   . Master Shallow, my Lord Shallow, be what thou wilt ; I am Fortune's steward—get on thy boots ; we 'll ride all night. O sweet Pistol ! Away, Bardolph ! Come, Pistol, utter more to me ; and withal devise something to do thyself good. Boot, boot, Master Shallow ; I know the young king is sick for me. Let us take any man's horses ; the laws of England are at my commandment. Blessed are they that have been my friends, *and woe unto my Lord Chief Justice !*

Lord Campbell thus comments : " Shakespeare has likewise been blamed for an extravagant perversion of law in the promises and threats which Falstaff throws out on hearing that Henry IV. was dead, and that Prince Hal reigned in his stead. But Falstaff may not unreasonably be supposed to have believed that he could do all this, even if he were strictly kept to the literal meaning of his words. In the natural and usual course of things he was to become (as it was then called) ' favourite ' (or, as we call it, *Prime Minister*) to the new king, and to have all the power and patronage of the crown in his hands. Then, why might not Ancient Pistol, who had seen service, have been made *War Minister ?* And if Justice Shallow had been pitchforked into the House of Peers, he

might have turned out a distinguished *Law Lord.*
By taking ' any man's horses ' was not meant *stealing* them, but *pressing* them for the king's service,
or appropriating them at a nominal price, which
the law would then have justified under the king's
prerogative of *pre-emption.* Sir W. Gascoigne was
continued as Lord Chief Justice in the new reign ;
but, according to law and custom, he was remov-
able, and he no doubt expected to be removed,
from his office. Therefore, if Lord Eldon could
be supposed to have written the play, I do not see
how he would be chargeable with having forgotten
any of his law while writing it."

3

III.

CRITICISM on the oceanic-minded Shakespeare is not like circumnavigating a desert islet ; 't is like coasting along and exploring a continent. This myriad-minded man * has left no form of human action or utterance ungilded by his genius. Capable of being all that he actually or imaginatively saw, this one man in his time played many parts, and, in all of them, he held, as it were, the mirror up to nature. So comprehensive was his genius for the delineation of character that, in his plays, the king and the beggar, the hero and the coward, the sage and the idiot, speak and act with equal truth. He entered into at will, and aban-

---

* '' Coleridge has most felicitously applied to him a Greek epithet, given before to I know not whom, certainly none so deserving of it, μυριόνους, the thousand-souled Shakespeare.'' —HALLAM's *Literature of Europe*, Part III., ch. vi.

In a note to ch. xv. of his *Biographia Literaria*, Coleridge says : ''Ἀνὴρ μυριόνους, a phrase which I have borrowed from a Greek monk, who applies it to a patriarch of Constantinople.''

doned at will, the passions which bless, and those that blast, other natures. He is the only writer who was as great in describing weakness as strength.

E. P. Whipple, in his *Literature of the Age of Elizabeth*,* after stating the few facts certainly known of Shakespeare's personal history, says : " Such is essentially the meagre result of a century of research into the external life of Shakespeare. As there is hardly a page in his writings which does not shed more light upon the biography of his mind, and bring us nearer to the individuality of the man, the antiquaries in despair have been compelled to abandon him to the psychologists ; and the moment the transition from external to internal facts is made, the most obscure of men passes into the most notorious. For this personality and soul we call Shakespeare, the recorded incidents of whose outward career were so few and trifling, lived a more various life—a life more crowded with ideas, passions, volitions, and *events* —than any potentate the world has ever seen. Compared with his experience, the experience of Alexander or Hannibal, of Cæsar or Napoleon, was narrow and one-sided. He had projected himself into almost all the varieties of human character, and, in imagination, had intensely realized and *lived* the life of each. From the throne of the monarch to the bench of the village alehouse, there were few positions in which he had not placed himself, and which he had not for a time

* Pp. 33, 34, 53.

identified with his own.   No other man had ever
seen nature and human life from so many points of
view; for he had looked upon them through the
eyes of Master Slender and Hamlet, of Caliban
and Othello, of Dogberry and Mark Antony, of
Ancient Pistol and Julius Cæsar, of Mistress Tearsheet and Imogen, of Dame Quickly and Lady
Macbeth, of Robin Goodfellow and Titania, of
Hecate and Ariel.   .   .   .   Shakespeare could run
his sentiment, passion, reason, imagination, into
any mould of personality he was capable of shap-
ing, and think and speak from that.   The result is
that every character is a denizen of the Shakespearian World; every character, from Master
Slender to Ariel, is in some sense a poet, that is, is
gifted with imagination to express his whole nature,
and make himself inwardly known; yet we feel
throughout that the 'thousand-souled' Shakespeare
is still but one soul, capable of shifting into a thousand forms, but leaving its peculiar birth-mark on
every individual it informs."

Schlegel, in his *Lectures on Dramatic Art and
Literature*, says : "Never, perhaps, was there so
comprehensive a talent for the delineation of character as Shakespeare's.   It not only grasps the
diversities of rank, sex, and age, down to the
dawnings of infancy; not only do the king and the
beggar, the hero and the pickpocket, the sage and
the idiot speak and act with equal truth; not only
does he transport himself to distant ages and for-
eign nations, and portray in the most accurate
manner, with only a few apparent violations of

costume, the spirit of the ancient Romans, of the French in their wars with the English, of the English themselves during a great part of their history, of the Southern Europeans (in the serious part of many comedies), the cultivated society of that time, and the former rude and barbarous state of the North ; his human characters have not only such depth and precision that they cannot be arranged under classes, and are inexhaustible, even in conception: No, this Prometheus not merely forms men, he opens the gates of the magical world of spirits ; calls up the midnight ghost ; exhibits before us his witches amidst their unhallowed mysteries; peoples the air with sportive fairies and sylphs : and these beings, existing only in imagination, possess such truth and consistency, that even when deformed monsters like Caliban, he extorts the conviction that if there should be such beings they would so conduct themselves. In a word, as he carries with him the most fruitful and daring fancy into the kingdom of nature; on the other hand, he carries nature into the regions of fancy, lying beyond the confines of reality. We are lost in astonishment at seeing the extraordinary, the wonderful, and the unheard of, in such intimate nearness."

Heine writes: " The scene of the action of Shakespeare's plays is the globe itself,—this is his unity of place ; eternity is the period of the action of his pieces,—this is his unity of time ; and in conformity with these two unities is the hero of his drama, who represents the central point,—the unity

of interest. Humanity is his hero, a hero continually dying and continually being born, continually loving, continually hating, yet loving more
than hating." *

Dowden writes : † " Shakspere does not seem
to feel that Dogberry and Verges are creatures of
another breed from himself. He stands, it is true,
at the opposite pole of humanity; nevertheless, a
potential Dogberry element existed even in Shakspere. 'Common people,' as Mr. Bagehot has
happily said, 'could be cut out of Shakspere';
just as the robust and prosaic statesman of Westmoreland could have been cut out of the great
spiritual thinker and poet of the Lake district.
Therefore, apart from the interest of sympathy, we
have a personal interest in understanding the common features of the most ordinary lives. Our own
life is akin to them, and may readily lapse into a
resemblance curiously exact. But as long as we
can smile at them we are safe; our sense of humor
is servant of our passion for perfection. We have
no need to grow impatient or indignant with those
grotesque portions of humanity; that would un-
necessarily disturb the balance of our lives and the
purity of our perceptions: we only need to understand them and to smile."

Shallow and Silence, the Gloucestershire justices, sit with Dogberry and Verges, Slender and

---

* *Wit, Wisdom, and Pathos from the Prose of Heinrich
Heine,* p. 63.

† *Shakspere: A Critical Study of his Mind and Art,* Am.
ed., pp. 315, 316.

Sir Andrew Aguecheek, high among Shakespeare's minor triumphs. One of the finest burlesque portraits that ever was drawn is Falstaff's delineation of Shallow, a portion only of the entire portrait being as follows : " This same starved justice hath done nothing but prate to me of the wildness of his youth, and the feats he hath done about Turn-bull street; and every third word a lie, duer paid to the hearer than the Turk's tribute. I do remember him at Clement's Inn, like a man made after supper of a cheese-paring. When he was naked, he was for all the world like a forked radish, with a head fantastically carved upon it with a knife. He was so forlorn that his dimensions to any thick sight were invisible; he was the very genius of famine; you might have thrust him and all his apparel into an eel-skin:—the case of a treble hautboy was a mansion for him—a court! and now has he land and beefs." Shallow is a garrulous old fellow, full of a sense of the greatness of his office, " a judge who ever carries the ermine with him off the bench, and lugs it laboriously around in ordinary life." Twenty Sir John Falstaffs shall not abuse Robert Shallow, esquire, " a gentleman born, who writes himself *Armigero*, in any bill, warrant, quittance, or obligation, *Armigero*," and who is, moreover, the *custos rotulorum* among the justices of the peace in the county of Gloucester. He is given to boasting of the hair-brained deeds and gallantries of his youth, which adventures, probably, were, for the most part, but fancies and figments of his rattle-box brain. His wit is wandering, and he has not the power of steady and concatenated thinking. His line of thought and speech is not straight, nor even curvilinear, but zigzag and angular. His talk is tautological, jumping, jerky, disjointed, and inconsequent, and abounds in commonplace reflections and impertinent digressions. As a more particular instance, take Shallow's account of his early life in London, and the inimitable and affecting, though most absurd and ludicrous, dialogue between Shallow and Silence on the death of old Double:

Shal. Come on, come on, come on, sir ; give me your hand, sir, give me your hand, sir : an early stirrer, by the rood !   And how doth my good cousin Silence ?

Sil. Good morrow, good cousin Shallow.

Shal. And how doth my cousin, your bed-fellow ? and your fairest daughter, and mine, my god-daughter Ellen ?

Sil. Alas, a black ousel, cousin Shallow ?

Shal. By yea and nay, sir, I dare say my cousin William is become a good scholar ; he is at Oxford still, is he not ?

Sil. Indeed, sir, to my cost.

Shal. He must, then, to the inns o' court shortly.   I was once of Clement's Inn,* where I think they will talk of mad Shallow yet.

Sil. You were called "lusty Shallow" then, cousin.

---

* Staunton, in his *Illustrative Comments* on *King Henry IV.*, says of Clement's Inn : This was so called, says Stow, " because it standeth near to St. Clement's Church, but nearer to the fair fountain called Clement's Well."   How long before 1479, nineteenth of Edward IV., it was occupied by students of the law is not known, but that it had been so inhabited for some time previously is quite certain ; and we have the testimony of Strype to show that in after-times the roisterers of the Inns of Court fully maintained the reputation which Shallow took so much pride in claiming for himself and his fellow

Shal. By the mass, I was called any thing ; and I would have done any thing indeed too, and roundly too. There was I, and little John Doit of Staffordshire, and black George Barnes, and Francis Pickbone, and Will Squele, a Cotswold man ; you had not four such swinge-bucklers in all the inns o' court again. Then was Jack Falstaff, now Sir John, a boy, and page to Thomas Mowbray, Duke of Norfolk.

Sil. This Sir John, cousin, that comes hither anon about soldiers?

Shal. The same Sir John, the very same. I saw him break Skogan's head at the court-gate, when a' was a crack not thus high ; and the very same day did I fight with one Sampson Stockfish, a fruiterer, behind Gray's Inn. Jesu, Jesu, the mad days that I have spent! and to see how many of my old acquaintance are dead!

Sil. We shall all follow, cousin.

Shal. Certain, 't is certain ; very sure, very sure : death, as the Psalmist saith, is certain to all ; all shall die. How a good yoke of bullocks at Stamford fair ?

Sil. By my troth, I was not there.

Shal. Death is certain. Is old Double of your town living yet ?

Sil. Dead, sir.

Shal. Jesu, Jesu, dead! a' drew a good bow ; and dead! a shot a fine shoot : John o' Gaunt loved him well, and betted much money on his head. Dead! a' would have clapped i' the

---

swinge-bucklers : " Here about this Church," he is speaking of St. Clement's, " and in the parts adjacent, were frequent disturbances by reason of the unthrifts of the Inns of Chancery, who were so unruly on nights, walking about to the disturbance and danger of such as passed along the streets, that the inhabitants were fain to keep watches. In the year 1582, the Recorder himself, with six more of the honest inhabitants, stood by St. Clement's Church, to see the lanthorn hung out, and to observe if he could meet with any of these outrageous dealers."

clout at twelve score ; and carried you a forehand shaft at fourteen and fourteen and a half, that it would have done a man's heart good to see.   How a score of ewes now ?

Sil. Thereafter as they be ; a score of good ewes may be worth ten pounds.

Shal. And is old Double dead ?

When Sir John asks the two justices whether they have provided him with half a dozen sufficient recruits, Shallow answers :   " Marry, have we, sir. Will you sit ?   .   .   .   Where 's the roll ? where 's the roll ? where 's the roll ? Let me see, let me see, let me see.   So, so, so, so, so, so, so ;   yea, marry, sir.   Ralph Mouldy !   Let them appear as I call ; let them do so, let them do so.   Let me see ; where is Mouldy ? "

When Falstaff says, " We have heard the chimes at midnight," Shallow responds : " That we have, that we have, that we have ; in faith, Sir John, we have ; our watchword was ' Hem, boys ! '*—Come, let 's to dinner ; come, let 's to dinner.—Jesu, the days that we have seen !—Come, come."   At another time the justice says to Falstaff, who asks to be excused from staying all night with him :

I will not excuse you : you shall not be excused ; excuses shall not be admitted ; there is no excuse shall serve ; you shall not be excused.—Why, Davy ! [*Enter Davy.*] Davy, Davy, Davy, Davy, let me see, Davy ; let me see ; yea, marry, William cook, bid him come hither.   Sir John, you shall not be excused.

---

* " There was an old rollicking song, whose burden, *Hem, boys, hem !* still lingered in Justice Shallow's memory.   Only one verse of this song is now extant."—STAUNTON.

In Shallow's orchard, Falstaff says:

Fore God, you have here a goodly dwelling and a rich.

Shal. Barren, barren, barren ; beggars all, beggars all, Sir John ; marry, good air. Spread, Davy ; spread, Davy ; well said, Davy.

Fal. This Davy serves you for good uses ; he is your serving-man and your husband.

Shal. A good varlet, a good varlet, a very good varlet, Sir John—by the mass, I have drunk too much sack at supper !—a good varlet.—Now sit down, now sit down.—Come, cousin.

Clarke, in his *Shakespeare-Characters*, thus comments : " It is impossible to conceive a stronger contrast, a more direct antipodes in mental structure than Shakespeare has achieved between Falstaff and Shallow ; the one all intellect, all acuteness of perception and fancy, and the other, the justice, a mere compound of fatuity, a *caput mortuum* of understanding. Not only is Shallow distinguished by his eternal babble, talking 'infinite nothings' ; but with the flabby vivacity, the idiotic restlessness, that not unfrequently accompany this class of mind (if such a being may be said to possess mind at all), he not only tattles on—'whir, whir, whir,' like a ventilator, but he fills up the chinks in his sentences with repetitions, as blacksmiths continue to tap the anvil in the intervals of turning the iron upon it. But Shakespeare has presented us with a still stronger quality of association in minds of Shallow's calibre, that of asking questions everlastingly, and instantly giving evidence that the replies have not sunk even skin-deep with them, rushing on from subject to subject, and returning again to those that have been dismissed. . . . As if it were not sufficient triumph for the poet to have achieved such a contrast as the two intellects of Falstaff and Shallow—in the consciousness and the opulence of unlimited genius, he stretches the line of his invention, and produces a foil even to Shallow—a climax to nothing—in the person of his cousin, Silence. Silence is an embryo of a man— a molecule—a graduation from nonentity towards intellectual being—a man dwelling in the suburbs of sense, groping about in the twilight of apprehension and understanding. He is the second stage in the *Vestiges ;* he has just emerged from the tadpole state. Here again a distinction is preserved between these two characters. Shallow gabbles on from mere emptiness ; while Silence, from the same incompetence, rarely gets beyond the shortest replies. The firmament of his wonder and adoration are the sayings and doings of his cousin and brother-justice at Clement's Inn, and which he has been in the constant habit of hearing, without satiety and nausea, for half a century."

Hazlitt, in his *English Comic Writers*, thus comments : " In point of understanding and attainments, Shallow sinks low enough ; and yet his cousin Silence is a foil to him ; he is the shadow of a shade, glimmers on the very verge of downright imbecility, and totters on the brink of nothing. He has been 'merry twice or once ere now,' and is hardly persuaded to break his silence in a song. Shallow has ' heard the chimes at midnight,' and roared out glees and catches at taverns and inns of court, when he was young. So, at least, he tells his cousin Silence, and Falstaff encourages the loftiness of his pretensions. Shallow would be thought a great man among his dependents and followers ; Silence is nobody—not even in his own opinion ; yet he sits in the orchard and eats his caraways and pippins among the rest. Shakespear takes up the meanest subjects with the same tenderness that we do an insect's wing, and would not kill a fly."

It has been lamented that we know so little of the man Shakespeare—that his true biography is so brief. More than a century ago, Steevens wrote : "All that is known with any degree of certainty concerning Shakespeare, is, that he was born at Stratford-upon-Avon ; married and had children there ; went to London, where he commenced actor, and wrote poems and plays ; returned to Stratford, made his will, died, and was buried." Dyce says : "Such is the remark made long ago by one of the most acute of his commentators ; and even at the present day,—notwithstanding some additional notices of Shakespeare which have been more recently discovered,—the truth of the remark can hardly fail to be felt and acknowledged by all, except by professed antiquaries, with whom the mere mention of a name, in whatever kind of document, assumes the character of an important fact."

Notwithstanding all the research into the external life of Shakespeare, and the commentary which, during the last hundred and fifty years and more has gathered around his Plays, " as the desert sands around the Egyptian Sphinx," all the facts respecting his personal history may be compressed within the compass of a quarto page of his writings —Parnassus crushed into a nutshell. But Shakespeare-lovers will probably continue to peep and botanize upon and around their idol's grave ; and will continue to turn over and over the lamentably small bundle of biographical straw from which every grain of truth and fact respecting Shakespeare's personal history seems to have been threshed long ago.

Though we can never know Shakespeare as we know Johnson by means of Boswell's book, yet we can know him if we study his works. Emerson, in his *Representative Men*, remarks : " Shakespeare is the only biographer of Shakespeare ; and even he can tell nothing, except to the Shakespeare in us. . . . What trait of his private mind has he hidden in his dramas ? One can discern, in his ample pictures of the gentleman and the king, what forms and humanities pleased him ; his delight in troops of friends, in large hospitality, in cheerful giving. . . . So far from Shakespeare's being the least known, he is the one person, in all modern history, known to us. What point of morals, of manners, of economy, of philosophy, of religion, of taste, of the conduct of life, has he not settled ? What mystery has he not signified his knowledge of ? What office, or function, or district of man's work, has he not remembered ? What king has he not taught state, as Talma taught Napoleon ? What maiden has not found him finer than her delicacy ?

What lover has he not outloved? What sage has he not outseen? What gentleman has he not instructed in the rudeness of his behavior?"

On the foregoing, Cushman K. Davis, in his *The Law in Shakespeare*, thus comments: "All this is true, but it is not the whole truth. We see a man who revered womanhood, who has given us the finest types of manhood, who was generous, gentle, blameless, who saw through shams clearer than Montaigne, who scourged lust, gluttony, lying, slander, cowardice, pedantry, and all personal meanness with more than the wit of Rabelais, and yet who was silent concerning those great agitations for personal right and liberty which so shortly after he died subverted the monarchy, put aside the peerage, overthrew the church, and forever established that the state is made for man and not man for the state." Mr. Davis further comments: "There is nowhere a hint of sympathy with personal rights as against the sovereign, nor with parliament, then first assuming its protective attitude towards the English people, nor with the few judges who, like Coke, showed a glorious obstinacy in their resistance to the prerogative. In all his works there is not one direct word for liberty of speech, thought, religion—those rights which in his age were the very seeds of time, into which his eye, of all men's, could best look to see which grain would grow and which would not. In all ages great men and great women have died for humanity, but none of these have been commemorated by him. The fire of no martyr gleams in his pages."

Corson, in his *Introduction to the Study of Shakespeare*, remarks : " We really know more of Shakespeare than we know of any other author of the
time, either in English or in European literature,
who was not connected with state affairs. The
personal history of a mere author, and especially
of a playwright, as a dramatic author, whatever his
ability, was frequently called, with no influence at
Court, was not considered of sufficient importance
to be recorded in those days, when the Court was
everything, and the individual man without adven-
titious recommendations, was nothing."

IV.

The Fat Knight "Leers" upon King Hal Passing by.—The "Sweet Boy" Sentences the "Greasy Knight."—The Chief Justice Sends Him to Prison.—A Judgment without "Cold Considerance."

THE last scene of Part Second of *King Henry IV.* is laid in a public place near Westminster Abbey. There two grooms enter and strew rushes in the path of the royal procession about to come from the coronation. Falstaff and his followers, who, all booted and spurred, have ridden posthaste from Shallow's house in Gloucestershire, enter; and, in a group, they press and push and thrust and squeeze and elbow and wedge their way well to the very front of the dense crowd—*arrectis auribus adstant*—assembled to see the newly-crowned King and his train pass by. The fat knight is almost breathless, but soon recovers his wind and is able to speak :

Fal. Stand here by me, Master Robert Shallow; I will make the King do you grace. I will leer upon him, as a' comes by; and do but mark the countenance that he will give me.

Pist. God bless thy lungs, good knight !

Fal. Come here, Pistol; stand behind me.—O, if I had had time to have made new liveries, I would have bestowed the thousand pound I borrowed of you. [*To Shallow.*] But 't is

no matter; this poor show doth better; this doth infer the
zeal I had to see him.

Shal. It doth so.

Fal. It shows my earnestness of affection,—

Shal. It doth so.

Fal. My devotion,—

Shal. It doth, it doth, it doth.

Fal. As it were, to ride day and night ; and not to deliber_
ate, not to remember, not to have patience to shift me,—

Shal. It is best, certain.

Fal. But to stand stained with travel, and sweating with desire to see him ; thinking of nothing else, putting all affairs
else in oblivion, as if there were nothing else to be done but
to see him.

Shal. 'T is so, indeed.

Presently the trumpets sound, and the many-
headed multitude roars with multitudinous tongue.
Thereupon enter the King and his train, the Lord
Chief Justice among them.　Sir John can no
longer be silent.

Fal. God save thy grace, King Hal ! my royal Hal.

Pist. The heavens thee guard and keep, most royal imp of
fame !

Fal. God save thee, my sweet boy !

King. My lord chief justice, speak to that vain man.

Ch. J. Have you your wits? know you what 't is you speak ?

Fal. My king ! My Jove ! I speak to thee, my heart !

King. I know thee not, old man : fall to thy prayers ;

　　　How ill white hairs become a fool, and jester !
　　　I have long dream'd of such a kind of man,
　　　So surfeit-swell'd, so old, and so profane ;
　　　But, being awak'd, I do despise my dream.
　　　Make less thy body hence, and more thy grace ;
　　　Leave gormandizing ; know the grave doth gape
　　　For thee thrice wider than for other men.

Reply not to me with a fool-born jest :
Presume not that I am the thing I was ;
For God doth know, so shall the world perceive,
That I have turn'd away my former self ;
So will I those that kept me company.
When thou dost hear I am as I have been,
Approach me, and thou shalt be as thou wast,
The tutor and the feeder of my riots ;
Till then, I banish thee, on pain of death,
As I have done the rest of my misleaders,
Not to come near our person by ten mile.
For competence of life I will allow you,
That lack of means enforce you not to evil ;
And, as we hear you do reform yourselves,
We will, according to your strengths and qualities,
Give you advancement.   Be it your charge, my Lord,
                              [*To the Chief Justice*]
To see perform'd the tenour of our word.
Set on.   [*Exeunt King, and his train.*]

As the King and his train move on, plump Jack
says to Justice Shallow, " I owe you a thousand
pound." The lean creditor beseeches the fat
debtor to pay in full, or, at least, to let him have
five hundred of the thousand due. Of course there
is not money enough in Sir John's purse—not even
so much as the "seven groats and two pence"
which his page not long before reported to be the
sum total therein ; and Falstaff " can get no remedy
against this consumption of the purse ; borrowing
only lingers and lingers it out, but the disease is
incurable.'' The knight asks Master Shallow not
to grieve at this ; and comforts that worthy by
saying that he will be sent for in private to the
King, and that he will be the man yet that will

make the justice great. But Shallow replies: "I cannot well perceive how, unless you should give me your doublet and stuff me out with straw." Sir John still insists that the young King's rough treatment of himself is only colorable, and that he will surely be sent for soon at night; and he ends by inviting Shallow, Pistol, and Bardolph to go with him to dinner.

Soon re-enter Prince John, the Chief Justice, and officers with them. Judge Gascoigne forthwith proceeds to "lay 'sweet Jack Falstaff' by the heels,' thus :·

Ch. J. Go carry Sir John Falstaff to the Fleet. Take all his company along with him.

Fal. My lord, my lord,—

Ch. J. I cannot now speak; I will hear you soon. Take them away.

Truly an evil plight to be in for one who, burning with high hopes, has just "leered" upon his royal Hal; a sad predicament for one who, but yesterday, declared himself to be Fortune's steward, rioted in visions of money and influence and pottle-pots of sack without limit, blessed his friends, cursed the Chief Justice, knew that the young king was sick for him—for him who has ridden day and night, and to-day stands "stained with travel, and sweating with desire to see him ['my royal Hal']; thinking of nothing else, putting all affairs else in oblivion, as if there were nothing else to be done but to see him ['my sweet boy']." Such a shock of disappointment would utterly crush most men; but plump Jack is not a man to be long depressed by any misfortune. The stormy waves of adversity may roll over the "greasy knight"; but the oil that's in him smooths and stills the troubled waters, and, cork-like, he soon comes up smiling, and gaily floats on the surface.

It appears that no specific charges were formulated against Falstaff; that he did not have his day in court; that the cross-grained and peremptory Chief Justice took him by surprise, would listen to no plea, shut his mouth, and at once hustled him off to the Fleet Prison. For this severe doom the Justice should be held responsible, and not the King, who has left the stage, and who had simply ordered that Falstaff should not come near him "by ten mile." He had also promised that the knight should have "competence of life," and had even held out the hope of "advancement" according to his strengths and qualities, in case he reformed himself. The "sweet wag," now become King, intimated however that there shall be "gallows standing in England" during his reign. The Chief Justice, evidently considering that the fat old reprobate had been let off too easily, in default of definite charges, took the responsibility of summarily punishing him on general principles, and thus made a sort of "Star-Chamber matter" of the old sinner's case. That Judge Gascoigne was a firm and upright magistrate, and dared to do his duty, is shown by his drastic treatment of Prince Hal "for striking him about Bardolph." Referring to his humiliation by the Judge, the King asked:

> How might a prince of my great hopes forget
> So great indignities you laid upon me?
> What! rate, rebuke, and roughly send to prison
> The immediate heir of England!   Was this easy?
> May this be wash'd in Lethe, and forgotten?

There is no finer or better exposition of the sacredness of judicial authority than the memorable defence which the Judge interposed:

> I then did use the person of your father;
> The image of his power lay then in me:
> And, in the administration of his law,
> Whiles I was busy for the commonwealth,
> Your highness pleased to forget my place,
> The majesty and power of law and justice,
> The image of the king whom I presented,
> And struck me in my very seat of judgment;
> Whereon, as an offender to your father,
> I gave bold way to my authority
> And did commit you.   If the deed were ill,
> Be you contented, wearing now the garland,
> To have a son set your decrees at nought,
> To pluck down justice from your awful bench,
> To trip the course of law, and blunt the sword
> That guards the peace and safety of your person:
> Nay, more, to spurn at your most royal image
> And mock your workings in a second body.
> Question your royal thoughts, make the case yours;
> Be now the father and propose a son,
> Hear your own dignity so much profan'd,
> See your most dreadful laws so loosely slighted,
> Behold yourself so by a son disdain'd;
> And then imagine me taking your part,
> And in your power soft silencing your son.
> After this cold considerance, sentence me;
> And, as you are a king, speak in your state

What I have done that misbecame my place,
My person, or my liege's sovereignty.

This defence prevailed, for the King replied:

You are right, justice, and you weigh this well ;
Therefore still bear the balance and the sword :
And I do wish your honours may increase,
Till you do live to see a son of mine
Offend you and obey you, as I did.
So shall I live to speak my father's words :
" Happy am I, that have a man so bold,
That dares do justice on my proper son ;
And not less happy, having such a son,
That would deliver up his greatness so
Into the hands of justice."   You did commit me :
For which, I do commit into your hand
Th' unstained sword that you have us'd to bear ;
With this remembrance,—that you use the same
With the like bold, just, and impartial spirit
As you have done 'gainst me.   There is my hand.
You shall be as a father to my youth ;
My voice shall sound as you do prompt mine ear,
And I will stoop and humble my intents
To your well practis'd wise directions.—
And, princes all, believe me, I beseech you ;
My father is gone wild into his grave,
For in his tomb lie my affections,
And with this spirit sadly I survive,
To mock the expectation of the world,
To frustrate prophecies and to raze out
Rotten opinion, who hath writ me down
After my seeming.   The tide of blood in me
Hath proudly flow'd in vanity till now ;
Now doth it turn and ebb back to the sea,
Where it shall mingle with the state of floods
And flow henceforth in formal majesty.

The Chief Justice, charged by the King "to see performed the tenour of our word," seems to have exceeded his authority, and pronounced against Falstaff a sentence too severe and without "cold considerance." Possibly his lordship's temper was warmed by the thought of his parting words to Sir John on a former occasion: "Now the Lord lighten thee! thou art a great fool." The King doubtless reversed the hard sentence soon afterward; for we find Falstaff and his friends all at liberty in the opening scenes of *King Henry V.*

V.

THE *Merry Wives of Windsor* is an offshoot
from the comedy of *King Henry IV.*, while
King Henry V. is the direct continuation of the
history. Tradition reports that Queen Elizabeth
was so well pleased with that admirable character
of Falstaff in the two parts of *Henry IV.* that
she commanded Shakespeare to continue it for one
play more, and to show Falstaff in love. It is also
said that this gross-minded old woman was so
eager to see the play acted that she commanded it
to be finished in fourteen days. Shakespeare did
not make a grievance of his task. He threw himself into it with spirit, and despatched his work
within the time appointed. Of course he could n't
make Falstaff really in love, or the man would
have been redeemed by it. But the gross-bodied,
self-indulgent old sinner, devoid of moral sense
and of self-respect, was past redemption. On his
appearance in the character of a lover, Johnson
remarks: "No task is harder than that of writing
to the ideas of another. Shakespeare knew what

the queen seems not to have known, that by any real passion of tenderness, the selfish craft, the careless jollity, and the lazy luxury of Falstaff must have suffered so much abatement that little of his former cast could have remained. Falstaff could not love but by ceasing to be Falstaff. He could only counterfeit love. Thus the poet approached as near as he could to the work enjoined him ; yet having, perhaps, in the former plays completed his own ideas, seems not to have been able to give Falstaff all his former power of entertainment."

Appleton Morgan, in his *Shakespeare in Fact and in Criticism*, writes : " Of course the fat knight, in amorous chase after a pair of petticoats, is no more ' in love' than previously with Dame Quickly or Doll Tearsheet. The pen that created Imogen and Desdemona, Perdita and Juliet, if seriously ordered to delineate a libertine controlled and ennobled by the passion that drives out self, would scarcely have failed to recognize a field for its genius. However, if Falstaff was still to titillate the fine humors of Elizabeth, he must be concupiscent always, but this time baffled, foiled and put to rout. And so, for the nonce, in a play for the eyes of a Virgin Queen and within the letter, even at the expense of the spirit of her royal orders, must wifely honor live outside of noble birth, and virtue walk in homespun." Mr. Morgan remarks further on this play : " The salaciousness Elizabeth wanted was all there, as well as the transformation scene, but at the end there is a rebuke to lechery and to lecherous minds not equivocal in its character. 'This is enough to be the decay of lust and late walking throughout the realm,' says Falstaff, and perhaps there is a reproof to the queen herself —who certainly deserved it—in the line, 'Our radiant queen hates sluts and sluttery,' that is scathing in its satire."

Dowden thus comments: "Shakspere dressed up a fat rogue, brought forward for the occasion from the back premises of the poet's imagination, in Falstaff's clothes; he allowed persons and places and times to jumble themselves up as they pleased; he made it impossible for the most laborious nineteenth-century critic to patch on the *Merry Wives* to *Henry IV.* But the Queen and her court laughed as the buck-basket was emptied into the ditch, no more suspecting that its gross lading was not the incomparable jester of Eastcheap than Ford suspected the woman with a great beard to be other than the veritable Dame Pratt." *

Elsewhere Dowden says: " Nor is he conceived in quite the same manner as the Falstaff of *Henry IV.* Here the knight is fatuous, his genius deserts him ; the never-defeated hangs his head before two country dames; the buck-basket, the drench of Thames water, the blows of Ford's cudgel, are reprisals too coarse upon the most inimitable of jesters. Yet the play is indeed a merry one, with well-contrived incidents and abundance of plain, broad mirth. A country air breathes over the whole—for which the Gloucestershire scenes of

------

* *Shakspere—His Mind and Art*, Am. ed., pp. 329, 330.

second *Henry IV.*, had prepared us. . . . Altogether, if we can accept Falstaff's discomfitures, it is a sunny play to laugh at if not to love."

In short, the sayings and doings of the fat knight in this comedy do not lead us to hold opinion with Pythagoras that the soul of " Jack Falstaff with his familiars, John with his brothers and sisters, and Sir John with all Europe," has wholly infused itself into the trunk of this lewdster, " old, cold, withered, and of intolerable entrails," who says of himself, " I think the devil will not have me damned, lest the oil that 's in me should set hell on fire"; who declares to Mistress Ford that "the firm fixture of her foot would give an excellent motion to her gait in a semi-circled farthingale "; who protests to her that he " cannot cog and say thou art this and that, like a many of these lisping hawthorn-buds, that come like women in men's apparel, and smell like Bucklersbury in simple time"; and who, disguised as Herne the hunter, with a pair of huge horns on his head, at last confesses, " I do begin to perceive that I am made an ass." No, no,—this fat and foolish rogue, who has no wit and eloquence, and who, instead of making a butt of others, is made a butt of by them, is not the incomparable jester of Eastcheap. "Sweet, kind, true, valiant, and old " Jack Falstaff, charged with the many misdemeanors committed by the oily old rascal who is the hero of the *Merry Wives*, could easily exculpate himself by proving an *alibi*.

Hudson writes: "That the free impulse of Shakespeare's genius, without suggestion or inducement from any other source, could have led him to put Falstaff through such a series of uncharacteristic delusions and collapses is to me well-nigh incredible." (See also Hazlitt's criticism of the play.)

Hartley Coleridge writes : " That Queen Bess should have desired to see Falstaff making love proves her to have been, as she was, a gross-minded old baggage. Shakespeare has evaded the difficulty with great skill. He knew that Falstaff could not be in love ; and has mixed but a little, a very little, *pruritus* with his fortune-hunting courtship. But the Falstaff of the *Merry Wives* is not the Falstaff of *Henry IV.* It is a big-bellied impostor, assuming his name and style, or, at best, it is Falstaff in dotage. . . . The merry wives are a delightful pair. Methinks I see them, with their comely, middle-aged visages, their dainty white ruffs and toys, their half-witch-like conic hats, their full farthingales, their neat though not over-slim waists, their housewifely keys, their girdles, their sly laughing looks, their apple-red cheeks, their brows the lines whereon look more like the work of mirth than years. And sweet Anne Page —she is a pretty little creature whom one would like to take on one's knee."

Clarke comments : " There are the two ' Merry Wives ' themselves. What a picture we have of buxom, laughing, ripe beauty ! ready for any frolic ' that may not sully the chariness of their honesty.' The jealous-pate, Ford, ought to have been sure of his wife's integrity and goodness, from her being so transparent-charactered and cheerful ; for your insincere and double-dealing people are sure to betray, some time or other, the drag that dishonesty claps upon the wheel of their conduct. The career of a deceitful person is never uniform. In the sequel, however, Ford does make a handsome atonement—that of a frank apology to the party whom he had abused by his suspicions ; and he winds up the play with the rest, not the least happy of the group from having an enfranchised heart. He says well :

> Pardon me, wife.   Henceforth do what thou wilt.
> I rather will suspect the sun with cold
> Than thee with wantonness.   Now doth thy honour stand,
> In him that was of late a heretic,
> As firm as faith.   .   .   .

Then, there is Page, the very personification of hearty English hospitality. You feel the tight grasp of his hand, and see the honest sparkle of his eye, as he leads in the wranglers with ' Come, gentlemen, I hope we shall drink down all unkindness.' If I were required to point to the portrait of a genuine indigenous Englishman, throughout the whole of the works of Shakespeare, Page would be the man. Every thought of his heart, every motion of his body, appears to be the result of pure instinct ; he has nothing exotic or artificial about him. He possesses strong yeoman sense, an unmistakable speech, a trusting nature, and a fearless deportment ; and these are the characteristics of a true Englishman."

Page has a sturdy English confidence in his wife's honesty, and says, upon hearing of Falstaff's proposed attempt upon her virtue, " If he should intend this voyage towards my wife, I would turn her loose to him ; and what he gets more of her than sharp words, let it lie on my head." Mrs. Page says of her good man, " He 's as far from jealousy as I am from giving him cause ; and that, I hope, is an unmeasurable distance." When she receives the fat knight's letter, she says : "·What, have I scaped love-letters in the holiday-time of my beauty, and am I now a subject for them ? Let me see." Having read it, she exclaims : " What a Herod of Jewry is this !—O wicked, wicked world ! One that is well-nigh worn to pieces with age to show himself a young gallant ! What an unweighed behaviour hath this Flemish drunkard picked—with the devil's name !—out of my conversation, that he dares in this manner assay me ? Why, he hath not been thrice in my company !—What should I say to him ?—I was then frugal of my mirth.— Heaven forgive me !—Why, I 'll exhibit a bill in the Parliament for the putting down of fat men. How shall I be revenged on him ? for revenged I will be." Presently in comes her friend Mrs. Ford, who has received the twin-brother of Falstaff's letter to Mrs. Page. The two gossips consult together and plot against this " greasy knight " as Mrs. Page calls him, and Mrs. Ford says : " What tempest, I trow, threw this whale, with so many tuns of oil in his belly, ashore at Windsor ? How shall I be revenged on him ? I think the best way

were to entertain him with hope, till the wicked fire
of lust have melted him in his own grease." When
Falstaff, dressed in woman's clothes, and persona-
ting the fat old woman of Brentford, makes his exit,
Mrs. Page says to Mrs. Ford: "Heaven guide
him to thy husband's cudgel, and the devil guide
his cudgel afterwards!" Though her sense of
humor prompts this lively remark, yet her sense of
justice, and also her wise kindheartedness, will not
see him beaten so unmercifully.

At what period in Falstaff's career he pursued
the Windsor wives cannot be certainly determined.
But the majority of recent critics agree in placing
the production of the play between that of second
Henry IV. and *Henry V.* Knight and Verplanck
think the knight experienced the witcheries of the
merry wives before his introduction in the historical plays, Halliwell between the two parts of
Henry IV., and Johnson between second *Henry
IV.* and *Henry V.* Hudson finds room for
Sir John's Windsor adventures somewhere in the
ten years covered by second *Henry IV.* Collier,
Dowden, White, and other critics consider the
comedy of the *Merry Wives* as having a certain independence of the histories, and not to
be brought into chronological relations to them.
As White remarks: "Shakespeare was not writing
biography, even the biography of his own characters. He was a poet, but he wrote as a playwright ;
and the only consistency to which he held himself,
or can be held by others, is the consistency of
dramatic interest. And if when he deals with his-

toric personages we find him boldly disregarding the chronological succession of events in favor of the general truthfulness of dramatic impression, with what reason can we expect to find him respecting that succession with regard to the time when such mere creatures of his will as Shallow, or Bardolph, Nym, and Pistol, lent money to or entered the service of Sir John Falstaff, or when Mrs. Quickly ceased to be maid, or wife, or widow? —if she were ever either. We must discard all deductions from the failure of the four plays to make a connected memoir of Falstaff and his friends and followers, as not only inconclusive but of no consequence."

Mistress Quickly, the housekeeper to Doctor Caius; or, as Sir Hugh Evans designates her, "his nurse, or his dry-nurse, or his cook, or his laundry, his washer, or his wringer," who acts as the very lively go-between for Falstaff with the two merry wives, and who courts Anne Page for her master, undertakes the same office for Slender, and moreover favors the suit of Fenton—this Mrs. Quickly is not mine hostess of the Boar's Head tavern; but she is a very pleasant, fussy, busybodying, good-natured, unprincipled old woman, whom it is impossible to be angry with. Her master, Doctor Caius, the Frenchman, and her fellow-servant, Jack Rugby, are very completely described. Rugby is rather quaintly commended by Mrs. Quickly as "an honest, willing, kind fellow, as ever servant shall come in house withal, and, I warrant you, no tell-tale, nor no breed-bate. His worst fault is, that he is given to prayer; he is something peevish that way: but nobody but has his fault." We have a sidelong glance into this busybody's character when Falstaff adopts her suggestion to send his page to Mistress Page: "Look you," says she, "he may come and go between you both; and in any case have a nay-word, that you may know one another's mind, and the boy never need to understand any thing; for 't is not good that children should know any wickedness: old folks, you know, have discretion, as they say, and know the world."

Sir Hugh Evans, ("Sir," a title which in those days was given to the clergy,) the Welsh parson, with his "pribbles and prabbles," and who, in speech, "makes fritters of English," is an excellent character in all respects. He is as respectable as he is laughable. He has "very good discretions and very odd humours." Nym, Bardolph, and Pistol are but the shadows of what they were; and Justice Shallow, who has lived "fourscore years and upward" and is in his dotage, should not have left his seat in Gloucestershire and his magisterial duties. In this play he has little of his former consequence left. But his cousin, Abraham Slender, makes up for the deficiency. "He is," as Hazlitt says, "a very potent piece of imbecility. In him the pretensions of the worthy Gloucestershire family are well kept up, and immortalized."

Little as he has to do, Slender is the character that most frequently floats before our fancy when we think of this comedy. We do not wish Anne Page to have been married to him, but in their poetical alliance they are inseparable. Some of the touches, which only Shakespeare's hand could give, are to be found in the character of Slender, as, " I 'll ne'er be drunk whilst I live again, but in honest, civil, godly company, for this trick ! If I be drunk, I 'll be drunk with those that have the fear of God, and not with drunken knaves "— which resolve, as Evans says, shows his "virtuous mind." We have a speaking portrait of Slender in the conversation between Mrs. Quickly and his man, Peter Simple : "He hath but a little wee face, with a little yellow beard, a Cain-coloured beard." He is "as tall a man of his hands as any is between this and his head ; he hath fought with a warrener. . . . He holds up his head, as it were, and struts in his gait." Master Abraham Slender's own estimate of himself is that he is "not altogether an ass"; but Mrs. Page, who declares that the doctor hath her good will, and none but he, to marry with Nan Page, says : "That Slender, though well-landed, is an idiot." Master Abraham does not hide his station in society, especially from the women, and takes care that Anne Page shall know that he "keeps three men and a boy yet, till his mother be dead"; and that he "lives like a poor gentleman born." He says this before Anne, not to her. Bashful even to sheepishness, he is yet closely observant of her, and remarks to Evans : "She has brown hair, and speaks small like a woman." Often he sighs and says gently to himself, "O, sweet Anne Page !" But she says sadly to herself :

> This is my father's choice.
> O, what a world of vile ill-favour'd faults
> Looks handsome in three hundred pounds a-year !

Slender is such a faint-hearted and shilly-shally suitor that he is compelled to borrow all the suggestions of his passion from his uncle :

Shal. She 's coming ; to her, coz. O boy, thou hadst a father !
Slen. I had a father, Mistress Anne ; my uncle can tell you good jests of him.—Pray you, uncle, tell Mistress Anne the jest, how my father stole two geese out of a pen, good uncle.
Shal. Mistress Anne, my cousin loves you.
Slen. Ay, that I do ; as well as I love any woman in Gloucestershire.
Shal. He will maintain you like a gentlewoman.
Slen. Ay, that I will, come cut and long-tail, under the degree of a squire.
Shal. He will make you a hundred and fifty pounds jointure.
Anne. Good Master Shallow, let him woo for himself.

Thereupon Justice Shallow departs ; and when Slender, *solus cum solâ*, is put in the embarrassing position of being allowed to woo for himself, the dialogue proceeds :

Anne. Now, Master Slender,—
Slen. Now, good Mistress Anne,—
Anne. What is your will?
Slen. My will ! 'od's heartlings, that 's a pretty jest indeed ! I ne'er made my will yet, I thank heaven ; I am not such a sickly creature, I give heaven praise.
Anne. I mean, Master Slender, what would you with me ?
Slen. Truly, for mine own part, I would little or nothing with you. Your father and my uncle hath made motions : if

it be my luck, so ; if not, happy man be his dole ! They can tell you how things go better than I can : you may ask your father.

But Mistress Anne loves neither her father's nor her mother's choice for her husband ; and rather than marry the latter, she says :

> Alas, I had rather be set quick i' the earth
> And bowl'd to death with turnips !

Master Fenton, a gay, wild young fellow, like Bassanio of *The Merchant of Venice*, loves sweet Nan. He meant to marry for money, but is won from it by love. In answer to his report of her father's objection to him, that " 't is impossible he should love her but as a property," Anne candidly says, " May be he tells you true," and he as candidly replies :

> No, heaven so speed me in my time to come !
> Albeit I will confess thy father's wealth
> Was the first motive that I woo'd thee, Anne,
> Yet, wooing thee, I found thee of more value
> Than stamps in gold or sums in sealed bags ;
> And 't is the very riches of thyself
> That now I aim at.

He 's frank, resolute, and lovable, and a friend of the host of the Garter Inn, and a friend, too, of the hostess, who describes him thus : " He capers, he dances, he has eyes of youth, he writes verses, he speaks holiday, he smells April and May." His beloved is thus sketched by Furnivall in his introduction to this play : " The sweetness of 'sweet Anne Page' is all through it.   A choice bud in the rose-bud garden of girls of Shakespeare's time, she is, this young heiress, not seventeen, pretty virginity, brown-haired, small-voiced, whose words are so few, yet whose presence is felt all through the play.   True to her love she is, ready-witted almost as Portia ; dutiful to her parents, so far as she should be, and then disobeying them for the higher law of love.   Her real value is shown by the efforts of three lovers to get her."

At the party, held at night at Herne's Oak in the park for the special benefit of Falstaff in the character of the "Stag at Bay," where all the actors were "mask'd and vizarded," we are not sorry that sweet Nan, dressed as the Fairy Queen, did not, as her father had commanded, slip away with Slender to Eton, there immediately to be married ; that Doctor Caius did not "shuffle her away," as her mother had appointed, and that his outcry was : "By gar, I am cozened ; I ha' married un garçon, a boy."   Alas for poor Slender, who says : "I went to her in white, and cried 'mum,' and she cried 'budget,' as Anne and I had appointed ; and yet it was not Anne, but a postmaster's boy."   But we are doubly glad that the young lover, gentle Master Fenton, with his eyes of youth and writing verses and smelling April and May, got the right Anne, and 'twixt twelve and one, slipped away with her to church where was a vicar, who straight did make the twain one.   The happy pair returns and the play ends, thus :

Page. How now, Master Fenton !

Anne. Pardon, good father !—good my mother, pardon !

Page. Now, mistress, how chance you went not with Master Slender?

Mrs. Page. Why went you not with master doctor, maid?

Fenton. You do amaze her ; hear the truth of it.

    You would have married her most shamefully,
    Where there was no proportion held in love.
    The truth is, she and I, long since contracted,
    Are now so sure that nothing can dissolve us.
    The offence is holy that she hath committed ;
    And this deceit loses the name of craft,
    Of disobedience, or unduteous title,
    Since therein she doth evitate and shun
    A thousand irreligious cursed hours,
    Which forced marriage would have brought upon her.

Ford. Stand not amaz'd ; here is no remedy.

    In love the heavens themselves do guide the state ;
    Money buys lands, and wives are sold by fate.

Fal. I am glad, though you have ta'en a special stand to strike at me, that your arrow hath glanced.

Page. Well, what remedy?—Fenton, heaven give thee joy !

    What cannot be eschew'd must be embrac'd.

Fal. When night-dogs run, all sorts of deer are chas'd.

Mrs. Page. Well, I will muse no further.—Master Fenton,

    Heaven give you many, many merry days !—
    Good husband, let us every one go home,
    And laugh this sport o'er by a country fire,—
    Sir John and all.

VI.

AFTER Royal Hal had given Sir John Falstaff a
nunc dimittis from the Fleet Prison, reassured him
that he should have "competence of life " lest lack
of means would enforce him to evil, and that
"advancement " would be given him according to
his strengths and qualities in case he reformed—in
such a pleasant predicament, it may reasonably be
supposed that Sir John intended to settle down
and pass his last years in careless jollity and lazy
luxury at the Boar's Head tavern in Eastcheap.
At this turning-point in his chequered and sack-
soaked career, he could no longer claim to be " in
the vaward of his youth." His friends had, years
before and in spite of his oft-repeated protests, set

down his name in the scroll of old men ; and his
enemies regarded him as too-too old, and nearing
the end of his graveward path. But what his age
was in fact, no chronicler can find out. He told
the Chief Justice that he was born about three of
the clock in the afternoon. Now, it is noteworthy
that he who was so precise as to the hour of his
birth, did not also mention the month, the day of
the month, and the year in which that important
event occurred. We shall not be far wrong, probably, if we set down 1340 as the year of Falstaff's
birth. "Why do you fix upon that year ?" asks
the agnostic critic, who is, of course, a stern stickler
for facts, and slams the door in the face of everything which he thinks has not been shown to be
certain. Listen. A year or two before the battle
of Shrewsbury, which was fought 21st July, 1403,
Sir John admitted to Prince Hal that his age was
"some fifty, or, by 'r Lady, inclining to three score."
Although Falstaff was not habitually truthful—was
indeed unrivalled as a truth-crusher—yet it may
reasonably be presumed that he did not then
overstate his age. Afterward, the Chief Justice
reproved him for calling himself young and hot-
livered, and asked him a dozen direct questions in
a string, all touching his age—the last being whether
every part about him was not blasted with antiquity. As the whole series of questions elicited
from Sir John no negative answer to any one of
them, it seems that, on this issue, judgment ought
to go against him. As Prince Hal was crowned as
King Henry V., 9th April, 1413, and on that day

the Chief Justice sent Sir John to the Fleet, he must, on this King's coronation-day, have been declining from three score and ten at least.

It is also permissible to suppose that when Falstaff was set at liberty, he thought himself, as defendant, finally free from " the rusty curb of old Father Antic, the Law " ; but it now seems that he was not. Although it is nowhere recorded that Judge Gascoigne ever again laid him by the heels, or even brought him in question for any felony or misdemeanor, yet it appears from a certain old, outlandish, and musty manuscript, which has luckily escaped " the tooth of time and razure of oblivion," and which has lately been discovered and deciphered, that, soon after he was let out of prison, he was apprehended and brought before Justices Shallow and Silence, and Abraham Slender as *amicus curiæ*, to be examined touching many and grievous public offences charged and formulated against him. It also appears from the manuscript aforesaid, and certain old letters and papers of the Shallow family, that the learned Welsh parson, Sir Hugh Evans, served as clerk of this court, Fang as sheriff, and Snare, Grabbe, and Ketchum as under-bailiffs ; that among the witnesses, both for the Crown and for the alleged culprit, were Peto, Corporal Nym, Lieutenant Bardolph, Ancient Pistol, Mistress Quickly, Doll Tearsheet, Master George Page and wife and son, William, Master Ford, *alias* Brook, and wife, Doctor Caius, and the host of the Garter Inn ; also, Justice Shallow's man, Davy, Slender's man, Peter Simple, and the recruits enlisted by Sir John, to wit, Ralph Mouldy, Simon Shadow, Thomas Wart, Francis Feeble, and Peter Bullcalf; and that the court was held at the Boar's Head tavern in Eastcheap, London.

In addition to what has already been written of the members of this court, it may be said that Falstaff, on his return from York, made a second visit to Master Robert Shallow in Gloucestershire. During this visit, and after a singularly characteristic and very amusing dialogue between the justice and his man, Davy, Sir John is left alone, and thus soliloquizes : " If I were sawed into quantities, I should make four dozen of such bearded hermits' staves as Master Shallow. It is a wonderful thing to see the semblable coherence of his men's spirits and his : they, by observing of him, do bear themselves like foolish justices ; he, by conversing with them, is turned into a justice-like serving-man. Their spirits are so married in conjunction with the participation of society that they flock together in consent, like so many wild-geese. If I had a suit to Master Shallow, I would humour his men with the imputation of being near their master ; if to his men, I would curry with Master Shallow that no man could better command his servants. It is certain that either wise bearing or ignorant carriage is caught, as men take diseases, one of another ; therefore let men take heed of their company. I will devise matter enough out of this Shallow to keep Prince Harry in continual laughter the wearing out of six fashions, which is four terms,

or two actions, and a' shall laugh without inter-
vallums." *

Moreover, Justice Shallow was distinguished for
loquacity, opiniatrety, and, as Macaulay says of
Dr. Sam Johnson, " the anfractuosities of his intellect and temper." Justice Silence—doubtless a
descendant of the Roman historian, Tacitus—was
noted for taciturnity ; and Master Slender was
famed for his extreme simplicity. It ought, however, to be here recorded in favor of 'Squire
Shallow and his cousin Silence, that it is not known
that either of these ancient worthies, with all his
oddities and weaknesses, ever, by his magisterial
misconduct, justified " the common resemblance of
the courts of justice to the bush, whereunto while
the sheep flies for defence against weather [storm],
he is sure to lose part of his fleece " (Bacon's
essay, *Of Judicature*) ; or answered the description
given by a member of the House of Commons in
1601, who defined a " justice of the peace " as
a creature that " for half a dozen chickens will
dispense with half a dozen penal statutes."

By way of preface to the report of the examination of Sir John Falstaff before the worshipful Jus-

---

* On this soliloquy Clarke comments : " The relish with
which Falstaff each time stays by himself to witticize upon
Shallow's peculiarities, the gusto with which he makes the
justice's leanness furnish him with as ample store of humour as
his own fatness, the shrewdness with which he penetrates the
truth of the relative qualities and positions of the country
magistrate and his serving-man, all show how thoroughly the
author himself enjoyed the composition of this thrice-admirable
comedy-portrait character."

tices Shallow and Silence upon the many charges preferred against him, it is meet that the strange story of the discovery of the manuscript notes of the trial, which, supplemented by certain curious letters and papers, constitute the only known record thereof, be now briefly told : Also, that an account be given of the translation of the manuscript, and a summary of the counts contained in the information filed against Falstaff. It is duly recorded that Robert Shallow, esquire, was " a gentleman born, who wrote himself *armigero*, in any bill, warrant, quittance, or obligation," and that his ancestors in Gloucestershire had so written themselves " any time these three hundred years." It may, therefore, be very reasonably inferred that, among his kith and kin and after the lapse of so many years, the office of justice of the peace had become so firmly fibred into and through the Shallow family as to cause many of the sons therein to become justices by heredity, and that, at least in its main branches, it has so continued, even unto this day. As Swedenborg says of some religious dogmas held by certain bigots, they are glued to their brains. So it was, and so it has continued to be, with the Shallow stock—the office of justice of the peace is glued to their brains, and hence it runs in the family. The oldest sons thereof, generation after generation, are born so. This famous family seems not to have had its *habitat* only in the county of Gloucester, but to be prevalent throughout Great Britain, and elsewhere in the English-speaking world. It has, in fact, forked, bifurcated and branched in all directions. Hence Shakespeare's description of the fifth age of the seven ages of man, is generic :

> . . . . And then the justice,
> In fair round belly with good capon lined,
> With eyes severe and beard of formal cut,
> Full of wise saws and modern instances ;
> And so he plays his part.

It is noteworthy that, in the case of Justice Shallow, this description does n't fit. He is not built that way. He is characterized neither by tough muscularity of mind nor of body. There is no rotundity in any part of his anatomy ; and the notion that his eyes could be severe, or that his beard— probably in his youth " a little yellow beard," like that of Abraham Slender—could be formally cut so as to give anything like judicial solemnity to his " little wee face "—such an idea is inherently absurd ; and besides, the make-up of the man's mind confutes the supposition that he could be " full of wise saws and modern instances."

Shallow, being an octogenarian justice at the time of Falstaff's trial, probably died soon after it took place ; but it may be presumed that he left a son to fill the official vacancy caused by his death. And doubtless this son begat a son who reigned in his stead after he slept with his fathers. And so, according to the book of the genealogy of the Shallow family, the heads thereof went on from the reign of King Henry V., generation after generation, begetting justices of the peace to a period within " the spacious times of great Elizabeth." Before this queen's reign the Shallow stock had been much improved by marriages outside of the Silence and the Slender families. Thomas Shallow, esquire, had married a wealthy woman of good sense and great beauty, Anne Page Fenton, a lineal descendant of gentle Master Fenton and his wife, " sweet Anne Page." Their eldest son was William, who married Rosalind Fenton, a descendant of a branch of the Fenton family long settled near Windsor. William Shallow and his wife Rosalind had three sons, Robert, Henry, and Hugh ; and two daughters, Anne and Elizabeth.

When James I. began to reign, the Shallows had greatly gentled their condition in mind, body, and estate. The bodies of some of them were heightened and rounded, broadened and beautified ; their intellects were enlarged and strengthened, their tempers sweetened, and their eyes brightened beneath foreheads not " villanous low." They also thought more and talked less—were not, as some of their ancestors had been, afflicted with an offensive flux of words without ideas. They no longer spoke in jerky, strident tones, which give the impression of inferior brain power. Many of the daughters were brightsome, brown-haired, and small-voiced like that sweet Anne Page for whom Master Abraham Slender had long before vainly sighed, and sighed.

During the last years of the reign of James I., the principal justice of the peace in the county of Gloucester was Thomas Shallow, who lived on an estate which had for ages been owned by his ancestors, and abode in "a goodly dwelling and a rich," wherein had dwelt the famous justice of Falstaff's time.   This Thomas was knighted by the King—it does not appear why.   Sir Thomas had two sons—the younger, Robert, a gifted and spirited scapegrace, was a student at Oxford, left the university without a degree, and became a law student at Clement's Inn.   Emulous of the name and fame of his great precursor and prototype, the "mad Shallow" who long before had been one of the foremost swinge-bucklers in all the inns o' court, this young Robert Shallow turned his back upon his books, led a roistering life, and became the protagonist of the young swash-bucklers of his time at Clement's Inn.   Still he contrived to pick up some "nice sharp quillets of the law," and also learned to smoke tobacco, in spite of the *Counterblast to Tobacco* written by his Majesty ("his Sowship," as the King's greatest favorite used to call him), to discourage its use.   He so doted on "divine, rare, superexcellent tobacco, a virtuous herb, if it be well qualified, opportunely taken, and medicinally used," * that he lived in a cloud of smoke, often.

---

* " Tobacco, divine, rare, superexcellent tobacco, which goes far beyond all the panaceas, potable gold, and philosopher's stones, a sovereign remedy to all diseases. A good vomit, I confess, a virtuous herb, if it be well qualified, opportunely taken, and medicinally used ; but as it is commonly abused by most men, which take it as tinkers do ale, 't is a plague, a mischief, a violent purger of goods, lands, health, hellish, devilish, and damned tobacco, the ruin and overthrow of body and soul."
—BURTON's *Anatomy of Melancholy*.

thought of Virginia where the plant grew, and
longed to join a company of " useless gentlemen "
who were about to go there.   After this prodigal
son had wasted his substance with riotous living,
he began to be in want.   And he left London and
walked into Berkshire, where, at the close of a long
day's journey, being weary, foot-sore, and hungry,
he sought and found food and shelter at the Sow-
and-Acorn Inn.   At this hostelry he fed and rested
several days, but having no money to pay for his
entertainment, either as man or beast, the thrifty
inn-keeper bristled up himself, waxed wroth, and
swore the impecunious young man into the office of
hogrubber, and forthwith sent him into his fields to
feed swine, and eat with them, and thereby pay for
his board and lodging.   There he found husks as
food very filling, but by no means satisfying.   When
he came to himself and seriously considered his
low estate, he pronounced upon his companions a
malediction, to the effect that the whole lot of
Berkshires, their owner included, might be be-
deviled, and, like the herd of devil-possessed
Gadarene swine, run violently down a steep place
into the sea, and be choked therein.   And then he
arose, shucked himself out of his environment, and
straightway went to his father's house in Gloucestershire.   Sir Thomas had compassion on his wayward
son, fell on his neck and kissed him, caused him to
be well clothed, bounteously fed, and delighted
with music.   But the young man soon grew weary
of humdrum life in the country, and eager to go
in search of adventures and riches beneath alien

stars. He daily besought his father to furnish him forth, and let him voyage to Virginia.

At this time the colonists had given up seeking a communication with the South Sea by ascending the Chickahominy, or some other stream which flows from the northwest ; nor did they any longer expect to find the Pacific Ocean just beyond the falls in James River. And the class of whom Captain John Smith wrote, "there was now no talk, no hope, no work, but dig gold, wash gold, refine gold, load gold,"—this sect of gold-finders had become extinct. The news reached Sir Thomas what great gains were to be got by cultivating tobacco in that colony, and that the settlers, in their eagerness for gain, had planted not only the fields, but the gardens, the public squares, and even the streets of Jamestown, and that Virginia was to be enriched by the culture of this valuable staple.

While the father was considering his son's petition, Robert went to London, where by great good fortune, he met his friend and fellow-student at Clement's Inn, Philip Wriothesly, a nephew of Shakespeare's early friend and patron, the popular Earl of Southampton, who was a leader in the London Company, and exulted in the anticipated glories of the rising state in Virginia, and who was about to send young Philip thither to seek his fortune. The nephew introduced Robert to his uncle. His lordship was well pleased with Master Shallow, and anxious that he should embark with young Wriothesly. Accordingly the earl wrote to Sir

Thomas on behalf of Robert, and also gave him a letter of commendation which proved to be of great service to him in the colony. Robert returned joyfully home. The father consented on his son's twenty-first birthday, gave him £500, plenty of good advice and his blessing, together with a certain huge iron-bound chest which had been for centuries an heirloom in the Shallow family, and into which it had been customary, from time to time, to toss and tumble all sorts of papers, documents, memoranda, and MSS., pertaining to that famous family. Robert, in his heedless and headlong haste to return to London, and set sail with his friend Philip, pitched and tumbled into this chest or trunk, and upon the *omnium gatherum* therein, his clothes, books, papers, keepsakes, and other articles of personal property, securely locked it, lost the key, bade farewell to his father and mother, brothers and sisters, took his trunk and travelled posthaste to London. He reached the city just in time to engage his passage with his friend on the *Queen Bess*, a ship belonging to the Virginia Company, and about to sail with new recruits and supplies for Jamestown. As emigrants the company had, here and there, in the skirts of England, Scotland, and Wales,

> Shark'd up a list of landless resolutes,
> For food and diet to some enterprise
> That hath a stomach in 't—

about one hundred and ten in all, consisting chiefly of vagabond and useless gentlemen, dissolute gallants, packed off to escape worse destinies at home, broken tradesmen, rakes and libertines, men more fitted to corrupt than to found a commonwealth, several goldsmiths, who still had lingering hopes of finding gold, and many "apprenticed servants" from England, who were to be sold for a certain number of years to the planters ; but among these emigrants were too few carpenters, husbandmen, gardeners, fishermen, masons, blacksmiths, "accomplished wood-cutters and diggers-up of trees' roots," and "honest laborers, burdened with wives and children."

Knox, in his *Fragment of Races*, states the following rash and unsatisfactory, but pungent and unforgetable, truths : "Nature respects race, and not hybrids." "Every race has its own *habitat.*" "Detach a colony from the race, and it deteriorates to the crab." On the foregoing, Emerson thus comments : "See the shades of the picture. The German and Irish millions, like the Negro, have a great deal of guano in their destiny. They are ferried over the Atlantic, and carted over America, to ditch and to drudge, to make corn cheap, and then to lie down prematurely to make a spot of green grass on the prairie." Surely there must have been "a great deal of guano" and little else in the destiny of such a cargo of emigrants ; but Robert and Philip were fated to embark with them, and, after a long and tempestuous voyage, to land in Virginia, and there to begin their struggle for life in the new hemisphere.

The colonists had found the soil so productive,

and the cultivation of tobacco so profitable, that
when Master Shallow arrived in Virginia, they " so
much doted on their tobacco " that they paid little
attention to commerce or the fisheries. Tobacco
had given animation to Virginian industry, and was
fast becoming not only the staple, but the currency
of the colony. Both Robert and his friend were
anxious to own land, settle upon and improve it,
become tobacco planters, and grow up with the
country. Philip went up the James River to a
plantation, which, in honor of Prince Henry, a
general favorite with the English people, had been
named Henrico ; and there he remained two or
three years without succeeding to his satisfaction.
Soon afterward he removed to a region which is
now Southampton County, and there settled upon
a large body of land that he purchased with money
generously furnished by his uncle, the Earl of
Southampton.

Robert was at first inclined to take, near the
mouth of the Appomattox River, the one hundred
acres of land to which he was entitled as a colo-
nist who had come at his own expense, and to add
largely thereto by the purchase of other lands ; but
he changed his plans. His father, having heard of
his good behavior, and being highly pleased with
his tendency to thrift, wrote him words of cheer,
and also sent him £1,000, with advice to buy good
and cheap lands, and lay the ground plan for a
large fortune for himself and the prosperous growth
of a transplanted branch of the illustrious Shallow
family. Robert followed his father's advice, and

bought of the London Company—paying at the rate of twelve pounds and ten shillings for every hundred acres—ten thousand acres of very fertile land in what is now Gloucester County, so named by its first settlers, who were mostly from the shire so named in Old England. By the way, they soon discovered the York River oyster, detected its fine flavor, and swallowed it without a thought of what Prof. Huxley says of this bivalve: "I suppose that when this slippery morsel glides along the palate few people imagine that they are swallowing a piece of machinery far more complicated than a watch." It appears, however, that their ignorance in this respect harmed them not.

Master Shallow's land was situated on the left bank of York River, and near the mouth thereof, and in the region, now so celebrated, where the youthful Lafayette hovered upon the skirts of Cornwallis, and the arms of France and the Confederacy were united to achieve the crowning victory of American independence. He soon bought several apprenticed white servants and two or three negroes, hired a number of men skilled in felling trees and digging up their roots, a carpenter, a mason, a blacksmith, and an honest laborer, burdened with a wife and children. Thus reinforced he settled upon his land, and began to improve it. In the rude husbandry of the time and place, he raised corn, horses, horned beasts, swine, and tobacco. He built his house upon the spot where, according to tradition, Powhatan and his breech-clouted council of grim warriors doomed Captain

John Smith to die, and Pocahontas clung firmly to his neck as his head was bowed to receive the strokes of the tomahawk, and by her fearlessness and entreaties persuaded the council to spare the agreeable stranger, who might make hatchets for her father and rattles and strings of beads for herself, the favorite child.* Perhaps Robert's house was like the mansion in which Washington was born, in Westmoreland County, Virginia: A rude farmhouse, steep-roofed, with low eaves, one story high, having four rooms on the ground floor, and others in the attic. There was a huge chimney at each end, which was built up outside the house.

Young Robert Shallow, having his own house, wanted a wife in it. He did not fall in love with

---

* Irving Browne, Esq., in his *Iconoclasm and Whitewash*, (pp. 15, 16,) says: "One of the most ruthless results of modern historical iconoclasm has heen the demolition of Pocahontas. About the prosaic and somewhat common name of John Smith, until recently, has entwined one of the sweetest of legends. But alas for faith in history and in human nature! and alas for some of the first families of Virginia! the fair fame of the lovely copper-colored maiden has received a deadly smirch from a prying investigator. We are now assured that the Indian princess was a mere camp follower of the whites, and of the most light and naughty behavior. Captain Smith was notoriously a very gallant man among the ladies, and it is not incredible that she had the strongest motive for rescuing the adventurer from the club of her father. Others say that Smith, who was a notorious liar, invented the story of his rescue. A writer in *Scribner's Magazine* points out the anachronistic, if not apochryphal, character of the painting of the baptism of Pocahontas, in the National Capitol at Washington. We are fain to dismiss Pocahontas with a sigh."

and propose to Lady Clara Vere de Vere, because
she was not then in the colony. He bought for a
wife Miss Angelica Penelope Dusenbury, and paid
for her the highest market price, one hundred and
fifty pounds of tobacco. She was the choicest of
the ninety "maids of virtuous education, young,
handsome, and well-recommended," sent out by
the London Company from England for planters'
wives. Robert and his Angelica loved each other,
were wedded, went to housekeeping, lived together
for half a century and upward—happily, 't is to be
presumed—and to them were born sons and
daughters. Thus was founded in " The Old Dominion," one of the genuine " F. F. V.'s "—a
family which was destined in due time to be in
some sort royalized by intermarriage with a family
having a strain of Pocahontas blood in its veins.

By and by, the judicial instinct was aroused in
Robert, and he longed to be a justice of the peace
in Gloucester County, Virginia. One lucky day
he chanced to fish out from among the papers and
documents in the chest which he had brought from
his old home, the commission of Solomon Shallow
as a justice of the peace in Gloucestershire, England. Instantly the idea occurred to him that he
might easily make himself a magistrate. This he
at once proceeded to do by a unique and ingenious
application of the statutes of amendment and
jeofails. It consisted of certain amendments of
the old and outlawed commission aforesaid, which
were effected by a careful erasure of the name
"Solomon " and the insertion of " Robert " in

place of it ; by removing the word " England " and writing " Virginia " in its stead ; and by making some other changes in the document which the necessities of the case at bar demanded. And so he became one of the king's magistrates *de facto* in the colony, and acted acceptably as such for many years, notwithstanding the bar sinister thus secretly emblazoned on his title to that office. Robert Shallow, justice of the peace, year after year, grew richer and richer, prouder and prouder, and before a score of years had passed since he settled in the colony he moved into a stately mansion built of imported brick, and having carved mahogany stairways, curiously panelled rooms, with richly decorated ceilings, and so forth. He was a staunch royalist ; was for many years a member of the House of Burgesses ; dreaded the general diffusion of intelligence ; and concurred with the Virginia governor, who, in 1671, wrote, " I thank God, there are no free schools, nor printing ; and I hope we shall not have, these hundred years ; for learning has brought disobedience, and heresy, and sects into the world, and printing has divulged them, and libels against the best government. God keep us from both." Moreover, like many other colonial gentlemen, he was fond of a manly out-of-door life, owned many negroes, kept open house, and was noted for his rough and generous hospitality. As to his religious views, they seem to have been well stated by that dogmatic divine, and tremendous theologaster, Mr. Thwackum, who, in Fielding's *Tom Jones*, thus speaks : " When I mention religion, I mean the Christian religion ; and not only the Christian religion, but the Protestant religion ; and not only the Protestant religion, but the Church of England." 'Squire Shallow died on his eightieth birthday, and was buried in the family cemetery on the Shallow plantation, and beside his wife who had died some years before. A steep hillock a mile east of that on which the mansion-house stood, and separated from it by a bosky ravine, was then crowned with tall and stately forest trees, among which were four gigantic, unwedgeable, and gnarled oaks, marking the corners of a small rectangular quadrangle. Under the shadows of those trees, and exactly in the centre of that quadrangle, Justice Shallow's grave was, and on his marble monument his effigy in high relief, and the following inscription :

Hic Jacet

ROBERTUS SHALLOW, Armiger :

Obiit, XXVI. Septembris,

MDCLXXXV,

Æt. LXXX.

Non opibus urna, nec mens

virtutibus absit.

On the eve of the American revolution the original Shallow family in Virginia had reached its zenith in mind, body, and estate. Soon thereafter its descent began, becoming more rapid as the years went by. At the time of the passage of the Kansas-Nebraska bill, it was nearing its nadir, and seemed about to peter out, so to speak. The patrimonial estate had so dwindled away, generation after generation, that hardly a hundred of the ancestral acres remained in the family ; and these were so plastered over and covered up by divers deeds and mortgages, drawn up with such infernal artifice and diabolical skill, that all the lawyers in Gloucester County were not able to decide, by a legal construction of their various conflicting clauses and conditions, to whom the land belonged, or whether it belonged to anybody at all. Near the ruins of the mansion built by him whose epitaph has just been quoted, stood a low, rambling, wooden, weather-beaten house, which was very old, in a tumble-down condition, deeply embowered in grapevines, and surrounded by jimson weeds of rampant and outrageous growth. The doors were off the hinges, old hats, trousers, and petticoats were stuffed into the broken windows, the roof of one wing had fallen in, and a huge chimney at one end of the house had toppled down headlong. The only negroes left on the plantation were Jupiter and his wife, Juno, both warmly attached to their master and mistress, and too aged and tottery to run away. Their master, William Shakespeare Shallow, was, in physical and psychical structure, the outcome of some queer law of reversional heredity which hinted at a remote period when his ancestors were perhaps in a polliwog state, and had "souls so dull and stupid as to serve for little else but to keep their bodies from putrefaction." * He was a little, wearish, old man, who had a bald pate,

---

* Dr. Robert South's sermon, "On the Education of Youth."

a frog-like forehead, large, green, glassy eyes with
a squint in one thereof, sail-like ears, a nimble
tongue, a croaking voice which was subject to sudden and ludicrous changes in its fundamental bass,
a weak and receding chin, and a bottle nose of
abnormal rubicundity. Moreover, he was splay-
mouthed, as well as splayfooted. Easy-going and
good-natured, slipshod and shiftless, he had an in-
superable aversion to all kinds of profitable labor.
To live seemed to him to mean nothing more than
to be, and to play pitch-and-toss with the realities
of life. Besides being in body the very genius of
famine, he was also the very genius of drouth, and
absorbed liquids as readily as a sponge—seldom,
however, sucking in a good sherris-sack, or a mint-
julep, because of his impecunious condition, but
imbibing whiskey and other vulgar drinks, commonly at the expense of somebody else. It was observed that intoxicating liquor never brought him
on all-fours, or lessened his good-nature ; and
curiously enough, it seemed to have no more effect
on him than it has on the bottle which contains it,
save that it doubled the nimbleness of his tongue and
aggravated the redness of his Bardolphian nose.
After he had taken a drink or two his chief delight
was to sit on a dry-goods box along with other
idlers, chew tobacco, let his tongue run at random,
and argufy on almost any subject, but particularly
on politics. In his profound political discussions,
he often quoted from the Richmond *Enquirer* as
his authority, and now and then referred to those
bewildering mysteries, the Kentucky and Virginia

Resolutions of 1798–9, which he had probably never read, and which he could not comprehend if he had. He was not usually fastidious in regard to facts which border on the marvellous ; and akin to this trait, a credulity, a readiness to believe the marvellous, tinged his whole character and made him a believer in ghosts, witches, and hobgoblins. He did not pay his debts, and it was impossible to collect them by law. Hence his creditors hyphenated his surname, removed the initial *e* of the word "esquire," suffixed it to his family name, and accented the second, instead of the first, syllable thereof ; and so he came to be called and known throughout Gloucester County as 'Squire Shall-Owe. Such a husband was a great grief—a mere incubus, as 't were—to his wife, who was a robustious woman of termagant temper and fearsome voice, and a lineal descendant from Dame Rip Van Winkle. Of course, he stood greatly in awe of his wife, as well he might, for she " ruled the roast," such as it was, and suffered him to domineer in his weak way outside of the house—the only side which, in fact, belongs to a thoroughly henpecked husband.

At last 'Squire Shall-Owe and his wife took the scant proceeds of the dregs of their estate in Virginia, and along with their old colored servants, Jupiter and Juno, who went willingly, emigrated to Kansas early in its Territorial days ; there, if possible, to grow green again and flourish anew beneath another and more hopeful sky. He purchased and settled upon a quarter-section of land in a sequestered situation, lying mostly between the forks of Owl Creek, in Avon township, Coffey County, and about seven miles north of Zenith City, then a puny place of much noise and notoriety, but destined to become—in the estimation of its inhabitants—the county-seat and metropolis of all the region round about it. He built a small house in a group of goodly trees growing on a bluffy tongue of land in the forks of the above-named stream ; and some years later, and after he had been several times terrified by fierce winds which swept up and down Owl Creek—doubtless seduced there by the long draw or ravine made by its high banks—he dug, close to his cabin, a deep cave as a refuge from wind and weather. A few acres of his land were arable ; the residue was best adapted to raising hogs, sheep, and cattle. But a change of sky and environment did not change his nature ; his inborn shiftlessness remained. His views of life were mostly retrospective, and, moreover, he was such a tireless talker about the Old Dominion that he was given the nickname of " Ole Virginny." In the year of the great drouth in Kansas, Jupiter and Juno died ; in the great grasshopper year the 'squire's wife died ; and 't is likely that he too would have died during that chill and starving time, had he not received aid in the form of cast-off clothes, bread, bacon, and beans.

When the Kansas prohibitory liquor law was at last rigidly enforced, 'Squire Shall-Owe began to " dwindle, peak, and pine," and to become, if possible, more moody, dry, dusty, shrunken, and shadowy than ever before. Like certain variable quantities in mathematics, he lessened more and more until he neared the vanishing-point. About noontide on a certain hot summer-day, he was seen in Zenith City, lingering long alone in the vicinity of Tom Todhunter's late " Cornucopia," where he was snuffing and sniffing the empty kegs and casks thereabouts, as if to refresh his memory, and brace himself up with thoughts of the thousands of drinks which he had taken at that dried-up fountain—the most of them not costing him a cent, as they had been treats, or, if counted against him, marked on the slate. Later in the day he was observed lurking near Jerry Jones's deceased distillery, or brewery, and inhaling the intoxicating reminiscences thereat. An hour before sunset he was seen astride of a sorry little mule belonging to Conrad Copenhaver, leaving town and hurrying homeward to his lonely castle, to escape an impending storm of wind and rain. Before midnight a cyclone swept with resistless and destroying fury through the Owl Creek country, and thereafter 'Squire Shall-Owe was seen alive no more. The next day two or three of the neighbors visited the wind-swept premises of the late owner, and found the trees uprooted and prostrate, the cabin and its contents utterly wrecked, and the frag- ments scattered afar to the four winds ; and, in a deep gulch distant about a furlong northeast from the site of the dwelling, Copenhaver's ass lay life- less. The dead donkey was securely tied by a rope halter to an apple-tree which had long stood near the door of the lowly mansion, not only comforting its owner with its fruit, but also serving as a hitching-post and a Kansas stable. Evidently the 'squire had reached home in time to tie the poor beast to this tree, which the cyclone tore up and transported, along with its four-footed appendage, to the spot where both were discovered. But the 'squire himself was not found, although the search for him was continued for several days. The next week Wilhelm Grohbengreaser went up the east fork of Owl Creek two or three miles, to look for some of his sheep which had been scattered by the recent storm. As he was about to return home from his fruitless search his attention was attracted to a convention of crows in session among the leafy and wide-spreading branches of an elm overhanging the stream ; but as his thoughts were chiefly of his lost sheep, he gave, at the time, only slight heed to this circumstance. He mentioned the fact, however, to two or three inquisitive and sympathetic neighbors ; and, on the following day, all went to discover why the crows were in council as reported. When they reached the spot, the crow convention, at sight of a shotgun shouldered by Grohbengreaser, at once adjourned *sine die*, and the members thereof, with caws, flew and alighted beyond its range. The nimblest man of the company climbed the tree in question, and found in a crotch formed by its trunk and a stout branch, and firmly fixed therein, what was left of the mortal remains of old 'Squire Shall-Owe. He whose pedigree reached back to the Robert Shallow who had settled in the Virginia colony almost three centuries before, reached back

to the illustrious Justice Shallow of Falstaff's time,
ran back even to the days of William the Conqueror
—this man had been seized by the cyclone, whirled
far aloft and lodged "up a tree" in the spacious
mediterranean State of Kansas. Thither had he
been translated by the tempest, like a dry and
withered leaf, the very last leaf on his genealogical
tree.

In the absence of the coroner, the facts were submitted to a high-prairie justice of the peace in Avon
township, and learned in "crowner's quest law,"
who decided that no inquest was necessary in the
case, for the reason that if the body found was not
the body of old Bill Shakespeare Shall-Owe, whose
body could it be? And so this sapient magistrate
cudgelled his brains no more about it. The funeral
was held at the Hardshell Baptist church on Duck
Creek—the Rev. Jedediah Goshorn preaching upon
the two texts, to wit : "All flesh is grass."—Isaiah,
xiv., 12 ; " He shall be buried with the burial of an
ass."—Jeremiah, xxii., 19. His double-barrelled
sermon was a very powerful one, and it hit and
brought down the congregation, so to speak. During
its delivery, even that octogenarian sinner, Andy
Shanklin, was heard snuffling a little, and seen
brushing a tear-drop or two from his eyes, giving
the sharp end of his fiery red nose a wring with his
fingers, to free it of the superabundant moisture,
and then wiping it on his rusty and greasy coat-
sleeve. The body of the deceased was buried
beside that of his wife, in the graveyard near at
hand—the graves of Jupiter and Juno being hard by.

Conrad Copenhaver—hoping, probably, to realize out of the decedent's estate enough to satisfy his own claim for the loss of his mule—without due authority, intermeddled somewhat with the few goods and chattels which the deceased left behind him. Certain creditors, aggrieved by the acts of this officious intruder, submitted their claims to a veteran pettifogger in Zenith City, Alexander Black-stone, who took the whole matter under considera-tion, and, at the end of a fortnight, handed down his opinion, written over an entire quire of fools-cap ; which foolscap opinion was to the effect that Copenhaver had, by his unauthorized and officious acts, made himself executor *de son tort*, and liable to pay out of his own pocket whatever deficiency of assets there might be for the satisfaction of claims against the estate. Nothing, however, for the benefit of complaining creditors, resulted from this opinion, as was to be expected.

In the cyclone cave in which poor Shallow had failed to find refuge from death, were discovered some of his worldly effects, as follows : A shirt and a half ; a ragged coat ; a threadbare and torn pair of trousers ; a pair of old boots ; a rusty razor ; a coarse comb ; a patent medicine almanac ; a box of Brandreth's pills ; several old numbers of the Richmond *Enquirer ;* a bottle of Perry Davis's pain-killer ; corks and corkscrew ; empty bottles ; and a jug or two. Under a lot of trumpery was found a small box wherein were papers and pam-phlets, and several books—among them *Hogg's Poems, Ram on Facts* (befittingly bound in sheep),

7

Edgeworth's *Essay on Irish Bulls*, and Ruskin's theological treatise, *On the Construction of Sheep-folds*. The 'squire had picked up these books with the expectation, perhaps, of reading something therein to his advantage and profit in the business of raising hogs, sheep, and cattle. In the box were also Wirt's *Life of Patrick Henry*, Swan's *Treatise for Justices*, and a well-printed copy of Shakespeare's Plays, with uncut leaves.

In a well-walled and carefully cemented niche in a corner of the cave, was found, securely locked, the iron-bound chest or trunk, which had been for ages in the Shallow family, and which Robert, the son of Sir Thomas Shallow, had brought with him when he emigrated to the Virginia colony. This chest, along with its ancient and mysterious contents, 'Squire Shall-Owe had doubtless brought to Kansas in its early days. According to report among his friends and neighbors, he took vigilant care of it, and stood greatly in dread of its insides. It appears that he was reluctant to touch this ancestral ark, or to rummage therein with his unconsecrated hands ; and it seems that he was as much in awe of it as certain African tribes are of a stone or a stick which they worship as a fetich. But Copenhaver feared it not. He, assisted by an ex-constable, who, like his employer, could n't read English, took the chest out of its niche, and, having no key to unlock it, broke it open, and held an inquest upon its contents. Finding nothing of value in his estimation, he turned over the trunk and everything therein to the schoolmaster of the district, who had a smattering of Latin and Greek, and was reputed to be a semi-Shakespearian scholar withal. He fumbled for a fortnight, at intervals, with the papers, documents and memoranda given over to him, but even he could make nothing of them. Becoming curious at last as to the mechanism of the chest, he made a careful inspection thereof, found that it had a false bottom, and therein discovered a long and narrow parchment roll, closely and quaintly written all over in black letter, and having a surface about equal to that of a roll or two of wall-paper, or to the superficies of half a dozen sheepskins, or thereabouts. After pottering a long while over the manuscript, and finding it to be all Greek to him, he at first thought of presenting it to the Kansas Historical Society ; but he finally followed the advice of a brother pedagogue and of the justice of the peace who had held the inquest on the remains of " Ole Virginny," and submitted it, along with all the papers turned over to him by Copenhaver and the ex-constable, to a select committee of seven wise men, each being a specialist, and all resident in and around Zenith City—said committee to have power, through its chairman, to send for persons and papers, and to employ, at its own expense, a stenographer, a chemist, a microscopist, an acidist, a photographist, a hermeneuticist, a volapükist, and so forth. The committee chosen to Anglicize the manuscript and to determine the question of its genuineness, was constituted as follows, to wit :

Edward Coke Fogg, legist ;
Richard Bentley Smyth, Egyptologist ;
Ahasuerus Jones, Assyriologist ;
Richard Porson Diaganma, Hellenist ;
Martinus Scriblerus, Latinist ;
Ignatius De Mudd, cryptologist ;
Joel Levi, a learned " Ebrew Jew," who was also
a studious cabalist and Talmudist.

On St. Swithin's day in the afternoon, all the
members of the committee, along with other *literati*
of Zenith City, met in and around Tom Todhunter's
grocery or juicery, *née* Cornucopia, which for
divers good and sufficient reasons had lately been
adjusted on wheels and moved from the main
street into a grove across the Neosho River, and
outside of the city limits.   After an hour of conviviality, they retired to the rear of this wheeled
academy, where they found seats on benches and
empty beer-kegs in the shade of a gigantic syca-
more tree.   Then and there these seven wise men
forthwith laid their heads together and proceeded
to tackle the important document which had been
intrusted to them.   They read it—or rather, tried
to read it—backwards, and forwards, and sideways,
and some parts thereof they read, or tried to read,
again and again ; and thus they continued, between
drinks, to puzzle and pother over it, and to become
more and more bewildered in their wits, until near
supper-time, when they adjourned for that day.
And in this way they continued to dawdle over the
manuscript, day after day—Sundays and rainy
days excepted—until about the middle of the dog

days ; and still they could make neither head nor tail of the text. Each of these wiseacres had a theory and views of his own in regard to the document ; and they all resembled certain German critics of Shakespeare, as described by Richard Grant White : " Like the western diver, they go down deeper and stay down longer than other critics, but, like him, too, they come up muddier." Of the seven scholars, Prof. De Mudd was the most opinionated and obstreperous. His theory was that the most important parts of the document are cryptographic, and, of course, indecipherable without the cipher. As a consequence, he was all the while on the lookout for cipher-words, which he believed to be lurking somewhere in the text ; but, after searching for a month, he failed to find even one of them. The key which could unlock the mysteries of the manuscript seemed to be lost beyond recovery. However, one sultry afternoon, and just as the disgusted chairman of the committee was about to roll up the manuscript, weight it with a heavy stone, and fling it into the turbid waters of the Neosho River, a lucky suggestion came from an unexpected quarter, and rescued the precious document from oblivion. 'T is said that once on a time, the cackling of a goose saved Rome. However that may be, the volapükist of the committee, George Psalmanazar Wopsle, who was lying on a grassy knoll in the shade of a tree, fighting flies and fanning himself, opened his mouth and spake in a maudlin way, and on this wise : " Hold on, old Fogg, don't toss that scrub document to the catfish in the Noshow just yet, though it does have a very ancient and fish-like smell. You seven wise men, don't give up the job of finding out what it all means, if it means anything, but fight it out on this line or t' other, if it takes all summer. I say, De Mudd, it 'pears to me that you 're the knowingest of this lot of litery fellers, but that 's not saying a great deal. You 've been all the time a-hunting for the key, or the ' cipher,' as you call it. Now, you old zeroist, why don't you look for it in the marginal notes as you call 'em, or in them monstrous long-tailed words you 've been talking so much about ? What do you suppose them words was put into this 'ere manuscript for, unless 't was to hide something or other ? I say, De Mudd, you just bring that tough old dokkyment straight here to me, and I 'll show you some words as long as the shadows of your long legs late in the afternoon of a midsummer day, and written alongside of the text ; I can't pronounce any of 'em, but I 'll point 'em out to you ; there 's one monstrous word—the longest in the lot, and made up of such queer letters —which the writer has coiled up in a sort of cipher or round-robin style, in a ring that, to my critical eyes, seems to have been made by the damp bottom of a beer-glass set on the parchment. Between you and me, De Mudd, I 've gazed at that spiral word with my naked eyes, and peered at it through a microscope, as well as through a beer-glass of im- mense magnifying power, and puzzled over it, and followed it round and round, until it has made my head swim ; and I 've felt just like that man who thought himself so wondrous wise that he jumped into a brier-bush and scratched out both of his eyes out, and then he saw his eyes was out. And so I can't see which is the head, and which is the tail, of that word; but it may be, it has neither; still, a cipher may be lurking in it somewhere. Think about it, De Mudd; and do you study them long words strung along the sides of the manuscript; study 'em with all yer might and main for a month, and I'll bet my head agin yours for a football that you 'll be able to spell out something or other outen this thing. You think I'm not much of a litery feller; maybe I'm not, in your way; but I've been a printer's devil, and I've set type for and even edited a country newspaper, and I say that a man that can spell well, even if he can't do anything else, he's a well-educated man. De Mudd, you just put out Am-bi-gu-i-ty t' me, and see if I can't spell it. Besides, I've read into Shakespeare considerable myself, and I've seen some of his best Plays played. Lay on Macduff, and be damned to you, sir."

Wopsle continued his remarks in a broken, rambling, and peremptory way, to the amazed committee now gathered around him; but, becoming queasy, he soon grew inarticulate with retching. When the volapükist had sufficiently recovered, he took the manuscript from De Mudd's hand, and soon found, perpendicularly written in the margin thereof, the following longitudinous word: "*Honorificabilitudinitatibus*"—which word, Doctor Scriblerus at once said, occurs in Shakespeare's *Love's*

Labour 's Lost, Act V., Sc. 1. He also remarked that this is outdone by Rabelais with the following word :
" *Antipericatametaanaparbeugedamphicribrationes.*"

And thereupon Wopsle pointed out several other long words similarly written, here and there, along the edges of the text. These the committee peered at silently for a long while. At last, Wopsle took the manuscript, and, looking as wise as a scholiast, poked his finger at the word which had perplexed and bewildered him so utterly. And then Professor Digamma put on his spectacles, looked thereon, and said, " 't is a Greek word " ; and, after studying it for a few minutes and scratching his head during the while, he declared that 't is a word of fourteen syllables, which was coined by Aristophanes and by him used in his comedy entitled *The Wasps*. Moreover, he said that the learned Voss has framed a German equivalent * for this sesquipedalian word, and that the German word, like the Greek, is an example of agglutination rather than technical etymological composition. He also remarked that Aristophanes concocted and used in his *Ecclesiazusæ*, a word which, in the Greek, consists of seventy-seven syllables, as the name of a dish composed of a great number of ingredients ; and that Richter quotes Forster as authority for a Sanskrit compound of one hundred and fifty-two syllables. And furthermore,

. . . . *Desunt*

. . . . *cætera.*

---

* *Morgendämmerungshändelmacherrechtsverderbmühwanderung.*

As 't was as natural for Digamma to speak Greek as 't is for a pig to squeak, there 's no telling how long he would have talked, had not a vivid flash of lightning, a deafening thunder-clap, and some drops of rain brought his remarks to an abrupt conclusion. Owing to the impending storm, the business of the day was brought to a close on the jump, as 't were, thus: The task of translating the manuscript, of supplying, so far as it was possible, the many gaps therein, and giving an opinion as to its worth or worthlessness, was given over to a sub-committee consisting of De Mudd, Digamma, Scriblerus, Fogg, and Wopsle—a sort of kangaroo committee, as it proved to be, for its chief strength and efficiency lay, not in its frontispiece, but rather in its tailpiece; and, as a consequence, the tail wagged not only itself, but also the head and the body as well. Wopsle, however, seems to have been made a member of the sub-committee at the special instance and request of the chairman thereof. It was ordered that a report be made, if possible, on or before the last of the dog days. Acting upon certain hints given by the word ABRACADABRA, written in its peculiar mystical manner and in an obscure corner of the document, De Mudd and Wopsle soon discovered, cunningly concealed in certain of the long words aforesaid, the all-important cipher-words—five in number, quincuncially arranged and running throughout the text—which words worked like a charm in revealing the mysteries of the manuscript, and with the certainty of the multiplication-table, the sublimity of the binomial theorem, and the luminosity of the famous "Problem of the Lights," which used to be in M. Bourdon's treatise on algebra. The joy of the Pickwickians after the Chairman of their Club had, by the payment of ten shillings, rescued from a rustic an uneven and broken stone whereon he had detected a strange and curious inscription of unquestionable antiquity, to wit,

×

BILST

UM

PSHI

S.M.

ARK,

did not surpass the joy of De Mudd and Wopsle when their sedulous search for the cipher-words was crowned with success. Doubtless their delight equalled that of Champollion when he had at last interpreted the famous Rosetta stone which had so long puzzled Egyptologists. George Psalmanazar Wopsle himself exhibited such extraordinary ingenuity in mending many of the holes in the text of the manuscript, and so much facility in turning obsolete words and archaic phrases into newspaper English, that De Mudd came to have as high an opinion of his genius in these respects as Dr. Johnson had of the character, talents, and piety of George Psalmanazar of Formosa with whom he used to discuss theological and literary matters in an alehouse in London, and of whom he asserted that he would "as soon think of contradicting a bishop." Although Digamma and Scriblerus worked in the background, so to speak, of the sub-committee, yet they did their duty faithfully and well by digging and delving in the graves of the dead(and "damned," ut dicebat iste $\pi\alpha\nu o\tilde{\nu}\rho\gamma o\varsigma$ Gulielmus Cobbett,*) languages, resurrecting the scraps thereof embraced in the text of the document, clothing them in the English language of to-day, and compelling them to tell the secrets of their prison-house. Fogg did little, but to object, except, and demur to almost everything that was done, and to wrangle daily with Wopsle.

The task of the sub-committee was finished, and its report made in due time. Among the many special findings of fact contained in said report, are the following: The manuscript submitted to the committee is, in many places, a palimpsest; fortunately, however, the erasures have been so slightly made that the subsequent writing—much of which is criss-cross—has not wholly obscured the first writing; but, unfortunately, there are many *lacunæ* therein. The text is a polyglot, mostly made up of law Latin, law Norman, and old English, all sprinkled and seasoned with bits of Greek and Hebrew; and the scholarly writer thereof seems to have been "at a great feast of languages, and stolen the scraps." The manuscript abounds in obsolete words, and archaic expressions; its style is quaint and pleonastic, and has the "damnable iteration" peculiar to legal

---

* James Russell Lowell, in "Notices of an Independent Press," prefixed to his *Biglow Papers.*

documents. In intervals of employment the clerkly hand has indented and illuminated the text with ornamental letters and grotesque figures and pictures, and listlessly scribbled marginal notes thereto. The clerk has, in school-boy fashion—merely to try his goosequill pen, perhaps—scrawled here and there in the margins several long Greek and dog-Latin words, "best fitted for Gargantua's mouth, but too great for any mouth of this age's size." The document purports to be the notes taken of the examination of Sir John Falstaff before Justices Shallow and Silence, with Master Abraham Slender as a friend of the court, in regard to a long list of public offences charged against him. These notes appear to have been mostly written by the learned Welsh parson, Sir Hugh Evans, as the clerk of this half-way court. It also appears that Fang served as the sheriff of said court, and Snare, Grabbe, and Ketchum as under-bailiffs ; and that the examination was held at the Boar's Head tavern, in Eastcheap, London.

Though there are many hiatuses in the manuscript, yet Wopsle has, with amazing critical acumen, often divined what is wanting and supplied it in the translation ; but the rest of the gaps therein have been left vacant because no member of the sub-committee has been able to guess what is lacking. Sir Hugh's notes end so suddenly that 't is surmised that the greater part thereof has been lost, or that the trial, for some unknown cause, came to an abrupt conclusion. The document appears never to have been duly filed in any public office.

The information or complaint filed against Sir John, seems to have been prepared on behalf of the King, by a pleader who clearly anticipated the three kinds of certainty which Lord Coke distinguishes. (Co. Litt. 303a.) The substance, essence, or rather, the quintessence, of the charges formulated therein—these charges being freed from verbiage, archaisms, and vermiculate rhetoric, and translated into plain, every-day English—is that Sir John Falstaff is a

> Tavern-haunter ;
> drunkard ; Bacchanalian ;
> bootlegger ; saloonist ;
> wine-bibber ; sack-butt ;
> huge bombard of sack ;
> [*Hiatus in MS.*]
> Incomparable liar ;
> omnipotent villain ;
> fat old rogue ;
> oily old rascal ; greasy knight ;
> whoreson round man ;
> gorbellied knave ;
> swinge-buckler ;
> braggadocio ; coward ;
> thief ; robber ; purse-taker ;
> murderer (of "men in buckram") ;
> [*Alter hiatus in MS.*]
> Idler ; vagabond ; dead beat ;
> swindler ; spendthrift ; cheat ;
> parasite ; peculator ;
> perennial debtor ; roisterer ;
> gormandizer ; lewdster ;
> flatterer ; slanderer ; tattler ;

scandal-monger ; blackguard ;
blatherskite ; conversationalist ;
[*Ingens hiatus hic in MS.*]
Profane swearer ; low Churchman ;
latitudinarian ;
Epicurean ; Ephesian ; Corinthian ;
abominable misleader of youth ;
old white-bearded Satan ; *
[*Hiatus valdè deflendus in MS.*]

Bringing Sir John Falstaff before such a court was very like arraigning Gulliver on articles of impeachment for high treason and other capital crimes alleged to have been by him committed in the empire of Lilliput. It appears that he did not care to employ counsel to defend him, but that he attorneyed his own case.

All of the members of the sub-committee, save one, agreed that the manuscript is genuine, probably authentic, and possibly of some literary value. After mature consideration by the entire committee, all of the members thereof, except two, concurred in the foregoing opinion : And it was ordered that the original manuscript and all the other documents and papers of the late 'Squire Shall-Owe which had been submitted to the committee, together with the translation of the manu-

---

* The new words in the foregoing translation of the information filed against Falstaff, as well as certain low and slangy, but expressive, Americanisms appearing here and there, in the report of Sir John's trial, were doubtless inserted therein by Wopsle, who seems to have been the ringleader of the translators of the manuscript notes of the trial aforesaid.

script, and the report thereon, be deposited among the archives of Zenith City—Edward Coke Fogg and Joel Levi, dissenting. They gave it as their opinion that the manuscript itself is a forgery and of no literary worth whatever ; hinted that George Psalmanazar Wopsle, aided and abetted by Ignatius De Mudd, had fabricated the greater part of the purported translation thereof ; sneered at the other members of the committee for their gullibility ; protested against filing the papers as aforesaid ; and insisted that such documentary trash should be tossed into a waste-paper basket, or, rather, reduced to ashes. But at this juncture, Wopsle, who was then half-seas-over—he 'd been a sailor-boy— good-naturedly interposed, and said : " Come, come, gentlemen of the committee, I hope we shall drink down all unkindness ; let 's all drink on my score, and to the memory of the old boy built like a Dutch lugger and having a round forecastle,* to wit, old Jack Falstaff." And all responded, " Ay, ay, sir," and drank accordingly, *iterum iterumque*, until one or two—perhaps three—of the seven sages aforesaid were seen to lurch considerably, and to be in great danger of shifting their cargo

---

* A sailor who had just come into port with a full pocket paid Stephen Kemble thirty pounds to have a performance of *Henry IV.* all to himself, with Kemble as " the old boy with the round forecastle, built like a Dutch lugger, and lurching like a Spanish galleon in a heavy sea." He chose the music to be played by way of overture, saw the play through, and gave vigorous expression to his appreciation of the Falstaff of the occasion.—*Chambers' Journal.*

and of being thrown on their beam ends. By and by, Tom Todhunter, looking lugubrious and as though he was choke-full of strange oaths which he would like to let fly at the merry crew thus liquored at his cost, slowly and solemnly made upon a slate a certain record which has endured even unto this day.

VII.

IT appears from the manuscript, discovered and deciphered as aforesaid, that about one hour before noontide, Sir John Falstaff, accused of being a tavern-haunter, a drunkard, a huge bombard of sack, a fat old rogue, a gorbellied knave, a braggadocio, a swindler, a lewdster, a vagabond, a thief, a profane swearer, a purse-taker, a highway robber, a murderer (of "men in buckram "), an incomparable liar, a coward, an omnipotent villain, etc., etc., etc., and accordingly apprehended for trial, was brought into court, then in special session for his examination in the great hall on the ground floor of the Boar's Head, in Eastcheap, and next door to the taproom of that renowned old tavern. Having made his obeisance to the worshipful Justices Shallow and Silence, and also to Master Abraham Slender as *amicus curiæ*, it was most gra-

8

ciously permitted the fat knight not to stand, but to sit in the very chair wherein he sat when Prince Hal said to him : " Do thou stand for my father, and examine me upon the particulars of my life " ; and Falstaff answered : " Shall I? content ; this chair shall be my state, this dagger my sceptre, and this cushion my crown." High on a bench behind a long table placed upon a dais at the farther end of the hall, and between two lofty windows which afforded an outlook into a small cemetery in the rear of St. Michael's church standing just back of the tavern, their worships exalted sat. A little to their left and upon a low stool resembling a dunce-block, sat Master Slender as the friend of the court. By an escritoire stationed in a nook in front of them, but depressed several steps so that their dignity might not be diminished, and their field of view obscured, there in an easy chair sat Sir Hugh Evans, the Welsh parson, who served as the chaplain and clerk of the court. At their left on a bench in the corner of the bar sat Sheriff Fang and the under-bailiffs. The right-hand corner of the hall had been partitioned into a closet for the use of the justices as a consultation room. The dock wherein Sir John Falstaff sat in his chair of state, and, throughout the trial attorneyed his own case, was directly in front of the magisterial seat, but so degraded from its level that plump Jack was compelled, in order to see the justices, to erect his head and eyes in much the same manner as Gulliver did on his return home after living among the Brobdingnagians. In a

day or two the dock was moved nearer to the court
and raised considerably, to enable the aged justices
to hear to better advantage ; and even after this
was done, they were often compelled to piece out
their long and ample ears by applying thereto their
half-closed hands as ear trumpets.   Within the bar
a few important witnesses and certain privileged
spectators were allowed to have seats during the
trial.   The Boar's Head tavern was full of guests,
and many strangers who were turned away by the
hostess, Mrs. Quickly, easily found entertainment
in Pudding Lane, Cock Lane, Billingsgate, at Pie
Corner, or elsewhere in the neighborhood of Eastcheap.   For Eastcheap, says the old chronicler,
Stow, " was always famous for its convivial doings.
The cookes cried hot ribbes of beef roasted, pies
well baked, and other victuals ; there was clattering of pewter pots, harpe, pipe, and sawtrie."

It appears from the clerk's notes of the examination, that it was conducted, not according to long
established rules or any code of procedure, but in
a colloquial style and in a free-and-easy way ; that
the defendant was allowed the largest liberty in the
introduction of evidence, and permitted to use the
Socratic method in the management of his defence.

The court being duly in session, Justice Shallow
directed Sir Hugh Evans to read to Sir John Falstaff the information filed against him, which was
accordingly done in about one hour. Sir John
slowly arose, and with cheerful effrontery, pleaded
generally, " Not guilty " ; and, after a short pause,
he said : " May it please your worships, you hear

all the matters and things charged against me in the information, denied : You hear—I deny all these matters from A to Ampersand." Then Justice Shallow, looking upon the defendant with judicial gravity and wisdom, said that, under the peculiar circumstances of the case, no "book-oath" would be administered to him ; and asked what special plea he would make to the charge of "tavern-haunting." Thereupon Sir John stated that his plea would be an oral one, and something in the nature of a plea by way of confession and avoidance. "Ay, marry, good Sir John," quoth the justice, "a plea by way of confession and avoidance ! It is well said, in faith, sir ; it is a very good phrase ; it is good ; yea, indeed, is it ; good phrases are surely, and ever were, commendable. Prithee, good Sir John, let us at once hear thee on the plea aforesaid, whatever such a plea may be. Gramercy ! I have not heard this good phrase spoken of since the mad days that I spent at Clement's Inn." Cousin Silence interrupted by saying, "That 's fifty-five year ago " ; and Master Abraham Slender, as the friend of the court, remarked, "Confession ! It comes of the Latin, *confessio*, from the deponent verb, *confiteri :* very good ; by these gloves, a good word for the knight to use." Then Justice Shallow said, " Let us hear, let us hear, let us hear ; yea, marry, good Sir John, let us hear, let us hear forthwith about your plea in confession and avoidance."

Thereupon Sir John stated to the worshipful justices in substance that he had no house of his own

and no wife ; that his profession had always been,
and that it now is, that of arms, and that, to use
the words of Ancient Pistol, "the world 's mine
oyster, which I with sword will open " ; that when
he went into Gloucestershire to enlist "a half a
dozen sufficient men " for soldiers, Robert Shallow,
esquire, one of the king's justices of the peace in
that county, inquired of Lieutenant Bardolph, who
had gone before himself, "How doth the good
knight ?"—meaning Sir John Falstaff—and he
further said, " May I ask how my lady his wife
doth ?" and that Bardolph answered, " Sir, pardon ;
a soldier is better accommodated than with a wife " ;
and then that wise justice replied approvingly, " It
is well said, in faith, sir ; and it is well said indeed
too.   Better accommodated ! it is good ; yea, indeed, is it. . . .   Accommodated ! very good ;
a good phrase."

Sir John further answered that he had not money
enough in his purse, and never did have, to enable
him to support a wife and children becomingly ;
that he " can get no remedy against this consumption
of the purse ; borrowing only lingers and lingers
it out, but the disease is incurable " ; that he has
not been able to pay the "thousand pound " long
ago lent to him by his good friend, wise and
generous Robert Shallow, esquire, whom Prince
Hal, after he was crowned king, ought to have
made " My Lord Shallow."

The knight further said that, in his view, a wife
and children are " impediments to great enterprises,
either of virtue or mischief " ; that he had followed

the advice of one of the Seven Wise Men of Greece, who made answer to the question when a man should marry—"A young man not yet, an elder man not at all," and that, in default of a wife and a house and a home of his own, he had been all his life long compelled to haunt taverns. Moreover, Sir John confessed, that, "since he perceived the first white hair on his chin he had weekly sworn to marry old Mistress Ursula"; and declared that if she was still crying heigh-ho for a husband, he was ready and willing to be at least handfasted to her, notwithstanding she 'd so long walked hand in hand with Time. At this point in the proceedings, Mistress Quickly, who, along with her bosom friend, that "honest, virtuous, civil gentlewoman," Dorothy Tearsheet, all frizzled and fucated, beruffled and bejewelled, and having on a frock of flame-colored taffeta, was sitting in Sir John's shadow, fanning herself and quietly listening to his testimony, hastily jumped up, angrily interrupted the knight and astonished the court and the spectators by saying : "Marry, if thou wert an honest man, the gross sum that thou owest me is thyself and a long score which I have against thee at the Boar's Head tavern, for moneys borrowed from time to time of me, for anchovies and a capon, for one half-pennyworth of bread and an intolerable deal of sack. Thou didst swear to me upon a parcel-gilt goblet, sitting in my Dolphin-chamber, at the round table, by a sea-coal fire, on Wednesday in Wheeson week, when the prince broke thy head for liking his father to a singing-man of Windsor, thou didst swear to me then, as I was washing thy wound, to marry me and make me my lady thy wife. Canst thou deny it? Did not good-wife Keech, the butcher's wife, come in then and call me gossip Quickly? coming in to borrow a mess of vinegar; telling us she had a good dish of prawns; whereby thou didst desire to eat some; whereby I told thee they were ill for a green wound? And didst thou not, when she was gone down-stairs, desire me to be no more so familiarity with such poor people; saying that ere long they should call me madam? And didst thou not kiss me, and bid me fetch thee thirty shillings? I put thee now to thy book-oath; deny it, if thou canst."

Many of the spectators murmured applause for the hostess of the Boar's Head, and one, bolder than the rest, cried out: "Sir John, for the bread you 've had, put a ha'penny in the slot. In your long life you must have been often left to hold the sack." This remark was greeted with an outburst of applause. Justice Shallow commanded silence, and directed the under-bailiffs, Grabbe and Ketchum, to arrest all guilty of a breach of the peace, and bring them before the court; but the officers caught nobody. Order being restored, the fat knight asked permission of their worships to hold a quiet confabulation with Mrs. Quickly, which was granted. He slowly rose from his chair, turned himself about, leaned upon the railing of his semicircular pen, looked smilingly down upon that irate landlady, and made a low courtesy to her. He rubbed his bald pate, chucked himself under the chin, and fumbled his gray beard; but at first, words seemed, like Macbeth's amen, to stick in his throat; and he made no denial of the promise to marry, which had just been, in a throng of words, so circumstantially stated by the fair interpleader. At last he said to her: "Come, an 't were not for thy humours, there 's not a better wench in England. Come, thou must not be in this humour with me; dost not know me? Come, come, I know thou wast set on to this. Ay, marry, I 'll take my book-oath that old Mistress Ursula never lived but in my thoughts; that she has never been anything more real to me than the shadow of a shade; and that she is only such stuff as dreams are made of." And then he leered so long upon Mrs. Quickly, that the heat of love seemed to dissolve the ice of age in him, and to thaw his frozen affections for the hostess of Eastcheap. Although she had long ago out-worn the gloss of her girlhood, yet Sir John called her pet names, as bird, dove, chick, duck, lamb, mouse, kid, honey, love, puss, pigeon, pigsney, sweeting, etc. And she was mightily pleased thereat, and hid her smiling face behind her fan, but furtively peeped over it at Falstaff.

This confab was closed by Justice Shallow, who abruptly said: "Let me see, let me see; by cock and pie, Sir John, the trial must go on. Attend." As the knight turned to face the court, Mrs. Quickly looked lovingly upward to the fat culprit in the dock, and said whisperingly to herself: "I have known thee these twenty-nine years, come peascod-time ; but an honester and truer-hearted man——" leaving her sentence thus unfinished, and ending it with what Andrew Lang calls " an amorous aposiopesis." *

The interview between Sir John and Mrs. Quickly having closed, Peto, who was called and sworn as a witness for the Crown, testified that, on a certain occasion, he went in great haste to the Boar's Head tavern, and notified Prince Hal that the King, his father, was at Westminster, and that twenty weak and wearied posts had come and brought further news of the rebellion in the north of England. He further stated that as he came along, " he met and overtook a dozen captains, bare-headed, sweating, knocking at the taverns, and asking every one for Sir John Falstaff."

" So, so, so, so," said Justice Shallow ; " let me see, let me see ; Peto, why did the dozen captains knock only at the taverns to ask for Sir John Falstaff ?   Let me hear ; let me hear."   Peto answered that he did n't know for certain why they did so. " Good Sir John," said the justice, " prithee, how answer you that ?"   " I give it up," said Sir John. The defendant, declining to cross-examine the witness, said that, by way of a comprehensive answer and defence to the charge of tavern-haunting, he desired to ask the court a simple question. Leave being granted, he asked their worships the follow-

---

* See the *Merry Wives of Windsor*, with illustrations by E. A. Abbey, and comments by Andrew Lang.—*Harper's Magazine*, December, 1889.

ing: "Shall I not take mine ease in mine inn?" *
This question seemed to stagger Shallow and
Silence, JJ.; and in their bewilderment they called
to their aid Master Slender, and these three put
their heads together in consultation over it. Seeing
the predicament in which the court stood, Falstaff
smiled, directed the clerk's attention to the triple
tribunal, and in a merry whisper said: " Prithee,
Sir Hugh, what famous pre-Raphaelite painting by
one of the old masters does the court now remind
thee of?" But the learned clerk could not tell,
and the knight answered: "Ay, marry; 't is the
picture entitled, 'When Shall We Three Meet
Again?'—the looker-on being the third of the

------

* Franklin Fiske Heard, in his *Shakespeare as a Lawyer*, remarks: " In *Riddle v. Welden*, 5 Wharton, 15, it was
decided that the goods of a boarder are not liable to be dis-
trained for rent due by the keeper of the boarding-house.
Chief Justice Gibson, in delivering the opinion of the court,
said that Falstaff 'speaks with legal precision when he demands,
"Shall I not take mine ease in mine inn?"' In early times an
inn signified a dwelling; and 'To take mine ease in mine
inne' was an ancient proverb, says Percy, not very different in
its application, from that maxim, 'Every man's house is his
castle'; for *inne* originally signified *a house* or *habitation*
[Sax., inne, domus, domicilium]. When the word *inne* began
to change its meaning, and to be used to signify *a house of
entertainment*, the proverb, still continuing in force, was applied in the latter sense, as it is here used by Shakespeare.

" An example of the use of the word, in its early significa-
tion, occurs in *Greene's Farewell to Folly* (1591): ' The beggar
Irus, that haunted the palace of Penelope, would *take his ease
in his inne*, as well as the peers of Ithaca.'"

asinine three. Hast thou not seen a large copy of this picture hanging in the tap-room of the Garter Inn at Windsor?" After the lapse of half an hour, Justice Shallow announced that he and his associates, being weary with their day's work, would take Sir John's question under advisement, and that the court would be adjourned until two o'clock in the afternoon of the next day. Thereupon the justices and Master Slender retired to the suite of rooms in the Boar's Head, to wit, the Half-Moon, the Pomegranate, and the Bunch of Grapes, which had been severally assigned to them during the term of court. Falstaff himself was soon surrounded by his friends and followers, and, still seated in the dock, held a mock court of his own, and without any of that aloofness of manner which marks most judges.

By and by, Bardolph, who was serving as a temporary tapster at the tavern, reported to the knight that, soon after the justices had gone to their rooms and in obedience to an order given, he sent to the Half-Moon a bottle of small beer, a pint of brown bastard, and a pottle-pot of sack, and scored the same against Justice Shallow ; that he promptly followed the drawers, Francis and Ralph, to see that the liquors reached their destination, to interview their worships, and to learn what he could of their sayings and doings. " Prithee, Bardolph," quoth the knight, " what tidings dost thou bring of the behaviour of these unwigged justices, and what did they say and do in the Half-Moon?" Bardolph answered that when he entered the room

Shallow seemed to be in consultation with his brother justice, and said: "Ay, marry, cousin Silence, we 've had a hard day's work; that we have; in faith, cousin, we have. Didst thou not find the bench whereon we sat blanked hard?" "Ay, forsooth, I did," quoth Silence. Thereupon Shallow said: "Sir John's question is indeed a hard one for us to answer; yea, indeed, is it; why should not any true man, and especially Sir John Falstaff, take his ease in his inn? Answer me that, cousin Silence." "Ay, forsooth, why should he not?" echoed Silence. "Let 's take this question under advisement," remarked Shallow; and then seeing Master Abraham Slender refreshing himself with the bottle of small beer, the justice said: "By the mass, cousin Slender, 't is felony to drink small beer, when thou canst drink sack; what saith the Apostle Paul to Timothy, his own son in the faith: 'Drink no longer water, but use a little wine for thy stomach's sake and thine often infirmities.' Cousin Silence, let 's crack a quart of sack together; let 's be merry; not too merry, however, for the pottle-pot hath drenched the judgment of wiser men than we. What saith the wise King Solomon? 'Who hath woe? Who hath sorrow? Who hath contentions? Who hath babbling? Who hath wounds without cause? Who hath redness of eyes? They that tarry long at the wine.'" Quoth Silence, "I have been merry twice and once, ere now." Bardolph further reported that when he left the Half-Moon, Slender had betaken himself to the brown bastard; that the justices were drinking by turns from a tankard, and that Silence was singing,

> "Be merry, be merry, my wife has all ;
> For women are shrews, both short and tall."

And thereupon Falstaff winked and smiled at Bardolph, and said : "I, too, am drouthy, and would moisten my clay and be merry ; thou boot-legger, thou red-nosed knave and knight of the burning lamp, my withered servingman turned into a fresh tapster, my faithful cupbearer for two and thirty years, canst thou accommodate me with a pottle of sack finely brewed, and with no lime in it ? Hast thou not brought for me such a pottle-pot from the tap-room of the Boar's Head? A pottle of sack finely brewed ! Very good ; gra-mercy, a good phrase." Bardolph, who was well whittled with liquor, made a profound bow to the fat knight, then straightened and bristled up him-self, and staggeringly responded : "Pardon me, good Sir John ; I have heard the words, ' a pottle of sack finely brewed.' Phrase call you it ? by this good day, I will maintain the phrase with my sword to be a soldier-like phrase, and a phrase of exceeding good command, by heaven. Accommo-dated with a pottle of sack finely brewed, that is, when a man is, as they say, accommodated ; or when a man is, being, whereby a' may be thought to be accommodated with a pottle-pot of sack finely brewed ; which is an excellent thing." And then he brought forth from a capacious side-pocket in his jerkin and handed up to Falstaff a quart bottle

of sack, which the thirsty knight clutched, uncorked, and forthwith drank a half-pint at least,
and then paused for breath preparatory to taking
a second swig therefrom. Just as Sir John was
about to kiss the bottle's mouth a second time,
Pistol impertinently interposed a question as to the
contents of the bottle. Falstaff paused a moment,
looked lovingly at the bottle, shook it, and said:
"No quips now, Pistol, I double charge thee; 't is
merely a *scire facias* to revive my dormant judgment."

The next day the court met pursuant to adjournment. Shallow, J., announced that they were
unable as yet to decide the question submitted by
the defendant, and, there appearing to be no good
reason why Sir John Falstaff should not take his
ease in his inn, that the further consideration of
the charge of tavern-haunting would be preter-
mitted for the present.

The court then took up the charge of drunken-
ness; the fat knight pleaded not guilty, declared
that he was ready for trial, and said to the presid-
ing justice: "I challenge any man to say that he
ever saw me drunk, or in any way the worse for
liquor; play out the play; I have much to say in
the behalf of that Falstaff." Lieutenant Bardolph
was then called as a witness for the Crown, but he
answered not. Under-bailiff Ketchum found him
at his post of duty in the taproom of the Boar's
Head, and hurried him before the justices in session. He brought his bottle nose along with him
—not a simple bottle nose, but one of a thousand

bottles, whose blushing honors were trophies of past victories, the colors won in tavern-campaigns. When he was sworn he sweated and showed some fear, for though he had all his life long been " full of strange oaths," he had never until this time been put to his "book-oath." Laying his huge hand upon the Bible, and bowing reverently, he kissed the sacred book with such a clamorous smack that all the court-room did echo. Justice Shallow said to the trembling witness : " Master Bardolph, thou hast been solemnly sworn to speak the truth, the whole truth, and nothing but the truth, in the matter in agitation between the Crown and Sir John Falstaff. Let me see, let me see ; where are the special questions which I, aided by my learned associates, have prepared for thee to answer under oath and without prevarication. So, so, so ; here are the interrogatories which the court propounds, and which Sir Hugh Evans will read to thee." The clerk then read the first question, as follows :

" A few days after the Gadshill robbery, were not you and Sir John together at the Boar's Head tavern ? If so, state on your book-oath whether the defendant did not then and there study and peruse your face, and comment thereon, as follows : ' I make as good use of it as many a man doth of a Death's-head or a *memento mori.* I never see thy face but I think upon hell-fire and Dives that lived in purple ; for there he is in his robes, burning, burning. If thou wert any way given to virtue, I would swear by thy face : my oath should be, ' By this fire, that 's God's angel ' ; but thou art altogether given over, and wert indeed, but for the light in thy face, the son of utter darkness. When thou rannest up Gadshill in the night to catch my horse, if I did not think thou hadst been an *ignis fatuus*, or a ball of wild-fire, there 's no purchase in money. O, thou art a perpetual triumph, an everlasting bonfire light ! Thou hast saved me a thousand marks in links and torches, walking with thee in the night betwixt tavern and tavern ; but the sack that thou hast drunk me would have bought me lights as good cheap at the dearest chandler's in Europe. I have maintained that salamander of yours with fire any time these two and thirty years ; God reward me for it.' "

Then Justice Shallow gazed with owl-like gravity upon the witness and said : " Ay, that is the question, and 't is a grave one ; what is thy answer ? Speak directly. I am, sir, under the King in some authority." Bardolph looked steadfastly at the justice, then at Falstaff, then at the justice, and hesitated so long that Shallow grew angry and began to reprimand him for his silence. But just at this moment the sun, breaking forth in all his splendor from behind a dark cloud, did dart his refulgent beams through the uncurtained windows full upon the malmsey nose and the crimson countenance of Bardolph, the reflection of which shot straightway up into the faces and eyes of the members of the court, and instantly blinded and bewildered them. They all jumped to the conclusion that the recalcitrant witness had played upon them the bad boy's trick of flashing into their faces the sun's rays by means of a bit of looking-glass. As soon as Shallow had collected his scattered senses, he wrathfully exclaimed against Bardolph, would not hear his explanation and defence, threatened to make a Star-Chamber matter of him, found him guilty of contempt of court, fined him forty marks, and, in default of a convenient prison, sentenced him to be confined forty-eight hours in the cemetery of St. Michael's church hard by, there to be fed only on bread and water. In obedience to the order of the court, shoulder-clappers Grabbe and Ketchum forthwith seized the witness and hustled him away to undergo his punishment. Thereupon the court adjourned for that day.

9

VIII.

THE court met early in the morning according to adjournment. After looking curiously around the room and holding a brief consultation with Silence and Slender, Justice Shallow fixed his lack-lustre eyes for a minute or two upon the defendant seated in the dock, and then said : "By my troth, good Sir John, it seems that the witness Bardolph is not present—is still in limbo because of his gross contempt of this honourable court yesterday ; nor do I at this moment see any other witness for the Crown to testify against thee. Let me see, let me see, let me see ; Sir John, what can now be done in thy case ? What canst thou say for thyself on the charge of being a wine-bibber, a drunkard, a lewdster, and so forth ? Ay, marry, Sir John, I've often heard thee called a Bacchanalian, a sack-butt, a huge bombard of sack, and the like. So, so, so ; there being nobody here at this hour to testify against thee, I give thee leave to speak for thyself ; let me hear, let me hear."

The knight slowly arose, stood awhile in a brown study, and then said : " May it please your worships, once on a time and at the Boar's Head tavern, Prince Hal, playing the part of the King his father, sat in the very chair from which I 've just risen, and questioned me, standing for Hal himself, upon the conduct of my life. Though that examination was had many years back, yet I well remember the dialogue between us. It ran substantially thus :

Prince. Now, Harry, whence come you ?

Fal. My noble lord, from Eastcheap.

Prince. The complaints I hear of thee are grievous.

Fal. 'Sblood, my lord, they are false;—nay, I 'll tickle ye for a young prince, i' faith.

Prince. Swearest thou, ungracious boy ? henceforth ne'er look on me. Thou art violently carried away from grace : there is a devil haunts thee in the likeness of a fat old man ; a tun of man is thy companion. Why dost thou converse with that trunk of humours, that bolting-hutch of beastliness, that swollen parcel of dropsies, that huge bombard of sack, that stuffed cloak-bag of guts, that roasted Manningtree ox with the pudding in his belly, that reverend vice, that grey iniquity, that father ruffian, that vanity in years? Wherein is he good, but to taste sack and drink it? wherein neat and cleanly, but to carve a capon and eat it? wherein cunning, but in craft? wherein crafty, but in villany? wherein villanous, but in all things? wherein worthy, but in nothing?

Fal. I would your grace would take me with you ; whom means your grace?

Prince. That villanous abominable misleader of youth, Falstaff, that old white-bearded Satan.

Fal. My lord, the man I know.

Prince. I know thou dost.

Fal. But to say I know more harm in him than in myself, were to say more than I know. That he is old (the more the pity), his white hairs do witness it ; but that he is (saving your reverence) a whoremaster, that I utterly deny. If sack and sugar be a fault, God help the wicked ! if to be old and merry be a sin, then many an old host that I know is damned ; if to be fat be to be hated, then Pharaoh's lean kine are to be loved. No, my good lord: banish Peto, banish Bardolph, banish Poins ; but for sweet Jack Falstaff, kind Jack Falstaff, true Jack Falstaff, valiant Jack Falstaff, and therefore more valiant, being, as he is, old Jack Falstaff, banish not him thy Harry's company, banish not him thy Harry's company: banish plump Jack, and banish all the world.

Prince. I do, I will.

" May it please your worships : I would on that occasion have spoken more good words in the behalf of that much-maligned Falstaff ; but, just as I was about to utter more, we heard a thunderous knocking on the tavern-door, and Hostess Quickly, Francis, and Bardolph went out to find

what in the devil's name the matter was.   Bardolph
soon ran back and exclaimed to Prince Hal, 'O,
my lord, my lord ! the sheriff with a most monstrous
watch is at the door to search the house ; for he
declares that a hue and cry hath followed certain
men unto this house, and that one of these men is
well known, to wit, a gross fat man, as fat as butter.'
Well, well, in this emergency I hid me behind the
arras as Hal had directed, and Bardolph, Peto, and
the rest walked up above.   Thereupon Hal met
master sheriff at the door, and, with a true face and
a good conscience, assured the officer that I was
not within, and gave his word that by dinner-time
next day he would send me to answer the sheriff,
or any man, for any thing I might be charged
withal."

Shal. Heigh, heigh ! Sir John, what was the
matter ? Why was the sheriff with a most monstrous watch at the door of the Boar's Head tavern ?
Why did he wish to search the house ? Prithee,
let me hear, let me hear.

Fal. [*Yawning.*] Heigh-ho-hum ! it tires me even
to think of it, and, zounds ! it tires me much more
to tell of and be cross-examined about it.

Shal. But let me hear ; say on, Sir John.

Fal. Well, well, I bethink me 't was something
touching the Gadshill misadventure of a few hours
before, whereby, as the sheriff said, two gentlemen
were robbed of three hundred marks ; but, may it
please your worships, that trifling matter no longer
stands on the docket against me.   The Chief
Justice and I, years agone, settled and dismissed

that case ; 't is now *res judicata ;* and, moreover, Hal told me that the money had been paid back again. Prithee, let bygones be bygones, and suffer me to return to the matters and things properly before the court.

Shal. So, so, so ; do so, do so, do so ; go on, Sir John.

Fal. Prince Hal—the mad wag—ever took a pride to gird at, nickname, and mock me ; and a multitude of the mirthful and mischievous things which he jestingly said about me have long been current among the common people, and, by the Lord, my good name hath been thereby most horribly hurted. Moreover, not a few of these untruths and slanders have found a lodgment in the information now pending against me. But, your worships, as I declared at the outset of this examination, I do now declare ; you hear all the charges laid against me, denied ; you hear, I deny them all, each and every one. Zounds ! I care not the sixteenth part of a baubee what the red-nosed under-skinkers, bottle-ale rascals, and mechanical salt-butter rogues have already blabbed here and there among vile vulgarians to hurt my good name, to besmirch my character, and to injure my reputation for sobriety, strict veracity, honesty, integrity, charity, chastity, and other Christian virtues too many to be now enumerated ; but let any mother's son of them be bold enough to appear in this court and testify against me, and, by the Lord, if I do not stare him out of his wits, or, outside of this court-room, predominate over and awe him with my cudgel, then hang me up by the heels for a rabbit-sucker, or a poulter's hare. Look you, Master Robert Shallow, in our young manhood, and when we were fellow-students at Clement's Inn, did we not read in the *Institutes of Justinian* that the maxims of law are these : To live honestly, to hurt no one, and to give every one his due ? And, by my troth, have we not always remembered these golden rules, and made them the guide of our lives ?

Shal. That we have, that we have, that we have ; in faith, Sir John, we have. O, Sir John, do you remember when we and little John Doit of Stafford-shire, and black George Barnes, and Francis Pick-bone, and Will Squele, a Cotswold man, and other Clement's Inn boys lay all night in the windmill in Saint George's field ? Ha ! 't was a merry night. And is Jane Nightwork alive ? doth she hold her own well ? If alive, she must be old ; she cannot choose but be old ; certain she's old ; and had Robin Nightwork by old Nightwork before I came to Clement's Inn. But, prithee, Sir John, in what book did you say that these maxims of law may be found ?

Fal. In the *Institutes of Justinian.* The Latin words in which these maxims are clothed no longer linger in my memory.* Well do I remember when we and other lively young men of Clement's Inn stayed all night in the windmill in Saint George's field ; but we did n't go there to study Justinian,

---

* " *Juris præcepta sunt hæc : honeste vivere, alterum non lædere, suum cuique tribuere.*"—Lib. I., Tit. I.

or to grind corn, but rather to be corned, and so forth. We were not such smugs and reading men as to go thither to pursue our legal studies. When we both were young and lusty, not only did we hear the chimes at midnight, but we painted the town a deep, deep red. Did we not, Master Robert Shallow?

Shal. That we did, that we did, Sir John. Jesu, the mad days that we have seen!

Fal. 'T is agreed, however, that we 've both striven all our lives long to be guided by the three golden rules aforesaid?

Shal. 'T is so, 't is so, 't is so agreed between us. Well, Sir John?

Fal. Though I 've struggled hard to be guided by the Justinian precepts, and also by the maxim that honesty is the best policy (or nearly so), and to be called and known by my familiars as " Honest John," yet I must confess that oftentimes I 've had as much as I could do to follow the precepts aforesaid and to keep the terms of my honour precise. I, ay, I myself sometimes, leaving the fear of God on the left hand and hiding mine honour in my necessity, have been fain to shuffle, to hedge, and to lurch. But I may say to your worship as I once said to Prince Hal : " Thou knowest in the state of innocency Adam fell ; and what should poor Jack Falstaff do in the days of villany? Thou seest I have more flesh than another man, and therefore more frailty."

When Hal—the naughty varlet—called me " a huge bombard of sack," and the long list of ill names aforementioned, was it for me to tell the heir-apparent that he lied in his throat? Was it for me to cudgel, or to lay violent hands upon, or even to touch, the true prince? Once or twice Hal called me a coward, and many times he said as much in a roundabout way. Though I am as valiant as Hercules, was it for me, a true knight and loyal subject of the king, to run my sword through the sacred body of the heir-apparent, or to seek on the field of honour reparation for the insult? God-a-mercy! 't would have been *leze majesty* for me to do so, in fact, high treason, for which crime I might have been drawn to the gallows; hanged by the neck, and then cut down alive; my entrails taken out and burned, while I was yet alive; my head cut off; my body divided into four parts; and my head and quarters disposed of at the king's pleasure. 'Sblood! sweet Jack Falstaff dragged on the ground to the gallows! kind Jack Falstaff hanged! plump Jack Falstaff embowelled! true Jack Falstaff beheaded! valiant Jack Falstaff's head and quarters placed at the king's disposal, and his head possibly posted up on a pole at Temple Bar to fear traitors! Think of that, Master Robert Shallow. When Hal called me a coward, he did but jest, for the very next morning after the Gadshill affair, he promised to procure for me a charge of foot in the wars then raging in England and Wales; and he kept his word, met me by appointment in the Temple Hall, gave me my instructions, together with money and order for the soldiers' furniture.

Shal. So, so, so, Sir John ; talking of soldiers and the wars warms my blood and reminds me of the mad days of my lusty youth. I have seen the time when with my long sword I would have made any four tall fellows skip like rats. Bodykins, Sir John, though I.now be old and of the peace, if I see a sword out, my fingers itch to grasp it. Good Sir John, we still have some salt of our youth in us ; we are the sons of women, Sir John.—But, let me see, let me see ; by my troth, have we not strayed away from the matters strictly before the court ? Let me see ; art thou not a sack-butt, a saloon itinerant, a bootlegger, and so forth ? How answer you that, Sir John ?

Fal. Whether I 'm a sack-butt, or a huge bombard of sack, is a question to be asked and answered ; but that I 'm a bootlegger, I utterly deny. I may say, however, that Bardolph, who has been in my service for so many years, may be something of a bootlegger, so to speak. I bethink me of many instances of his duteous services as such, and notably of one case writ large and indelibly in my memory.

Shal. Prithee, let me hear, let me hear, Sir John.

Fal. May it please your worship, fair and softly; Master George Page and his wife, and Master Ford and his wife—are they present in court ?

Fang. They are not, Sir John ; they 're absent with leave of the court.

Shal. Peace, Sheriff Fang, peace ; last evening I excused them all, and gave them leave to return to Windsor for a few days. Urgent business called

Master Ford home, and Mistress Ford does so dote on her husband that she must needs go along with him. Master Page and his wife were sent for because of the sore sickness of their beloved daughter, the wife of Master Fenton.

Slen. [*Aside.*] O, sweet Anne Page! 'od's heartlings, I had rather than forty shillings I had my Book of Songs and Sonnets here, and also my Book of Riddles which I lent to Alice Shortcake a long time ago.

Shal. By my troth, Sir John, I long to hear of Bardolph's great services to thee as thy cupbearer; let me hear, let me hear.

Fal. Once on a time—'t is no matter when or where—I said to Bardolph, " Go fetch me a quart of sack ; put a toast in 't ; go brew me a pottle of sack finely, simple of itself, with no eggs in its brewage." The unexpected had happened ; an emergency had arisen in my career. I had been most grievously tricked and made a preposterous ass of ; and I well deserved to have my brains taken out and buttered and given to a dog for a New Year's gift.

Shal. So, so, so, Sir John ; what was the matter ? What had befallen you ? Let me hear, let me hear.

Fal. You shall hear, Master Robert Shallow. One fine summer morning between eight and nine of the clock, and when one Master Ford, *alias* Brook, had gone a-birding, I visited Mistress Ford at her house as she had appointed. Presently in came one Mistress Page, and gave intelligence of the approach of that peaking Cornuto Ford ; and, in her invention and Ford's wife's distraction, they pursuaded me, in a horrid funk and in a devil of a hurry, to creep into a buck-basket.

Shal. A buck-basket?

Fal. By the Lord, a buck-basket! rammed me in with foul shirts and smocks, socks, foul stockings, greasy napkins; so that there was the rankest compound of villanous smell that ever offended nostril. Being thus crammed into the basket, a couple of Ford's knaves, his hinds, were called forth by their mistress to carry me in the name of foul clothes to Datchet-lane. They took me on their shoulders, met the jealous knave their master in the door, who asked them once or twice what they had in their basket. I quaked for fear, lest the lunatic knave would search it; but fate, ordaining he should be a cuckold, held his hand. Well; on went he for a search, and away went I for foul clothes. I suffered the pangs of three several deaths: first, an intolerable fright, to be detected by a jealous rotten bell-wether; next, to be compassed, like a good bilbo, in the circumference of a peck, hilt to point, heel to head; and then, to be stopped in, like a strong distillation, with stinking clothes that fretted in their own grease. Think of that,—a man of my kidney,—think of that,—that am as subject to heat as butter; a man of continual dissolution and thaw: 't was a miracle that I scaped suffocation. And in the height of this bath, when I was more than half stewed in grease, like a Dutch dish, was I thrown into the Thames, and cooled, glowing hot, in that surge, like a horse-shoe; think of that,—hissing hot,—think of that, Master Robert Shallow. The rogues slighted me into the river with as little remorse as they would have drowned a blind bitch's puppies, fifteen i' the litter : and you may know by my size that I have a kind of alacrity in sinking ; if the bottom were as deep as hell, I should down. I had been drowned, but that the shore was shelvy and shallow,—a death that I abhor ; for the water swells a man, and what a thing should I have been when I had been swelled ! I should have been a mountain of mummy. And then think of the disgrace to which I 'd been subjected by having been thus fired into the Thames just as though the buck-basket, including me in its contents of an offensive and suffocating smell— faugh !—were a stinkpot flung on board of an enemy's vessel during a naval battle,—think of that, your worship. By the Lord, after such a *water*-ordeal* to cure me of concupiscence and other little ailments to which I 'm subject ; after such a baptism to wash my sins away, confirm my faith, and hearten me to chant the Psalm of Mercy

---

* Sir William Blackstone, in his *Commentaries*, says: " Water-ordeal was performed, either by plunging the bare arm up to the elbow in boiling water, and escaping unhurt thereby ; or by casting the person suspected into a river or pond of cold water : and, if he floated therein without any action of swimming, it was deemed an evidence of his guilt ; but if he sunk, he was acquitted. It is easy to trace out the traditional relics of this water-ordeal, in the ignorant barbarity still practised in many countries to discover witches by casting them into a pool of water, and drowning them to prove their innocence."—Book IV., chap. xxvii.

in the old and orthodox church of the Ephesians *
[jolly companions], of which I've been of the
vestry, off and on, time out of mind—in such an
emergency in my life, and at a time, too, when I
was completely water-logged and my belly was as
cold as if I'd just swallowed snow-balls to cool my
reins, did I not do myself right in ordering Bardolph to fetch me forthwith a pottle-pot of sack
finely brewed, and to put a toast in 't? God-a-
mercy! in the calamitous condition in which I
then was, if sack and sugar be a fault, God help
the wicked.

Sil. Do me right, and dub me knight, Samingo!
Is 't not so?

Shal. Peace, cousin Silence, peace. Ay, marry,
Sir John, you did yourself right in that case; you
did indeed too. You might well and duly have
ordered Bardolph to bring you not only a pottle of
sack, but even a gallon or two; yea, indeed.

---

* *Prince.* Is your master here in London?

Bardolph. Yea, my lord.

Prince. Where sups he? doth the old boar feed in the old
frank?

Bard. At the old place, my lord, in Eastcheap.

Prince. What company?

Page. Ephesians, my lord, of the old church.

Prince. Sup any women with him?

Page. None, my lord, but old Mistress Quickly and Mistress
Doll Tearsheet.

Prince. What pagan may that be?

Page. A proper gentlewoman, sir, and a kinswoman of my
master's.

King Henry IV., Part II., Act II., Sc. 3.

Fal. Give me a cup of sack, Francis ; tarry not at all ; away, thou rogue, away.

Fran. Anon, anon, Sir John.

Fal. Heigh ! back so soon ? Well done ! thou 'rt thrice welcome, fleet-footed Francis.

Fran. Anon, anon, sir.

Fal. [*Drinks.*] I bethink me of another emergency in my chequered career, which, if the court please, it in some sort now jumps with my humour to tell of.

Shal. Let me hear, let me hear ; go on, Sir John.

Fal. On a certain dark night on the prick of twelve, and when I, disguised as a stag, was lying down on my face at Herne's oak in Windsor Park, I prayed fervently that Heaven would defend me from that Welsh fairy, Parson Evans, disguised as a satyr, lest he should transform me into a piece of cheese, stick me on a toasting-fork with a slice of bread, hold me close to a hot fire, and make a Welsh rabbit of me. Though all my life long and after the most straitest sect of our religion I have lived an Ephesian of the Ephesians, yet I 've not forgiven thee, Sir Hugh, for commanding the fairies at Herne's oak to trip around me, and pinch my arms, legs, back, shoulders, sides, and shins, and to burn the ends of my fingers with their lighted tapers. On that dread night methought I heard the queen of the fairies sing :

> With trial-fire touch me his finger-end :
> If he be chaste, the flame will back descend
> And turn him to no pain ; but if he start,
> It is the flesh of a corrupted heart.

The fairies burned me as their leader had directed,
and, tripping around me, they sang a scornful
rhyme, and pinched me to keep their time. Oh,
oh, oh ! I liked not that Welsh movement cure for
sinful fantasy, lust, and luxury. Such heroic treatment for unchaste desires is not warranted by
anything I 've read in Galen or Hippocrates.

Evans. Sir John Falstaff, serve Got, and leave
your desires, and fairies will not pinse you. Are
you not given to fornications, and to taverns and
sack and wine and metheglins, and to drinkings
and swearings and starings, pribbles and prabbles?
I am of the church and can give you goot advice.
Got pless you, Sir John, old as you pe, and pig as
you pe, you must pe porn again. 'T is an old and
true saying, " 'T is nefer too late to mend."

Fal. Marry, and amen, master parson, thou
knowest that love is omnipotent ; that Jupiter became a bull because of Europa, and a swan for the
love of Leda ; * that other hot-blooded gods, as
well as demigods, are reported to have cut many a
curious caper because of love. When even gods
and demigods have hot backs, what shall poor men
do ? Thou knowest, moreover, that Nature may

---

* In *The Winter's Tale* (Act IV., Scene 4) Florizel says to
Perdita :
The gods themselves,

   Humbling their deities to love, have taken
   The shapes of beasts upon them : Jupiter
   Became a bull, and bellow'd ; the green Neptune
   A ram, and bleated ; and the fire-rob'd god,
   Golden Apollo, a poor humble swain,
   As I seem now.

be driven out with a pitchfork, but she 'll surely come back ; *Naturam expellas furcâ*—Sir Hugh, though thou 'rt one that makes fritters of English, yet thou 'rt clerkly ; I prithee, help me out with the Latin, which I 've quite forgot.

Evans. I will, Sir John. Horace says, in one of his Epistles, *Naturam expellas furcâ, tamen usque recurret.* Got pless you, Sir John, your translation is goot, fery goot ; but if you please, I 'll give another version :

> Drive Nature out with might and main,
> She 's certain to return again.

Fal. Sir Hugh, your translation is good, very good ; 't is better and more poetical than mine. Give me a cup of sack, Francis ; I am a rogue, if I 've drunk to-day.

Fran. Anon, anon, sir.

Fal. [*Musing awhile.*] Back so soon, my little Ganymede ?

Fran. Anon, anon, sir.

Fal. Give me the cup, boy. [*He drinks.*] You rogue, there 's lime in this sack : there is nothing but roguery to be found in villanous man, and in villanous boy as well.

Fran. Anon, anon, sir ; O Lord, Sir John, I 'll be sworn on all the books in England that there 's no lime in the sack ; for I heard Tom Toss-Pot, the tapster, say to Ralph who drew it, " Mark me, thou rogue, there 's never to be any lime in Sir John's sack."

Fal. Your worship, I prithee, what time of day is it ?

Shal. St. Michael's clock hath just stricken ten. Didst thou not hear it, Sir John ? Marry, and amen, we should note the fleeting hours and not sneeze at the sun.

Fal. Once on a time I asked the most comparative, rascalliest, sweet young Prince Hal what time of day 't was ; and he retorted : " Thou art so fat-witted, with drinking of old sack and unbuttoning thee after supper and sleeping upon benches after noon, that thou hast forgotten to demand that truly which thou wouldst truly know. What a devil hast thou to do with the time of the day ? Unless hours were cups of sack, and minutes capons, and clocks the tongues of bawds, and dials the signs of leaping-houses, and the blessed sun himself a fair hot wench in flame-coloured taffeta, I see no reason why thou shouldst be so superfluous to demand the time of the day."

Shal. By the mass, Sir John, though we hold our own well, yet we are old, old, old ; yea, indeed, we must be old ; we cannot choose but be old ; certain we 're old ; therefore 't is better for us to time ourselves by St. Michael's clock, or the sun, or the moon, or the planet Saturn, or the Seven Stars, or Capricorn, or even by the sun-dial in the Boar's Head garden, than to reckon time in the wenching way Prince Hal spoke of. Is 't not so, Sir John ? Why should we old men make believe that we are young and hot-blooded, when in fact every part about us is blasted with old age ?

Fal. [*Aside.*] Which reminds me of a certain occasion when I besought Doll Tearsheet, seated

on my knee, to kiss me ; and thereupon I over-
heard some one behind me snigger and say to his
companion, " Saturn and Venus this year in conjunction !　What says the almanac to that ? "
'T was Hal thus speaking to Poins, as I soon
discovered.

Shal. So, so, so, Sir John ; I would fain hear
thy opinion of sack ; and do thou discourse
thereof as an expert, and as one having full knowledge and authority in the matter. I give thee
leave to speak at large thereon ; prithee, let me
hear, let me hear.

Fal. Before reviewing the sack-stained current
of my long life, and then directly answering your
worship's question, I 'll begin by briefly speaking
of my family, which, by the way, is a very ancient
and honourable one. In the second and lesser
volume of *Domesday Book* it appears that many
centuries ago a certain Falstaff held freely from
the king a church at Yarmouth, and that—

Shal. Domesday Book !　Ay, marry, Sir John,
I 've not seen that ancient book since I was a student at Clement's Inn ; but I was not allowed to
look therein, for it was kept at Westminster in the
Exchequer under three locks and keys. A certain
Falstaff held a church, you say, Sir John, a church,
forsooth ?　Was that Falstaff named John ?　Let
me hear, let me hear.

Fal. But, your worship, I 've not only seen
Domesday, but have carefully read therein everything that relates to Norfolk and Suffolk ; and I
regret to say that the Falstaff I 've mentioned was

not named John. His Christian name was Nicholas ; and, moreover, he was a priest so holy and a man so jolly that he was called and known the country round as " good Saint Nicholas." The names, Nicholas and John, have, from a time when the memory of man runneth not to the contrary, run in the Falstaff family ; and, what is most remarkable, those named Nicholas have almost always been of the church, while those named John have generally been little better than of the wicked. When, long ago, I fretfully said to Bardolph that if I 'd not forgotten what the inside of a church is made of, I was a peppercorn, a brewer's horse, then I was thinking with some remorse of the church of St. Nicholas at Yarmouth, which has been for ages a familiar landmark in our family. In plain sight of its steeples and moss-grown towers, I went to school, played hopscotch, whipped top, plucked geese, and was often breeched for playing truant, or for mauling Priscian's head.* Latin was the main branch taught in the school which I attended. It was Latin, year in and year out, summer and winter, morning and evening ; only Latin, and that continually. Even at play outside the school-rooms, the boys were often persecuted by being called upon to English some

---

* Priscian, a famous old grammarian who wrote a great work entitled *Institutiones Grammaticæ*. It may fairly be said that from the beginning of the 6th century until recently Priscian has reigned over Latin grammar with almost as generally recognized an authority as Justinian has over Roman law. Hence, one who violates the rules of grammar is said to *break Priscian's head.*

Latin lines, or by being asked some questions in their accidence. And the manner of teaching was usually as dull as the matter of it was monotonous. No effort was made to make the study of Latin interesting and profitable, or to wake up the wits of boys who had no taste whatever for languages. *Mehercule!* Latin—that dead and damned language—did make me so tired at the Yarmouth grammar-school that my old bones ache whenever I think of it. But when I was a schoolboy, I picked out of the dry rot of Priscian's grammar a sweet and juicy proverb which has since been one of the guides of my life.

Shal. Good Sir John, prithee, let me hear, let me hear that proverb.

Fal. 'T is this : *In vino veritas.* And thus plainly appears one reason why in my eager search for the truth, I 've so often had my nose in a cup of wine, and—

Sil. A cup of wine that 's brisk and fine—

Shal. Peace, cousin Silence, peace ; go on, Sir John.

Fal. 'T was of the Yarmouth church I was thinking when I told the Chief Justice I 'd lost my voice with whooping, hallooing, and singing of anthems—when a boy I used to sing in the choir of St. Nicholas's church. And when the surly Chief Justice, on another occasion, asked me what foolish master had taught me my manners, and I answered that, if my manners became me not, he was a fool that had taught them me, I then had in my mind's eye old Doctor Dionysius Digamma, the head-master of the Yarmouth grammar-school founded by Sir Thomas Falstaff during the reign of King Edward the First, surnamed Longshanks. 'Sblood! what a tyrant old Digamma was, and how he used to breech the boys, often for the most trivial causes. One winter morning the Doctor commanded a poor little squint-eyed and hare-lipped lad, named Tommy Funk, *alias* "Funky," to decline the noun "cat" in English ; and this is the way Tommy did it :

> " Nominative, a cat ;
> genitive, of a cat ;
> dative, to or for a cat ;
> accusative, a cat ;
> vocative, O cat—"

"Stop right there, thou little ignoramus," thundered out the magister to trembling Tommy ; "know this, that the vocative of cat is 'puss' or 'pussy' throughout these three kingdoms. Though thou 'rt worthy of the cat o' nine tails, I 'll but breech thee with birches," which he forthwith did. The very next day the doctor flogged my fag, a low-browed, broad-bottomed boy named Hugh Bardolph—nicknamed "Nosey" because of his huge amorphous nose—for failing to repeat the Paternoster correctly ; and, by the Lord, before Nosey's tears were dry, this *plagosus Orbilius**— as some of the boys in the higher forms called the head-master—walloped him again because he 'd

---

* " *Non equidem insector delendave carmina Livi*
Esse reor, memini quæ plagosum mihi parvo
Orbilium dictare."—*Hor.*, Book II., Epistle i.

failed to recite truly certain of Priscian's rules. Poor Nosey had no taste for, and was sickened by, daily gnawing the dry bones of a stone-dead language. He soon burned all his school books, and ran away from home, vowing that he 'd never touch another book in his life, and he seems so far to have kept his resolve. When I first came to London, I found Bardolph out at heels, and at once took him into my service.

Shal. So, so, so, Sir John ; was your fag at school any relation of Lieutenant Bardolph now imprisoned in the cemetery of St. Michael's church for contempt of this court yesterday ? Let me hear, let me hear.

Fal. By my troth, they 're one and the same Bardolph who, as boy and man, has been my faithful fag for forty years and upward. As I am a gentleman, I do assure your worship that he intended no disrespect to this honourable court by his behaviour yesterday as a witness ; and therefore I pray your worship to consider him as purged of his supposed contempt, and to order him to be set at liberty. Methinks I read in your worship's looks a denial of my prayer ?

Shal. Not so, not so, not so, Sir John, i' faith ; but let me hear, let me hear your reasons for your request.

Fal. The trouble in this contempt case lies wholly in Bardolph's face ; 't is mostly in the nose of him. Of course, this court may rightly take judicial notice of his red nose, which is, *prima facie*, an everlasting bonfire-light, and also of his face, which makes me think of hell-fire, and is worthy of the " Knight of the Burning Lamp," as I long ago dubbed him. When I once asked Bardolph to amend his face, and did gird at him about it, he took fire and hotly said to me, " 'Sblood, I would my face were in your belly ! " and I could only reply, " God-a-mercy ! so should I be sure to be heart-burned." Well, well, poor Bardolph's face being as it is, and he being before you as a witness, the blessed sun's rays were, by an inexorable law of anacamptics, reflected from his face as from a mirror, and they chanced to be turned into the very eyes of the members of this honourable court, thereby blinding, bewildering, and angering them. Only this, and nothing more. As I am a gentleman, ill-starred Bardolph played no trick upon your worships, and was as innocent of malicious mischief as a naked, new-born babe.

Shal. Hem, hm, hm, it may be so, it may be so ; Sir John, as you pray, so 't is ordered ; Sir Hugh, so record the fact ; Sheriff Fang, let Bardolph loose ; go on, Sir John ; 't was about the Yarmouth school, was 't not ?

Fal. I was speaking of the character of the head-master of the Yarmouth grammar-school. Doctor Digamma's ordinary nickname among the boys was " Old Yarmouth " ; but, zounds ! they took care not to call him so in his hearing.

Shal. So, so, so ; Sir John, why was the Doctor so named by his disciples ? Let me hear, let me hear.

Fal. Your worship, there were reasons as plentiful as blackberries why the boys called the Doctor "Old Yarmouth"; but the only reason that I can now think of is because his wide mouth was so drawn downwards and aslant in its right corner that he could neither whistle, nor blow out a candle, nor becomingly kiss his homely wife, whose mouth—*mirabile dictu*—was similarly askew in the left corner thereof. And the Doctor's son John and his daughters three—*horresco referens*—all had crooked mouths, so help me God.

Shal. Hem, hm, hm, so, so, so, Sir John; will you now be put to your book-oath as to the truth of these statements?

Fal. I will, your worship, twelve times over; and, besides, I can prove the fact by Bardolph, and also offer in evidence my old copy of Priscian's grammar, on a fly-leaf of which are authentic portraits of the whole family—the same having been made by my favourite chum at school, who had naturally a good eye, a knack for drawing, and a most wonderful genius for making faces. By the way, I bethink me that that school-book of mine is not in London, and never was. It, along with other books and relics of my boyhood, is probably in a certain old oaken chest marked with the name " Jack "—cut on the lid by myself—which chest, I 'm sure, is in the cockloft of the house wherein I was born, and in which some of my brothers and sisters are doubtless still living. If your worship yearns to see the Digamma family portraits I 've spoken of, I suggest the issuance of a *subpœna duces tecum*, commanding some one of my brothers or sisters resident in Norfolk to come before this court as a witness and to bring with him, or her, the Priscian's grammar aforesaid. Moreover, I 'll give Grabbe, or whoever goes with the writ, a letter of commendation, which may be of some service to the sheriff.

Shal. Let me see, let me see, Sir John ; by my troth, that dusty and dog-eared old grammar has nothing in the world to do with the case before this court ; 't is neither here nor there ; I 'll send the sheriff on no such wild-goose chase to get it ; let it stay in the cockloft where you say it may be found. Sir John, suppose the book to be in court, what would it prove ?

Fal. Your worship, I give it up.

Slen. Ay, Sir John, you spake some Latin words a little while ago ; but 't is no matter, I understand them ; I, too, have studied Latin. Prithee, did you study Euclid at the Yarmouth grammar-school ?

Fal. I did, Master Slender, until I reached the *Pons Asinorum*, which—not deeming it safe, and not wishing to make an ass of myself—I refused to cross, and went around it. 'T was not built for such boys as I was. But I 've known that rickety old bridge to be safely crossed by many a lad who had hardly enough intellect to enable him to play a good game of jackstraws, or of pushpin. I prithee, Master Slender, did you ever cross the bridge in question ?

Slen. Ay, by these gloves, I 've crossed and re-crossed it many a time ; it keeps my wits from wandering ; but by this hat, I am not altogether an ass.

Shal. Peace, cousin Slender, peace. So, so, Sir John, is n't Yarmouth a seaport town and famous for fish, especially for herrings? Let me see, let me see ; the sea, the sea, I 've never seen the sea. By my troth, I 've never travelled farther from Gloucestershire than London. Sir John, where is Yarmouth? Is n't it on an island off Ramsgate? Is n't it where Yarmouth bloaters come from? . . . . *Hiatus in MS.*

Fal. My family is not only ancient and honourable, but 't is also a ramigerous one which has bifurcated and branched in various directions. And to-day there are Falstaffs who sit under the shade of their genealogical tree originally planted in Norfolk long before the Norman Conquest.

Shal. Did you say, Sir John, that the Falstaffs are a ramigerous family? So, so, so ; did any of 'em ever keep sheep? I 've heard of a certain farmer Falstaff who owns a large estate near Barson in Warwickshire ; but much of his land is rough and poor ; he has, however, grown rich by raising sheep. He 's a little quiver old fellow ; and 't is said that he drinks no wine, and seldom smiles. Is he of your family? Let me hear, let me hear.

Fal. Belike the man of whom your worship speaks is named Fastolfe, not Falstaff. Zounds, I 've never seen, nor so much as heard of, a trueblooded Falstaff who drank no wine, and who degraded himself and the family name by becoming a baaing shepherd, and letting his wits go a-woolgathering all his life long.

Shal. No offence, Sir John, i' the world ; no

offence whatever. Did the Falstaff who founded your family come over to England with William the Conqueror?

Fal. I rejoice to say that he did not. The Falstaff family had been firmly rooted among the Northfolk in East Anglia long before that bastard king, Wilhelmus Conquestor, was born, and from a time when the memory of man runneth not to the contrary.

Shal. So then, Sir John, your family is not from France to England?

Fal. By the Lord, no. The name Falstaff is of Scandinavian origin. Johannes Olaf Falstaff, the reputed founder of our family in England, was doubtless a Dane, a worshipper of Odin, and probably a pirate, who of course drank as well as he fought. He seems to have been dubbed a knight when he was a very young man—I know not for certain for what. He married a noble Norweyan lady, who, nominally at least, converted him to Christianity in spite of his inborn Scandinavian thirst. Before his conversion, as well as after, he believed with St. Augustine, that the soul never dwells in a dry place—that drought kills it * ; and, of course, he continued to drink in accordance with this belief. It may reasonably be presumed that he was primsigned, but never baptized,—

Shal. " Primsigned," did you say, Sir John? I 've been baptized, but I 've never been primsigned that I know of. I never heard of that strange

---

* *Anima certè, quia spiritus est, in sicco habitare non potest.*

word when I was at Clement's Inn. Is it a law term? What does it mean? Prithee, let me hear, let me hear.

Fal. Marry, and amen, your worship, when we were students at Clement's Inn, the boys there had little or no use for the word " primsign," which means to mark with the sign of the cross. This pious performance was regarded by the Norsemen as a sort of compromise between their old religion and the new, and was supposed to secure a certain favour from Christ the White without wholly forfeiting the good-will of Odin and his wife Frigg, and of the other old gods and goddesses.

This Sir John's wife was a sea-king's daughter, and traced her descent from the Haarfager family. She was a woman of wonderful vigour both of mind and body, and firm in her faith in Christ the White ; and her zeal for the conversion of the Odinites was akin to that of Olaf Tryggvesson, who, in his heroic and rigorous efforts to Christianize his kingdom, during his reign of only five years, made it very unsafe for his subjects to be anything else but Christians, and soon scarcely left a man of note unbaptized in Norway. Sir Johannes Olaf Falstaff, by hook and by crook, grew rich in goods, lands, tenements, and hereditaments, lived to be old, died at peace with the Church and in the odour of sanctity, and was buried hard by Yarmouth. His wife died on the following Childermas day, and was laid to rest beside him. And there had been born unto them seven sons and three daughters,—

Shal. Seven sons and three daughters, did you

say, Sir John?   Let me see, let me see, by my troth, the very same number of sons and daughters that were born unto Job.

Fal. Did I say seven sons and three daughters, your worship?

Shal. Indeed, Sir John, you said so.

Fal. Then I misspoke and made a grievous error in the census of the original Falstaff family ; for unto Sir John the First and his wife were born eleven sons and seven daughters.   The sons were christened as follows, to wit :   Johannes, Nicholas, Christian, Guttorm, Olaf, Erik, Haakon, Harold, Hamlet, Hardicanute or Hardiknut, Sweyn, Snorre, and Sigurd ; and the daughters were christened as follows, to wit :   Agnes, Angelica, Bertha, Barbara, Christina, Dorothea, Griselda, Jemima, Matilda, Tabitha, Ulrica, and Winifred.

Shal. So, so, so, so, so, so, so many children, Sir John?   Let me see, let me see ; the children of youth are, as the Psalmist saith, as arrows in the hands of a mighty man, and happy is the man that hath his quiver full of them.

Slen. Od's heartlings, Sir John, you said at first that unto Sir John Falstaff the First were born seven sons and three daughters ; and then you said there were eleven sons and seven daughters ; but, by these gloves, you 've just named thirteen sons and twelve daughters as the sum total of his children, if I 've counted them aright.   That 's a pretty jest indeed !   That 's meat and drink to me, now.

Sil. Ha, ha, ha ! very singular good, i' faith !

Shal. Hem, hm, hm !   Sir John, if what you 've

said about the children of Sir Johannes Olaf Falstaff be true, then, by the mass, he must have had his quiver full of arrows and have been a happy man ; yea, indeed. Let me see, let me see ; did he, like that famous archer, old Double, draw a good bow and make a fine shoot? [*To Silence.*] Is old Double of your town living yet?

Sil. Dead, sir.

Shal. Jesu, Jesu! old Double dead! He could have clapped i' the clout at twelve score ; and carried you a forehand shaft at fourteen and fourteen and a half, that it would have done a man's heart good to see. And is old Double dead?

Sil. He 's still dead, sir ; died a dozen year ago.

Shal. Certain, 't is certain ; very sure, very sure ; death, as the Psalmist saith, is certain to all ; all shall die. By the mass, Sir John, when you were a young man, I knew you to be a good backsword man ; but, bodykins, good Sir John, until now I knew not of your skill in archery—particularly in drawing a long bow as to the number of arrows in the quiver of Sir John Falstaff the First.

Fal. May it please your worships, I 'll be put to my book-oath that there were born unto the original Sir John Falstaff at least a baker's dozen of sons, and a dozen daughters, be the same more or less ; nay, more, I 'll swear by my grandfather's seal-ring which was given to me as a tooth-gift *—of which

---

* Hjalmar H. Boyesen, in a note to Chapter IX. of his *Story of Norway*, says : "It was customary to give to infants of high birth a thrall or some other valuable gift when it got its first tooth. This gift was called a tooth-gift."

ring, along with three or four bonds of forty pound
a-piece, my pocket was long ago picked on a certain night when I 'd fallen asleep behind the arras
in the Boar's Head tavern—I say that I 'll swear by
my grandfather's seal-ring that in my opinion a
strict census of the children lawfully begotten by
Sir John Falstaff the First would reveal at least
half a score more than those I 've mentioned.   I
care not so much for the bonds I was robbed of ;
but, by the horned shoes * of my great-great-grand-
father, I would not, for a thousand pound, have lost
my grandfather's signet-ring.   When I, at the age
of twenty, or something earlier, left home to ride o'
horseback to London, to enter as a student at
Clement's Inn, and there to become acquainted
with Master Robert Shallow, I wore that precious
ring on the forefinger of my left hand.   Then I was
not, as now I am, a bed-presser, a horseback-breaker,
a huge hill of flesh ; then my figure was shapely,
and I had all the grace and activity of youth ; then
I was not an eagle's talon in the waist ; I could have
crept into any alderman's thumb-ring, and, by 'r
Lady, I could have seen mine own knee : a plague
of sighing and grief ! it blows a man up like a

---

* " Horned shoes " were first introduced in the reign of
William Rufus, 1090, by " Robert the Dandy."   Robert's
shoes were long and pointed, the toes being turned up and
twisted like a ram's horns.   On this account history frequently
refers to him as " Robert the Horned."   In the reign of
Richard II., 1390, the dandies of London wore shoes with toes
from one foot to eighteen inches in length, with the point or
" horn " turned up and fastened to the garter by a gold or silver chain.—GEORGE PSALMANAZAR WOPSLE.

bladder. I wore my grandfather's seal-ring for two and thirty years, and until my hands grew pudgy, and my fingers so fat that 't was too small for any of 'em. When I could no longer wear it, I still piously kept it as a talisman, and commonly carried it in the pocket nearest my heart. I 've never trusted it in the hands of any woman, not even in the hands of old Mistress Ursula herself. My grandfather's seal-ring was to me a priceless heirloom ; and, by the Lord, I 've sorrowed more over its theft than King Gyges could have grieved over the loss of his magic ring which he dropped into the sea. In lamenting the loss of this souvenir, so many years worn by me and by my father and by my grandfather, I 've often wept silently, and sometimes I 've drenched myself with my tears. Ah ! welladay ! luck has been against me ever since that ring was picked from my pocket when I fell asleep at the Boar's Head as aforesaid.

Shal. Hem, hm, hm, Sir John ; let me see, let me see ; did not Prince Hal say to thee that that ring was but a trifle, some eight-penny matter, and that 't was copper? I prithee, let me hear, let me hear.

Fal. Indeed, your worship, Hal may have so said to me ; but, if he did, 't was in jest. But, unknown to the prince, there was inset in that ring a most precious stone, to wit, an amethyst, which I do devoutly believe, as the old Greeks and Romans believed, has the power to prevent intoxication. But, zounds, unless your worships wish Sir John Falstaff the First to go on begetting sons and daughters, world without end, ask me not to revise and repeat his family record. I prithee, let me go on and briefly tell the history of those whose names I 've given.

Shal. Go on as you please, Sir John.

Fal. Johannes, the eldest son, took a wife, trod in his father's footsteps, and, in all respects, sustained and strengthened the dignity and power of the Falstaff family. Nicholas and Christian became priests, and Haakon, a monk ; Olaf, Erik, Harold, and Hamlet were all well wived, and lived long and prospered in Norfolk ; Guttorm, who was a scaly, amphibious fellow, and alternately fisherman and pirate, at last went to the dogs, as 't were, for he fell out of a boat and was drowned off the Isle of Dogs ; Gottfried, when fap, fell into the fire and got fried to death ; Sweyn, Snorre, Sigurd, and Hardicanute or Hardiknut (Hardnut, rather), were all scapegraces, who sailed away with the Vikings, and were never heard of more. There is a tradition in our family that they were all drawn into the wonderful and terrible Maelstrom on the coast of Norway, and went down among the krakens at the bottom of the Arctic Sea. Agnes, Christina, and Griselda became nuns ; Angelica, Dorothea, Bertha, Matilda, Ulrica, and Winifred were all happily husbanded—the first two having their homes near Norwich, the second two not far from Bury St. Edmunds, and the third two near Colchester in Essex ; Barbara and Jemima died in their infancy ; and Tabitha sat in the chimney-corner, year after year, purring her life away. But one summer day poor Tabby mysteriously disappeared, never to return. According to a tradition in our family, this is how it happened : A sea-king seized her as she was walking alone and disconsolate on the seashore, carried her on board of his ship, and sailed away to the Isle of Man, or to the tempest-haunted Hebrides, the Orcades, Orkneys, Ireland, Iceland, Thule, or the Lord knows where. There is another tradition concerning Tabitha's disappearance ; 't is as follows : Freya, the Northern Venus, forsaken by her husband Odd, ever hoping for his return, and travelling far and wide in search of him, took Tabby up into her chariot drawn by cats, and in which she drives over the sky. There are tears in my mind's eye as I think of this catastrophe.

By the way, from off our family tree in its early days there fell this chestnut, which, roasted and re-roasted,.has often wrinkled the faces and shaken the sides of many a Falstaff, and which has been carefully kept as an heirloom, as 't were, in our family even unto this day.

Shal. A chestnut, a chestnut as an heirloom, did you say, Sir John ? What sort of a chestnut could that be ? Let me hear, let me hear.

Fal. You shall hear, Master Robert Shallow ; marry, and amen, 't will do your old heart good to hear. One winter night Hardnut, surcharged with liquor as usual, walked into his father's room, and seeing a bottle of sack on the corner of the mantelpiece, he poured out a dose into a cup, took a sip therefrom, and spat it out into the open fire. His father looked up at the moment from a game of draughts which he was playing with a friend, and, not having seen Hardnut take the drink, but seeing the expectorated liquid flame bluely up from the coals, cried out in astonishment : " God-a-mercy, my son, if your spit 's as bad as that, the sooner you swear off from drinking sack the better ! " . . .

. . . . *Hiatus in MS.*

Shal. Let me see, let me see, Sir John, dinner-time is coming on apace, and yet I 've not heard your opinion of sack.

Fal. I 'll soon give it, your worship. 'T is a well-founded tradition in the Falstaff family that every son therein named John, if his age was some fifty, or inclining to threescore, was a goodly portly man and a corpulent, and had a cheerful look, a pleasing eye, a most noble carriage, and virtue in his looks ; and that, because of his congenital Scandinavian thirst, he was never a sneak-cup. The fact should not be forgotten that the warlike Norsemen, who in early times invaded England and established themselves therein, were as much renowned for drinking as for foining and fighting. They have, however, long been reproached because 't is said and believed that even their religion encouraged an implacable hatred of their enemies ; for in the future state, their deceased heroes, at their drinking-bouts in Valhalla, drank wine out of the skulls of their enemies ; * but this belief has no firm foundation in fact and rests only

---

* Isaac Disraeli, in his *Amenities of Literature*, explains the origin of this popular error.—Vol. I., p. 44, note. Am. ed.

upon wild songs sung by crazy scalds. And now, your worship, let me breathe awhile.

Shal. Do so, do so, do so, Sir John.

Fal. Zounds, my throat is parched, and I feel like a whale in a flurry on dry land. God-a-mercy! 't is a long time between cups of sack. Some sack, Francis.

Fran. Anon, anon, sir.

Fal. Back so soon! good boy, give me the cup. [*He drinks.*]

Fal. May it please your worship : A good sherris-sack hath a two-fold operation in it. It ascends me into the brain ; dries me there all the foolish and dull and crudy vapours which environ it ; makes it apprehensive, quick, forgetive, full of nimble, fiery, and delectable shapes ; which, delivered o'er to the voice, the tongue, which is the birth, becomes excellent wit. The second property of your excellent sherris is the warming of the blood ; which, before cold and settled, left the liver white and pale, which is the badge of pusillanimity and cowardice ; but the sherris warms it and makes it course from the inwards to the parts extreme. It illumineth the face, which as a beacon gives warning to all the rest of this little kingdom, man, to arm ; and then the vital commoners and inland petty spirits muster me all to their captain, the heart, who, great and puffed up with this retinue, doth any deed of courage ; and this valour comes of sherris. So that skill in the weapon is nothing without sack, for that sets it a-work ; and learning a mere hoard of gold kept by a devil, till sack commences it and sets it in act and use.

Hereof comes it that Prince Harry is valiant ; for the cold blood he did naturally inherit of his father, he hath, like lean, sterile, and bare land, manured, husbanded, and tilled with excellent endeavour of drinking good and good store of fertile sherris, that he is become very hot and valiant.   If I had a thousand sons, the first humane principle I would teach them should be, to forswear thin potations and to addict themselves to sack.*

Do not your worships well remember my second visit to Justice Shallow in Gloucestershire, and what a merry time we had in his orchard, where in

---

* Sir Theodore Martin, in his *Translation of the Odes of Horace*, says in his note to Ode XXI., of book third : " This joyous panegyric of the virtues of wine will hold its own against anything which has been written on the subject.   Horace's views were akin to those of The Preacher—' Give strong drink unto him that is ready to perish, and wine unto those that be of heavy hearts.   Let him drink and forget his poverty, and remember his misery no more.'   Burns in his own vigorous way echoes unconsciously the very words of Horace :

> ' Food fills the wame, and keeps us livin',
>   Tho' life 's a gift no worth receivin',
>   When heavy dragg'd wi' pine and grievin' ;
>   But, oil'd by thee,
>   The wheels o' life gae down-hill, scrievin',
>   Wi' rattlin' glee.

> ' Thou clears the head o' doited lear ;
>   Thou cheers the heart o' drooping care ;
>   Thou strings the nerves o' labor sair,
>   At 's weary toil ;
>   Thou even brightens dark despair
>   Wi' gloomy smile.' "

an arbour, we had an after-supper, and ate last
year's pippins of his own graffing, with a dish of
caraways, and so forth, particularly the etceteras ?
On that joyful occasion, I specially commended
his serving-man and husbandman, Davy, who
waited on us. In response, Justice Shallow said :
" A good varlet, a good varlet, a very good varlet,
Sir John—by the mass, I have drunk too much sack
at supper !—a good varlet—now sit down, now sit
down.—Come cousin."   The hospitable host urged
us all to be merry, many healths were drank and
wishes spoken for long life, which moved Justice
Silence to sing,

> " Do nothing but eat, and make good cheer,
>   And praise God for the merry year ;
>   When flesh is cheap and females dear,
>   And lusty lads roam here and there
>   So merrily,
>   And ever among so merrily."

And Justice Shallow said, " Be merry, Master Bardolph " ; and to my page, " My little soldier there,
be merry " ; and thereupon Justice Silence, ever
so merrily, sang,

> " Be merry, be merry, my wife has all ;
>   For women are shrews, both short and tall :
>   'T is merry in hall when beards wag all,
>   And welcome merry Shrove-tide.
>   Be merry, be merry."

At the end of this song, I remarked, " I did not
think Master Silence had been a man of this mettle." " Who, I ? " said the singer, " I have been
merry twice and once, ere now."   When Davy

pledged Bardolph—"A cup of wine, sir!" Silence chimed in with, "A cup of wine, that 's brisk and fine." And later on in the sweet o' the night, good Master Silence boozily warbled,

> " Fill the cup, and let it come ;
>   I 'll pledge you a mile to the bottom."

But the culmination of this scene of conviviality was when the songster accepted my pledge to a bumper, and I replied, " Why, now you have done me right," and he responded,

> " Do me right,
>   And dub me knight ;
>   Samingo ! *   Is 't not so ?"

" 'T is so," said I ; and Silence piped, " Is 't so ? Why, then, say an old man can do somewhat."

And now, may it please your worships, since I have refreshed your memories of that scene of revelry by night, long years ago, in an arbour in the orchard of that gentle gentleman, Master Robert Shallow, esquire, and hard by his goodly dwelling, I may be permitted to add that when that merry party broke up, Sir John Falstaff, the defendant in this action, made the following order, to wit : " Carry Master Silence to bed."

Sil. Good Sir John, that 's twenty year or more

---

* " Do me right " · A common expression in drinking healths. " And dub me knight " : It was the custom in the time of Shakespeare to drink a mighty bumper kneeling, to the health of one's mistress. He who performed this exploit was dubbed a *knight* for the evening. " Samingo " · A boozy abbreviation of " San Domingo," which was a common burden of drinking-songs.—ROLFE.

ago ; but, old as I am, I well remember the sweet o' that night, indeed, sir, I do ; and a merry heart lives long-a ; be merry, be merry. 'T is merry in hall when beards wag all. Do, ra, mi, fa, sol, la— tra la, tra la-a-a-a-a ! Ah! I cannot quaver and sing as I could twenty year ago. Alas, I lost my voice with singing of songs that merry, merry night in cousin Shallow's orchard, and, by my troth, I 've never since found so much as a demisemi- quaver of it. Tra la, tra-la-a-a-a-a !

Shal. Peace, cousin Silence, peace ; I prithee, sing not here in court ; let us confer a little, along with cousin Slender, about the business before us ; let us do so, let us do so.

Fal. [*Aside.*] Come hither, Francis.

Fran. Anon, anon, sir.

Fal. [*Aside.*] Bring me a cup of sack, good Francis, that I may moisten my clay while that precious pair of justices are piddling over my case. If I have drunk to-day, then I am no two-legged creature, and nothing but a bunch of radish.

Fran. O Lord, Sir John, I 'll be sworn upon all the books in England,—

Fal. Francis ! away, thou whoreson, upright rabbit, away !

Fran. Anon, anon, sir.

. . . . *Hic pauca*
. . . . *desunt in MS.*

Shal. By the mass, Sir John, 't is now high noon by St. Michael's clock ; 't is so, 't is so, 't is so. This court is adjourned until two of the clock in the afternoon of to-day.

Thereupon Justice Shallow arose, wiped the sweat from his brow, and whispered to himself, " Beshrew my heart, if I do not wish I were fairly rid of this examination, my hands washed clean thereof, and I safely back to my dwelling-house in Gloucestershire. I am a-weary with sitting on this hard bench on such a hot day, and suffering the pangs of thirst. But, by my troth, I 'll soon hear the clinking of pewter ; 't is so, 't is so, 't is so, indeed."

In a few moments Justices Shallow and Silence, Master Slender and Sir Hugh Evans, betook themselves to their respective rooms in the Boar's Head ; and it seems, according to the manuscript, that they came no more to the court-room during that day.

PUNCTUALLY at the afternoon hour to which the court had adjourned, Sir John sat serenely in the prisoners' dock, twiddling his thumbs, gazing in the direction of the taproom of the Boar's Head, sniffing the air from that quarter, and humming to himself a ballad of the olden time when Arthur was a worthy king. But Justices Shallow and Silence came not, and were in default for the residue of the day. Presently he lapsed for a brief season into a meditative mood, from which he was aroused by the noisy entry of Francis, playfully pursued by his fellow-drawer Ralph. "How now, Francis," said Sir John, "what a devil dost thou here in this sacred temple of Themis, thou naughty varlet? Seest thou not, pictured on the wall behind the judgment-seat, that cold, stately, and severe goddess who hath her eyes bandaged as if to play hood-man-blind with Law and Justice? It becomes thee to be quiet and reverent in this court-room. Give me a cup of sack, rogue; zounds, if I have drunk to-day, then am I a Jew else, an Ebrew Jew."

Fran. Anon, anon, sir.

Fal. Back so soon! boy, give me the cup.

Sir John took the cup handed up to him, and kissed it as Titan kisses a dish of butter, pitiful-hearted butter, that melts at the sweet tale of the sun. While in the act of wiping his mouth and mustachios, his wandering eyes caught sight of the recruits furnished him by Justice Shallow, to wit, Ralph Mouldy, Simon Shadow, Thomas Wart, Francis Feeble, and Peter Bullcalf, all of whom had that day dined together at free-lunch counters, here and there, in Pudding Lane and at Pie-Corner, and were then leaning in a row upon the railing which enclosed the bar of the court, and gazing in open-mouthed astonishment upon himself. At his beck this squalid squad of scarecrow soldiers came before him for review. "'Sblood!" said Sir John, " I am a chewet, a whoreson, impudent, embossed rascal, all filled up with guts and midriff, if I did not think that every mothers' son of you had long ago become food for powder and filled a pit on that royal field of Shrewsbury * as well as better soldiers could have done. Zounds! I reported to Sir Walter Blunt that I had led you, along with my other ragamuffins, where you were all well peppered and filled with lead ; that there were not three of my hundred and fifty left alive ; and that the survivors, if any there might be, were for the town's end, to beg during life. Let Sathanas make a carbonado of me, and broil me to death on a gridiron as St. Lawrence was, if I ever looked to see any of you left alive after the battle of Shrewsbury, wherein that hot termagant Scot, Douglas, nearly embowelled me, and paid me scot and lot too. Zounds ! which one of these ragamuffins is Mouldy ? Where is he ?

Mouldy. Here, an 't please you.

Fal. Is thy name Ralph Mouldy ?

Mouldy. Yea, sir.

---

* Old Jack's remembrance seems to have been very strangely at fault here. Mouldy and the other " sufficient men " were provided by Justice Shallow for service as soldiers in Yorkshire ; but as to the battle of Shrewsbury, they were not " in it."—WOPSLE.

Fal. "T is the more time thou wert used. Prick him, Bardolph.

Mouldy. I was pricked well enough before, an you could have left me alone ; my old dame will be undone now for one to do her husbandry and drudgery. You need not to have pricked me ; there are other men fitter to go out than I.

Fal. Go to ; peace, Mouldy ! thou shalt go. Mouldy, it is time thou wert spent.

Mouldy. Spent ! good Sir John, I have already seen and fixed good Master Corporate Captain Bardolph, for my old dame's sake, to stand my friend and save me from going to the wars ; she has nobody to do anything about her when I am gone ; and she is old, and cannot help herself.

Fal. Go to ; well, stand aside ; stay at home till thou 'rt past service. Where 's Simon Shadow ?

Shadow. Here, sir.

Fal. Shadow, whose son art thou ?

Shadow. My mother's son, sir.

Fal. Thy mother's son ! like enough, and thy father's shadow ; so the son of the female is the shadow of the male. It is often so, indeed ; but much of the father's substance ! Yea, marry, let me have thee to sit under ; thou 'rt like to be a cold soldier. Shadow will serve for summer ; prick him, Bardolph, for we have a number of shadows to fill up the muster-book. Stand aside, Shadow. Thomas Wart ! Where 's he ?

Wart. Here, sir.

Fal. Is thy name Wart ?

Wart. Yea, sir.

Fal. Thou art a very ragged wart. It were superfluous to prick thee down ; for thy apparel is built upon thy back and thy whole frame stands upon pins. But, go to ; Wart, thou shalt go to the wars. Francis Feeble ! Where 's he ?

Feeble. Here, sir.

Fal. What trade art thou of, Feeble ?

Feeble. A woman's tailor, sir.

Fal. Wilt thou make as many holes in an enemy's battle as thou hast done in a woman's petticoat ?

Feeble. I will do my good will, sir ; you can do no more.

Fal. Well said, good woman's tailor ! well said, courageous Feeble ! thou wilt be as valiant as the wrathful dove or most magnanimous mouse. Prick the woman 's tailor well, Bardolph, and prick him deep ; let that suffice, most forcible Feeble.

Feeble. It shall suffice, sir. But, by my troth, I care not ; a man can die but once : we owe God a death. I 'll ne'er bear a base mind : an 't be my destiny, so ; an 't be not, so. No man is too good to serve 's prince ; and let it go which way it will, he that dies this year is quit for the next.

Fal. Well said ; thou 'rt a good fellow.

Feeble. Faith, I 'll bear no base mind.

Fal. Peter Bullcalf ! yea, marry, let 's see Bullcalf.

Bullcalf. Here, sir.

Fal. Fore God, thou 'rt a likely fellow, a good-limbed fellow, young, strong, and of good friends. Bardolph, come prick me Bullcalf till he roar again.

Bullcalf. O Lord ! good Sir John, I am a dis-eased man.

Fal. What disease hast thou ?

Bullcalf. A whoreson cold, sir, a cough, sir, which I caught with ringing in the king's affairs upon his coronation-day, sir.

Fal. Come, thou shalt go to the wars in a gown ; we will have away thy cold ; and I will take such order that thy friends shall ring for thee.

Bullcalf. But, Sir John, I've already fixed good Master Corporate Bardolph, for four Harry ten shillings in French crowns in hand paid him, to stand my friend, as well as Mouldy's friend, and free us from going to the wars. In very truth, good Sir John, I had as lief be hanged, sir, as go : and yet, for mine own part, sir, I do not care ; but rather, because I am unwilling, and, for mine own part, have a desire to stay with my friends ; else, sir, I did not care, for mine own part, so much.

Fal. Go to ; well, stand aside, Bullcalf, and stay at home and grow till thy cough hath ceased and thou 'rt fit for service. I will none of thee. And yet, if Justice Shallow were here, he 'd declare Mouldy and Bullcalf to be by far the likeliest of this lot of pusillanimous tatterdemalions, and object to freeing them from going to the wars. But Master Shallow being absent, wilt thou, Master Peter Bullcalf, tell me how to choose a man ? Care I for the limb, the thews, the stature, bulk, and big assemblance of a man ! Give me the spirit, Master Bullcalf.—Here 's Wart ; you see what a ragged appearance it is : a' shall charge you and discharge you with the motion of a pewterer's hammer, come off and on swifter than he that gibbets on the brewer's bucket.—And this same half-faced fellow, Shadow ; give me this man : he presents no mark to the enemy ; the foeman may with as great aim level at the edge of a penknife. And for a retreat, —how swiftly will this Feeble, the woman's tailor, run off ! O, give me the spare men, and spare me the great ones.—Bullcalf, put me this staff as and for a caliver into Wart's hand. Hold, Wart, traverse ; thus, thus, thus ; come, manage me your caliver. So : very well ; go to ; very good, exceeding good. O, give me always a little, lean, old, chopt, bald shot.—Well said, i' faith, Wart ; thou 'rt a good scab : hold, there 's a tester for thee ; but, I prithee, keep it not in thy pouch, but give it to a barber for shaving those lantern-jaws of thine.

And now, Peter Bullcalf o' the green, a word in your ear, sir. Fore God, I am sorry for thee because thou 'rt a diseased man. Are there not doctors and doctors who can phlebotomize thee, and salivate thee, and dephlogisticate thee, and do for thee various other tricks of that sort, and at the last medicine away thy whoreson cold and cough, caught long ago, and, as thou sayest, in the king's service ? What has been done to heal thee ? I prithee, tell me.

Bullcalf. Good Sir John, I 've tried all sorts of doctors, and though they all promised to cure me, yet not one of them has ever done me any good by his treatment ; and now my last state is worse than the first. And so we three—my cold, my cough, and I—go on and on together, and I, day after day, am coughing my way into my coffin. One of my doctors gave me hocus-pocus boluses as big as gooseberries ; another, pills as little as. mustard seeds ; another pounded and pommelled me as if I were a beefsteak ; another filled and bloated me with water which I abhor either to drink of, or to wash myself with ; another dosed me with syrup which he called the Elixir of Life ; another fed me with a nasty gruel made thick and slab ; another put me in a sweat-box and anointed me with opodeldoc and rubbed it in till I howled with pain ; another put a prickly porous-plaster all over my chest as though 't were a breastplate ; another soaked a red woollen rag in some sort of liniment and tied it around my weasand ; and still another gave me no medicine, i' faith, but tried to cure me by faith and the laying on of his hands. And the last doctor I 've had, Dr. Pillgarlic, told my good dame to scrape the bark from some shrub or other —I 've quite forgot its name—then to steep this bark, make the decoction strong, and often give me thereof to drink when 't was piping hot all that I could hold. And, moreover, this doctor said that if the bark had been scraped up, the tea thereof, made and taken as directed, would act as an emetic ; but, if it had been scraped down, 't would act as a cathartic. My good dame made the tea and filled me therewith. It soon threw me into a great sweat ; but it wrought neither up nor down, and put me in such misery and pain that I almost gave up the ghost. Alas, alas ! my good dame, who had lately slipped her calf and was in consequence distraught and often forgetful, had scraped the bark both ways. In very truth, sir, I 'd as lief be hanged as take any more doctor's stuff. I prithee, Sir John, tell me what to do.

Fal. Look you, Peter Bullcalf, I have read in Galen and Hippocrates and other mediciners, and in the alchemists as well, and have studied physianthropy generally ; and so I 've become something of a medicaster myself. I now give it as my opinion that if all the skimble-skamble stuff set down and described in the pharmacopœia could be thrown into the sea, 't would be all the better for mankind, and all the worse for the fishes. Zounds ! do thou dismiss all doctors, throw physic to the dogs, and have none of it. Give the druggers the go-by. For it hath lately been discovered that as a drug diminishes in quantity so its potency increases ; and especially is 't so when the drug is mentalized with a high attenuation of belief or faith. When I think of the dynamic nature of a pellet, unmedicated save by a molecule of ipecacuanha, for example, but mentalized with the highest attenuation of belief, and then taken into the human stomach—when I think of the potentiality of such a globulet invisible to any thick sight, and so lodged within a man, by the Lord, good Peter Bullcalf, though I am no coward, yet am I horribly afeard, and do I shake and quake with terror. Francis !

Fran. Anon, anon, sir.

Fal. Fetch me a cup of my magistral, my cure-all, for all the natural shocks and ills that I 'm heir to. Away, Francis, away !

Fran. Anon, anon, sir. O Lord, Sir John, what do you mean?

Fal. Some sack, Francis.

Fran. Anon, anon, sir.

.   .   .   . *Hic pauca verba*

.   .   .   . *desunt in MS.*

Fal. Mark me, Peter Bullcalf, it hath been but lately discovered that all diseases and suffering are mere beliefs, images of mortal thoughts superimposed on the human body, and appearing thereon by the consent of the mind; that mind, not matter, cures disease; that a change of belief changes all the physical symptoms, and determines a case for better or for worse; that all disease is the result of hallucination, and can convey its ill-effects no further than mortal mind maps out; that the evidence of the senses is not to be accepted in the case of sickness any more than it is in case of sin; that evil is an awful unreality; that sickness is a growth of illusion, springing from a seed of thought, either thy own or another's; that disease is a fear expressed not so much by the lips as the functions of the body, and that, mitigate this fear, and you relieve the oppressed organ; that pain is a figment of the imagination; that decrepitude is an illusion; that there is no need of dying, for death is an illusion; that all is mind, and that there is no matter.

"Since these things are so,"* as Cicero so often says, do thou, Peter Bullcalf, suffer me to prescribe in thy case. What is wanting in thee is more belief

---

* *Quæ quum ita sint.*

or faith, and less medicine ; add to thy faith, and
subtract from thy medicine ; aggravate the former
a thousand fold—raise it even to the nth power ;
but divide and subdivide and diminish the latter
accordingly. Make and hourly take an unmedicated pellet—surely thy good wife will give thee a
bit of bread to make the globulets of ; or, in default
of some crumbs of bread, do thou always keep
about thee a ha'pennyworth of sugar-candy, and
mentalize it with a very high attenuation of belief,
a belief as tenuous as the dream of the shadow of a
shade of a surmise of a suspicion of a supposition,
or as ethereous and metaphysical as a chimæra buz-
zing *in vacuo*, and endeavouring to devour second
intentions ; and when thou hast thus mentalized
the sugar-candy, do thou slightly lick thereof at
least threescore and ten times a day, all the while
believing that thou hast no whoreson cold and
cough, and, by the Lord, thou 'lt soon have them
both away, and the late Peter Bullcalf o' the green
will be himself again. Ay, marry, medicate thyself
in the way I 've told thee of, and thou canst soon
serve as a sort of bullbeggar to all the bad children
in thy bailiwick ; nay more, and something better,
for thou 'lt early become as fully cornuted and robustious as any town-bull or young bull of Bashan, or
even Apis himself, and wilt bellow and roar so that
't will do any man's, or woman's, heart good to hear
thee ; and to me, peradventure thou 'lt joyfully cry,
in thy most sonorous tones," Bless thee, bully doctor,
bless thee." Zounds ! do thou take old Jack's sovereign remedy for a whoreson cold and a cough, and

also a good sherris-sack, and they 'll together soon
and surely make thee well and enable thee to roar
and roar again and as loudly as the Devil is said to
have done when, having poked his head into St. Dun-
stan's cell, the saint seized Old Nick by the nose
with a pair of red-hot pincers, and held him there
till Lord Harry made the whole neighbourhood re-
sound with his bellowings.*   An you do not, then
am I a soused gurnet, a deboshed fish, a shotten
herring.

I bethink me of another matter of concern to
thee, brave Bullcalf. Fore God, thou richly deserv-
est a pension for ringing and roaring on behalf of
His Majesty, Hal's father, upon his coronation-day.
'T was so doing in the king's affairs that solely and
proximately caused thee to become a diseased man,
was 't not ?

Bullcalf. Yea, good Sir John, that was it, that
was the very cause, indeed, sir, 't was. Before that
day, I 'd never caught a cold, sir, nor had a cough,
sir, nor been a diseased man, sir. In very truth,
sir, I 'd never been sick a day in my life, sir, nor an
hour, sir. No man is too good to serve his master,
the king ; an it be my fate to die for his sake, sir,
it must be so, sir : a man can die but once, and he
that dies this year, will not die the next. Is 't not
so, Sir John ? But, as I 've said, sir, that cold and
cough caught me by the scruff o' my neck, as 't
were, and they together are fast hustling me into
my grave, sir, a young man and of good friends, as

____

*Hume, *Hist. Eng.* Vol. I., ch. 2.

I am, sir, and long before my time, sir. Though I 'd not thought of it before, it doth now seem to me that the king ought to do something for me, sir, for 't was in his service that I took my death-cold, and my cough, sir. I suppose that the king whom I served on that day, whatever his name may be, is reigning yet ? An he be, I may get my pension before I die. Good Sir Doctor—no, good Sir John, I mean—an thou 'lt fix and mix the medicine, I 'll take it as thou hast told me, sir. In very truth, sir, I 'd as lief be hanged to-day at sunset, sir, as die this year ; and yet, for mine own part, sir, I do not care so much ; but rather, because I am unwilling, and, for mine own part, have a desire to stay with my friends on this earth many years, sir, and with my dame, sir, though she be a shrew, sir, and hath a sharp tongue, sir, which hath often caused me to have a desire, at once, to go to heaven, or to go to——

Fal. Go to ; peace, brave Bullcalf, peace ; an it had been good King Arthur in whose affairs thou didst so loyally ring and roar, that worthy king would long since have allowed thee a pension sufficient for thy needs as an invalid, would have knighted thee and granted thee a coat-of-arms whereon is emblazoned a bull rampant, a cow couchant, a bull calf levant, a pitch-fork standant in a dunghill, a bar sinister, and so forth ; and, peradventure, His Majesty would have made thee a lordkin called Lord Nebuchadnezzar, and chosen thee as a member of his household under the name and style of My High and Mighty Master and Lord-

Keeper of the King's Bull-Pen, with all the honours and emoluments appurtenant unto the ancient and honourable office aforesaid. But, alas, alas! poor Peter, thou didst not serve Arthur when he was approved king and crowned, but quite another. The wearers of crowns are generally forgetful and ungrateful. King Henry the Fifth is not what Prince Hal was to me, and has not allowed me a competence for life, nor given me advancement according to my merits and as he promised on his coronation-day.

At this moment Sir John wildly threw up his arms, made a wry face, as though suffering acute pain, and exclaimed, "Oh! ah! eh! God-a-mercy!" Great drops of sweat beaded his forehead, while several big round tears coursed one another down his ruddy Roman nose in piteous chase. He suddenly lifted his right foot from the floor, stood tremblingly on the other for some seconds, then sank into his chair, and thus soliloquized:

"A pox of this gout! or, a gout of this pox! for the one or the other plays the rogue with my great toe. 'T is no matter if I do halt; I have the wars for my colour, and my pension shall seem the more reasonable. A good wit will make use of anything. I will turn diseases to commodity; and my motto shall be the gamblers' motto, that success consists not so much in having a good hand, as in playing a poor one well. One of the few fundamental legal principles which I picked up when I was a student at Clement's Inn, is this one:

In jure non remota causa sed proxima spectatur ; but
this maxim does not, forsooth, always hold good in
the matter of securing an invalid's pension because
of disease alleged to have been contracted during
service as a soldier on the king's side in the wars.
If, for example, John o' Noakes, or Tom Styles, or
John Doe, or Richard Roe, hath served his sovereign as a soldier, and if, moreover, he hath a good
wit, he may turn almost any disease or bodily infirmity which he hath, to his advantage in getting a
pension for the loss of an eye, or a tooth, or a toe,
or a finger ; or, because he hath the gout, a cough,
the asthma, a diarrhœa, the dyspepsia, insomnia,
neuralgia, sciatica, scrofula, a vertigo, the lumbago,
or some other disease whose name ends with the
interjectional sound of *oh, ah,* or *eh,* or which has
otherwhere in its name these, and the like, syllables
of sorrow, pain, fear, dread, or horror. The pension which I applied for soon after the battle of
Shrewsbury, not so much, however, on account of
my valorous deeds therein as because I—though
I 'm not a swallow, an arrow, nor a bullet, nor
have I, in my poor old motion, the expedition of
thought—had speeded with the very extremest
inch of possibility, and had foundered ninescore
and odd post-horses in reaching Gaultree Forest
in Yorkshire, and there, travel-tainted as I was, and
sorely galled in my seat, and, with my girdle
broken, and all my entrails beshaken, churned,
and, as 't were, turned topsy-turvy, by long and
hard horseback riding, I had, in my pure and
immaculate valour, taken Sir John Colevile of

the Dale prisoner, a most furious and valorous enemy. But what of that? he saw me, and yielded at once; so that I may justly say, with the hook-nosed fellow of Rome, I came, saw, and overcame. Zounds, not a penny of the pension so long due me, so long delayed and greatly needed, has found its way into my purse, although as soon as I 'd delivered my famous rebel prisoner into the power of Prince John of Lancaster, and he 'd sent Colevile with his confederates to York to be there presently beheaded, I besought his grace that what I 'd done in the behalf of the king, his father, might not be bedwarfed, but that it might be booked with the rest of that day's deeds of valour; or, by the Lord, I 'd have it in a particular ballad else, with mine own picture on the top on 't, Colevile kissing my foot. And, moreover, I besought his grace to let me have right, and let desert mount; asked for leave to go through Gloucestershire and there visit my particular friend, Master Robert Shallow, esquire; and entreated that, when he 'd returned to court, he would ever stand my good lord, let me shine as well as others, and befriend me there. Prince John then bade me farewell, saying that he, in his condition, would speak better of me than I deserved; but, welladay! spoken words are often mere wind which bloweth where it listeth; and princes' promises are too often false, and prove to be no better than wind-broken words—only these and nothing more. A fool, a wretched fool, a knotty-pated fool, was I to hang my hopes of advancement on Prince John's favour, for that same sober-blooded boy did not love me ; but that was no marvel, for he drank no wine. He's never spoken well of me at court, though his brother Thomas, Duke of Clarence, there reminded him that he should speak me fair ; nor has he done anything that might do me good. That demure and boyish prince has never come to any proof ; and to him poor old Jack is to-day as a back number of a newspaper, or as an almanac of a dozen years agone, read no more and altogether forgotten ; or, like unto a handbill, or a street-ballad, which has become the sport of the winds, and may, peradventure, be brought to base uses at the last. But, by the Lord, 't will will be no neck-and-neck race between Prince John of Lancaster and Sir John Falstaff in their desire and struggle to have their names writ large and booked forever in the world's remembrance. If I, in the clear sky of fame, do not in aftertimes o'ershine Prince John as much as the full moon doth the cinders of the element, which show like gilt two-pences, like pins' heads, believe not the word of the noble. Poh ! that pin-headed prince's name and fame will be no more remembered than the shapes of clouds at midnight a twelvemonth back. For so many years hath my pension, long past due me for doing on that royal field of Shrewsbury, in Gaultree Forest, and elsewhere, such deeds in arms as Turk Gregory never did nor could, been in arrears that to-day it amounts to a good round sum ; an 't were paid, I would not in my old days be distracted and oppressed with poverty. Zounds ! I pray that cruel necessity may not drive me upon the London streets, force me to doff a greasy and stinking skullcup, hold forth a beggar's grimy hand, and beseechingly cry, *Date obolum Belisario : vacuus venter præcepta non audit, poscit, appellat.* Had I now in my possession my pension, with all proper arrearages, beshrew my heart, if I do not soon marry Mistress Ursula Griselda Distaff, if, indeed, she be above ground and unhusbanded, can abide me, and will gladly have me for a *de facto* husband. By my troth, I 've not seen her for a score of years at least. ˙Is she rich ? No. Am I rich ? No. Is she young ? No-o. Am I young ? No-o. Is she beautiful ? No-o-o. Am I handsome ? No-o-o. Hath she ever had the heartache ? I don't know. Have I ever had the heartache ? She does n't know. What fad, if any she hath, hath she ? Cats. Have I any fad ? and, if yea, what is 't ? Scat ! and sack and sugar, and so forth. Is she not a she-bear ? Ay and no, too ; that 's what the name Ursula means ; but what 's in a name ? She 's never hurt me by her hugging, no, no-o. Am I a he-bear ? I 'm often called ' Old Grizzly,' a nickname which, I confess, in some sort sorts well with my shape, looks, and clumsy carriage of myself ; but that I am bearish by nature and in the humours of my blood, I utterly deny. Is she not a prim, pragmatical old virgin, who hath kept her virtue by her until it hath turned sour ? Yea and nay, too ; I know not. Is she subject to fits of the vapours ? Would she fall into a swoon because of a declaration of love or the presence of a mouse ? Am I not an intolerant and intolerable old bachelor, who, all his life long, hath not been too virtuous for cakes and ale, sack and sugar, and divers etceteras? Yea, marry; but, if that man, sweet, kind, true, and old Jack Falstaff, should be lewdly given, he deceiveth me; for, I see virtue in his looks; that is to say, the outlines of virtue without the details. Are Ursula's bonnets bewitching, and her gigot-sleeved gowns always marvels of good taste, and the envy of her female friends? So 't is said. Does my dress become me? Not always; zounds! not when I was withered like an old apple-john, and my skin hung about me like an old lady's loose gown; nor when those mischievous Mesdames Page and Ford, once upon a time, dressed me in the big gown and thrummed hat and muffler of old Mother Pratt, the fat woman of Brentford, in which disguise was I, a noble knight, alas, alack! so grievously cudgelled by jealous Master Ford, *alias* Brook, that out of me was melted and tried, drop by drop, enough lard to liquor a dozen pair of fishermen's boots. Is Ursula fat, fair, and still forty? 'T is said that she is eating plentifully of water-cresses to bring back the bloom of her complexion. Does she use perfumes that she may smell as sweet as a rose?* Is she more than common tall? or is she short and dumpy? Doth she take long-metre, or short-metre, steps? Hath she a feline face? hath she doves' eyes? is she shrill-tongued or low? and are her hands such as old Greek sculptors gave their god-

---

* *Mulier tum recte olet ubi nihil olet*, saith Plautus.

desses, or such as may be likened to the hands of the Madonna? Is her nose as the tower of Lebanon which looketh toward Damascus? Is her temper tart and encroaching? and hath she a habit of nagging and of giving gratuitous advice? Would she probably prove to be a kicksy-wicksy wife? By the way, is the old, old woman—Ursula's mother—yet alive? doth she still live? She doth, she doth, she doth. . . . .

. . . . *Hiatus in MS.*
What is Mistress Ursula Griselda Distaff about? Some inches less than an ell Flemish, I suppose, for I 'm told that she hath a wasp-like waist. What am I about? Two yards and more. We two, we too-too old two,—would we, could we, make a happy match, and, at last united in the holy bonds of wedlock, rub along, scrub along, and scratch along together —with no burns and blisters for ourselves, and no total loss to some happy home fire insurance company—for better for worse, for richer for poorer, in sickness and in health, each loving and cherishing the other, till death do us part? Being an inexpert in all matters matrimonial, I don't know; but I 'm inclined to think that this match will never go off —will never show even a spark. They do say, however, that matches are made in heaven; but, zounds! I 'm sure that all of them were not made there; for not a few of 'em are tipped with brimstone, and seem, presumptively at least, to have been made somewhere else. Some so-called happy matches leave in their trail phosphorescent streaks and a sulphurous smell, and other hints of their Tarta-

rean origin. *Quære :* Are not many matches made in Hades ? So end my quips and catechism.

"An I were well wived, and were I myself worthy in every way of a good wife, I 'd hereafter take mine ease, not in mine inn, but at mine own fireside. And, moreover, I 'd quoit the Devil downstairs, like a shove-groat shilling, kick him out of my door (if my gouty great toe would permit me to do it), forbid the future circulation of that evil and malignant spirit in and around my house, have holy water sprinkled by a priest all over my premises, put up a God-bless-our-home card over my mantel-piece, and cause to be painted by one of the old masters, upon one entire wall of my dining- and wining-room, a picture, as large as life, of that superannuated elephant, Sir John Fustilugs, on horseback, having a drawn sword in his hand, hallooing his terrible name to the enemy in flight and dimly visible in the distance, and shouting and singing, 'God save the King'; and, marry, and amen, I 'd purge, and leave sack, and live cleanly, as a noble old knight should do.

"Ancient writers do report that in Rome, under the Cæsars, every man might have a statue, and if he had no friends or clients to give him one, he might put it up and pay for it himself. And so, if there 's nobody who cares enough for me to give me a statue, by the Lord, I 'll put up one at mine own cost ; an I do, it shall be of brass, of course, and of heroic size, and I shall appear as riding o' horseback at high speed, and up a hill perpendicular ; and at the base of my statue, there shall be a statuette of Prince John of Lancaster represented as bare-headed, kneeling, and in the act of kissing my foot. But, hold up ! old Jack, bethink thyself. To set up the statuette aforesaid, may be to commit treason—constructive treason—and so to rear the crest of disloyalty as to attack even majesty itself. Therefore, I 'll none of it. But othergates, shall Sir John Falstaff, in the world's wide eye, be like the loftiest Alp—seen, but not surmounted and crossed, by great Hannibal—and this same Princeling John of Lancaster shall be as a mole-hill, unnoted by the multitude, and daily trodden under foot of men."

Sir John paused in his speech to rest and breathe awhile ; but soon seeing that the five ragamuffins aforesaid were still standing before him, and that they were all ill at ease and astonished at his eccentric behaviour, he slowly arose, and leaning upon his staff to afford relief to his gouty toe, resumed his remarks :

Fal. Be not amazed, gentles ; look you, Peter Bullcalf o' the green, what was I last talking to thee about ? 'T was of the pension justly due thee because of the whoreson cold and the cough which thou caughtest in the king's service upon his coronation-day, was 't not ?

Bullcalf. Yea, Sir John ; that was it, sir.

Mouldy. Yea, Sir John, 't was of Peter's pension that thou wast talking. By my troth, I am a diseased man, and deserve to have a pension, as much as Bullcalf. I do not care for mine own part so much ; but my dame is, as I 've said, old, and cannot help herself.

13

Shadow. Good Sir John, I, too, am a diseased man, and deserve to have a pension, whatever good thing that may be.

Wart. And I, too, Sir John.

Feeble. And I, too, Sir John.

Fal. Ye pitiful, small-beer, bottle-ale rascals, ye lunch-fiends, feeding, here and there, in London, upon crusts of rye and barley bread, cold and broken meats, mouldy stewed prunes, dried cakes, and cheese that hath served as bait for mouse-traps; ye cankers of a calm world and a long peace, ten times more dishonourable ragged than an old faced ancient,—and so ye all beg for pensions because of diseases contracted while in the king's service, forsooth! Listen. Ye slaves as ragged as Lazarus in the painted cloth, where the glutton's dogs licked his sores,—ye are all soldiers with hearts in your bellies no bigger than pins' heads; such soldiers as had as lieve hear the Devil as a drum; such as fear the report of a caliver worse than a struck fowl or a hurt wild-duck. Never until now hath mine eye seen such a squad of scarecrows, such sodden faces, shaking nether lips, eyes bright as coddled gooseberries, noses illumined with hell-fire, paunches ale-swelled, doublets liquor-stained, hats crushed from having been much slept in, raiment ruinous, shoes such as allow the toes to peep through the over-leather, feet of uncommon fetor, faugh!—the tapster having taken from you the money which should have been paid the tailor and the cobbler, the grocer and the butcher; and then, God-a-mercy, think of your miserable wives, and of your children gotten in drink. The good hostess of the Boar's Head would say of my speech to you, as she once said to swaggering Pistol : "By my troth, these are very bitter words." I grant you, ye beggarly and cowardly knaves, that my words to you are very bitter ; but, by the Lord, are they not altogether true ? How now, Francis ?

Fran. Anon, anon, sir.

Fal. Give me a cup of sack, boy, to make my eyes look red, that it may be thought I have wept ; for I have spoken in King Cambyses' vein.

Fran. Anon, anon, sir.

The sack was soon fetched, and the fat knight, after draining the cup, cast at it a knowing and reminiscent look, and mused a little while thereon as though 't were the identical " parcel-gilt goblet " upon which, according to the vehement declaration of Dame Quickly, he had, once upon a time, sworn to make her his lady, his wife. He suddenly aroused himself from his meditation, glanced with a merry glint at Francis and the ragged recruits, and thereupon continued his conversation :

Fal. I am a rogue if I have drunk to-day ; come hither, Francis, and stay within my call; what o'clock is 't, Francis ?

Fran. Anon, anon, sir ; St. Michael's clock is upon the stroke of four.

Fal. Stand hard by me, Francis, and do not thou lose a word of what is spoken.

Fran. Anon, anon, sir.

Fal. Francis, thou hast fewer words than a parrot, and yet thou art the son of a woman ; thy industry is up-stairs and down-stairs, and in going to and from the taproom ; belike, then, thy speech is mostly made up of ' Anon, anon, sir ' and of tavern-reckonings. Is 't not so, sirrah ?

Fran. Anon, anon, sir ; yea, sir, Sir John.

Fal. Zounds ! Mouldy, Shadow, Wart, Feeble, and last, but not least, Peter Bullcalf o' the green, what earthquake hath hoisted and hurly-burlied you all out of your neglected and for-gotten graves in Gloucestershire, and tumbled you up to London, to wicked London ? D' ye think that ye 've risen from the dead, and that the great day of judgment is at hand ? Ye whore-son caterpillars, bacon-fed knaves, what are ye all here for ?

Omnes. We have come hither as witnesses for the Crown against one Sir John Falstaff.

Fal. Ye droughty, dirty dogs, would ye, one and all, drink ?

Omnes. Ay, marry, would we ; will your worship stand for each of us a pot of ale, or beer, or wine ?

Fal. That will I ; and each and every mother's son of you shall lap on my score. Most forcible Feeble, what wilt thou drink ?

Feeble. A pot of small beer, sir ; or, for God's sake, sir, a cup of horse-radish ale which I drink at home whenever I can get it, for I 'm troubled with the gravel.

Fal. Go to ; with the gravel in thy broken shoes, and between thy dirty and earthy toes——

Feeble. Nay, good Sir John, not there, but with the gravel in my——

Fal. I see, I see, most forcible Feeble ; 't is the gravel in thy structure, in thy mental make-up, that troubles thee withal. Yea, marry, 't is that which makes thee so gritty and of so invincible a spirit ; or, courageous Feeble, was 't not thy gravel which caused thee to run away—to scratch gravel, as they say—from the wars on the eve of a battle ?

Feeble. It may have been so, sir ; 't was my destiny just then to be sorely taken with my old complaint, and, distraughted 'twixt pain and duty, I ran home, as though the devil was after me, to drink a cup of horse-radish ale ; i' faith, 't was not because I 'm a coward, sir.

Fal. Well said, courageous Feeble ; thou 'rt not a bad fellow after all.

Feeble. Oh ! oh ! ooh ! ah !

Fal. Zounds ! What 's the matter ? What ails thee, poor Feeble ?

Feeble. Oh ! ooh ! good Sir John, I 'm gravelled again. Oh ! ah ! ooh !

Fal. Francis ?

Fran. Anon, anon, sir.

Fal. Go fetch forthwith for Feeble a cup of horse-radish ale. Away, boy, away.

Fran. Anon, anon, sir ; O Lord, Sir John, till now I 've never heard of horse-radish ale. I 'm cocksure that 't is not kept on tap at the Boar's Head, nor at any other tavern in Eastcheap.*

---

* Samuel Pepys, in his *Diary and Correspondence*, under date of 16 September, 1664, writes, among other things, as follows :

"Met Mr. Partiger, and he would needs have me drink a

But, anon, anon, sir, I 'll go for it.

Fal. Boy, stay a little; hem, hm, hm, a pot of small beer,—will not that poor creature suffice, poor Feeble?

Feeble. It shall suffice, sir; eigh! io! I feel much better, sir.

Fal. Go to, Feeble. Well, Wart, what wilt thou drink?

Wart. A pint of brown bastard.

Fal. The very drink for thee, thou whoreson caterpillar. And thou, Shadow, what thin potation for thee?

Shadow. A pot of the very smallest ale, sir.

Fal. And thou, Mouldy?

Mouldy. A cup of white bastard for my stomach's sake, good sir.

Fal. And thou, Bullcalf?

Bullcalf. A pottle-pot of sack, sir, and a ha'pennyworth of sugar-candy, sir, for my cold, sir, and my cough, sir.

Fal. Go to; well said, Peter; the sack, pure and simple, will take care of itself, and, forsooth,

---

cup of horse-radish ale, which he and a friend of his, troubled with the stone, have been drinking of, which we did, and then walked into the fields as far almost as Sir G. Whitmore's, all the way talking of Russia, which, he says, is a sad place ; and, though Moscow is a very great city, yet it is from the distance between-house and house, and few people compared with this, and poor, sorry houses, the Emperor himself living in a wooden house ; his exercise only flying a hawke at pigeons, and carrying pigeons ten or twelve miles off, and then laying wagers which pigeon shall come soonest home to her house."

do thee no harm at all ; but, Bullcalf, at thy peril, touch not thy tongue unto the sugar-candy with the intent to lick thereof, until thou hast first strictly mentalized it in the manner I 've told thee of. Mark me, Peter. [*Addressing himself.*] Sweet Sir John Sack-and-Sugar, I prithee, what wilt thou ?

Fal. A good sherris-sack is good enough for me. Francis ? Come hither, Francis.

Fran. Anon, anon, sir.

Fal. Mark, Francis ; hast thou heard what each and all of these gentles would drink on my score ? hark ! Francis—on my score ?

Fran. Anon, anon, sir ; I 've heard every word, Sir John.

Fal. And dost thou remember every word, rogue ?

Fran. Anon, anon, sir ; I do, Sir John.

Fal. Then tell the chief tapster of the Boar's Head to send hither, speedily, a leash of drawers, thyself included, bringing the various potations which these guzzlers all athirst would freely swallow ; and also tell him to mark on the slate the reckoning for everything against Sir John Falstaff. Away, Francis, away.

Fran. Anon, anon, sir.

The drawers, Tom, Dick, and Francis, presently entered, bringing the liquors bespoken, which they handed round as Sir John directed.

Fal. Attention ! gentlemen ; are your calivers all in good order, and duly charged ?

Omnes. Yes, good knight, they are, but we are not.

Fal. Attention! company; and now, ye knaves, at the word of command, sip not like a proud Jack, or a forsooth of the city; chirrup not like sparrows in the morning sunshine on the roof; lap not like dogs, though dogs ye be; but drink like tinkers, drink deep like Corinthians, lads of mettle, good boys; dye scarlet like all the good lads of Eastcheap; an you breathe in your drinking, cry "Hem, boys!" Attention, company; eyes! right; present! arms; take! aim.

> Old King Cole was a merry old soul,
> And a merry old soul was he;
> He called for his pipe, and called for his bowl,
> And he called for his fiddlers three.

Go, to, gentles; would ye fain hear the fiddlers three?

Omnes. Nay, nay, not now, good Sir John.

Fal. Well said; then, attention! company. Here 's to the health of our generous sovereign, Old King Cole, that merry old soul. Long may he live, reign, and prosper; and may there always be found myriads of subjects to love, honour, and obey that monarch of mirth. Fire away, gentlemen!

[*All drink according to command.*]

[*Enter Davy.*]

Fal. Good morrow, Davy.

Davy. Good morrow, Sir John; an 't please your worship, there 's one Pistol at the door, and would speak with you.

Fal. Tell him to come in; thou 'rt a good varlet, Davy.

[*Exit Davy.   Enter Pistol.*]
How now, Pistol !   What news ?

Pistol. Sir John, God save thee !

Fal. Welcome, Ancient Pistol.   What wind blew thee hither ?

Pistol. Not the ill wind which blows no man to good.

> Sir John, I am thy Pistol and thy friend,
> And helter-skelter have I rode to thee,
> And tidings do I bring, and lucky joys,
> And golden times, and happy news of price.

Fal. I pray thee now, deliver them like a man of this world.

Pistol. A foutra for the world and worldlings base !   I speak of Africa and golden joys.

Fal. O base Assyrian knight, what is thy news ? Let King Cophetua know the truth thereof.   My Pistol and my friend, once more I say, if thou hast any tidings, I prithee now, deliver them like a man of this world.

Pistol. Sweet knight, I kiss thy neif ; but,—

Fal. Peace, mine ancient ; mark me, and mark me well, good Pistol.   Thou and I are growing old ; though old we do wax, yet we 're not exactly old, but older.   I remember me that once on a time Prince Hal, that mad wag, set a dish of apple-johns before me, and told me there were five more Sir Johns, and, putting off his hat, said, ' I will now take my leave of these six dry, round, old, withered knights.'   It angered me to the heart, for I never could endure an apple-john, the more especially if 't was old and withered. Look thou upon my bald crown and my white beard : yea, marry, my bald crown is not so pitifully bald, nor is my white beard so very white. And I 've long since noted not a few gray hairs which have snuggled in and among the curly and abundant black locks that cover and adorn thy bullet head ; so that it has come to pass that thy black hair is not so very black. There 's also a touch of gray in thy all-abroad and flamboyant mustachios, measuring at least an ell from end to end, and, along with the long tuft of hair on thy lower lip and chin, forming the rude outlines of a cross ; the which, however, is much less notable than that 'devil's mark,' to wit, a large inky-black mole perching malignly upon thy left eyebrow. This grayness—is 't caused by lapse of years ? or, by thy much speaking, and that, too, in a bombastic style ? Thy speech and thy mustachios—both need to be curtailed. Prithee, good Pistol, perpend my words : Time, which cools our blood, lessens the heat of, and plays the devil with, our livers, dims our eyes, dulls our ears, stiffens our limbs, and abates our natural force,—time should tame our tongues as well. As we grow older, let us think more and talk less ; let 's clothe our thoughts in words so simple, plain, unaffected, and intelligible that he who hath ears to hear us, may not be driven to the lexicon to find out what in the devil we mean.* When I was a lad at the

------

* John M. Mason, D.D., in an essay, entitled *Qualifications of the Christian Ministry*, says :

"Men of great literature, and even of good manners, who

Yarmouth grammar-school, I read in Quintilian of a teacher of rhetoric, whose constant admonition to his pupils was, " darken, darken ! " as the readiest mode of gaining admiration. Mine ancient, let us not darken our thoughts by words without knowledge. In a word : Let 's call a spade a spade ; yea, marry, let 's say what we have to say like men of this world. " How forcible are right words ! " as

---

never offend against modesty, make most absurd mistakes in delivering to one audience discourses fit for another of entirely different character. They are very apt to do so, if they have allowed themselves to be absorbed· in a particular theme. Their favourite must be the favourite of all the world. Abstruse demonstrations, which years of study have rendered familiar to themselves, must, of course, be evident to the mechanic and the husbandman. An English divine, who was deeply enamoured of the study of *Optics*, and was a very distinguished proficient in all its *minutiæ*, could scarcely preach on a text in the Bible without sliding into his darling discussions. Accordingly, having to preach to a plain country congregation in Kent, he lectured them with much pith and animation on his *dioptrics* and *catoptrics*, his *refractions*, *reflexions*, and *angles of incidence*. They were greatly edified, no doubt, and the preacher was much delighted. It happened, however, that in going from church to the house of a substantial farmer, his host thus accosted him . '*Doctor, you have given us an excellent sermon to-day ; but I believe you made one mistake.*' '*Mistake !.*' exclaimed the Doctor. '*Sir, that is impossible, it was all demonstration !*' '*True, your Reverence,*' quoth Hodge, '*but them there things that you preached so much about you called Hop*STICKS ; *now in our country, here in Kent, we call 'em Hop-*POLES.' We think we have heard in the course of our lives, sermons nearly as well adapted to time and place, and quite as instructive to the people."— *Works*, Vol. IV., pp. 254, 255.

Job saith ; but Elihu, one of Job's miserable com-
forters, saith of that perfect and upright man,
" He multiplieth words without knowledge."   And
I remember me that Solomon saith, "A word spoken
in due season, how good is it ! "   Moreover,—

Pistol. Sir John, God save thee !   Art not thou
the very Devil citing Scripture for his purpose ?

Fal. Ah, no more of that, Pistol, an thou lovest
me.   Zounds ! I would not have thee go off so
soon ; don't discharge thyself—shoot off thy mouth,
as 't were—upon me just yet.   Peace,—

Pistol. My good knight, 't is true that old we
do wax ; but I 'll not have away with even one
particular hair of my mustachios, growing gray
though they be ; neither can I curtail my speech,
nor tie my tongue.   .   .   .

> My knight, I will inflame thy noble liver,
> And make thee rage.   Tidings do I bring that
> Thy Doll, and Helen of thy noble thoughts,
> Is in base durance and contagious prison ;
> Hal'd thither
> By most mechanical and dirty hand.—
> Rouse up revenge from ebon den with fell Alecto's snake,
> For Doll is in.   Pistol speaks nought but truth.

Fal. I will deliver her.   Sweet Pistol, I do
greatly fear that thy liver hath gone wrong and is
inflamed, and that thou mayst become atrabilious
and go off the hooks any day.   I prithee, let me
ask thee a question.

Pistol. So do, Sir John.

Fal. Is life worth living? How answerest thou that?

Pistol. Good knight, I give it up.   Prithee, tell me.

Fal. The answer is easy and at hand : That depends on the liver.* By my troth, there 's nothing the matter with my liver : it 's all right, and has always been on its good behaviour and done its duty faithfully and well. To me, then, life has always seemed worth living, and no more so than when, in the dreadful battle of Shrewsbury, I came so near losing it ; but I fell down before my enemy, Douglas, as if I were dead, and by counterfeiting dying, I thereby lived.

Pistol. Pish !

Fal. Pish for thee, Pistol ! Knowest thou not that the better part of valour is discretion ? 'T was by that better part that I then and there saved my life. I am old, I am old ; yet, God-a-mercy, I 'm full loath to lose my grip of life, and breathe my last.

Pistol. Sir John, thy Pistol would gladly revoke his " Pish ! " to his sweet knight ; 't was but a flash in the pan ; his liver, not his heart, was at fault.

Fal. Mine ancient Pistol, 't is as if that word had not been spoken by thee to me.

Pistol. My knight, from my heart of hearts do I thank thee. And now, prithee, lend me thy sword, and ask not wherefore.

Fal. Nay, before God, mine ancient, thou get'st not now my sword ; for in obedience to the command of the wise and worshipful Justice Shallow, I wear it not in this sacred temple of Themis ; but take my pistol if thou wilt.

---

* Sir John seems to have anticipated Mr. Thomas G. Appleton, of Boston, who answered the conundrum, " Is life worth living ? " by saying that " It depends on the liver."

Pistol. Prithee, good knight, give it me. What, is it in the case?

Fal. Ay, Pistol; 't is hot, 't is hot; there 's in 't that which will sack a city. Look you, there 's in that case a good familiar creature, if it be well used, and, if opportunely taken, it maketh glad the heart of man; yet hark, in thine ear, Pistol, there 's within that casket an invisible spirit that can hurt a man, give him grievous bodily wounds, ay, past all surgery; there lurks within an enemy that a man may put into his mouth to steal away his brains—petty larceny in many cases—and thereby, with joy, revel, pleasure, and applause, transform himself into a beast. Often there 's in that case a disembodied devil that can tangle the feet, throw upon all fours, or all flat upon the ground, and kill at forty rods.

[*Pistol draws out of the case a bottle of sack.*]

Thus, Pistol, have I charged thee; do thou at once discharge upon thyself, but not with the intent to kill thyself.

Pistol. By Bacchus, Pistol, moisten thy gullet, both for thy present extreme thirst, and for every degree of thirst to come; keep running after a dog, and he will not bite thee; drink always before the thirst, and it will never come upon thee. Ancient Pistol, may the distilled damnation within this horse-pistol be shot into every nook, corner, and concavity of thy lean and lank body. Fear I broadsides? No, let the fiend fire, for some sack have I; and, sweetheart, lie thou here. [*Laying down his sword.*]   And now, thou arid and adust Bezonian, chirp no longer over thy cup, but drink, or die.

[*Pistol drinks the bottle dry.*]

Fal. My Pistol, look thou upon these beggarly caitiffs, these tattered prodigals, lately come from swine-keeping, from eating draff and husks in Gloucestershire : These be they who have come to London town to testify on behalf of the Crown against Sir John Falstaff, against me ! and to show that I am, forsooth, a tavern-haunter, a drunkard, a sack-butt, a fat rogue, a cheat, a thief, a robber, a liar, a lewdster, a profane swearer, a perennial debtor, a buffoon, a braggadocio, no gentleman, a coward, and, I know not what else. 'Sblood ! I, Sir John Falstaff, not a man of honour ! I, no gentleman ! I, a coward ! Perdition seize these bacon-fed knaves, who have come hither from eating horsebread, salt fish and mutton, roasted turnips and onions, and turnip leaves for greens and salads, and from drinking stinking pond-water and broth made of goose-grass, or of nettles which they 'd stolen out of the hedges and ditches by the wayside. Where 's my sword ? Zounds ! 't is well for these vermin that 't is laid, as 't were, in pawn. By the way, I must confess that from my youth up I 've had as much as I could do to keep the terms of mine own honour precise. What is Honour ? A word ! What is that word, Honour ? Air. A trim reckoning !—Who hath it ? He that died o' Wednesday. Doth he feel it ? No. Doth he hear it ? No. Is it insensible, then ? Yea, to the dead. But will it not live with the living? No. Why? Detraction will not suffer it :—therefore I'll none of it. Honour is a mere 'scutcheon ; and so ends my catechism.

Pistol. Shall these dunghill curs confront Sir John Falstaff, and bay that sweet knight as if he were a base-born beggar, no gentleman, and a coward? Then, Pistol, lay thy head in the Furies' lap, and let the welkin roar. Cerebus, Cophetua, King Cole, Arthur, Harry the Fifth—puff ! a foutra for thine office—kings, all of them ; under which king, Bezonians? Speak, or die. To Pluto's damned lake, by this hand, to the infernal deep, with Erebus and tortures vile also. Hold hook and line, say I. Down, down, dogs! down. Die men like dogs !

Fal. 'Sblood !

Pistol. What ! shall we have incision ? shall we imbrue ?—[*Snatching up his sword.*]

> Then death rock me asleep, abridge my doleful days !
> Why, then, let grievous, ghastly gaping wounds
> Untwine the Sisters Three ! Come, Atropos, I say !

Fal. God-a-mercy ! peace, brave Pistol ; by thy hopes of salvation, slay not these slaves ; sheath thy sword.

Pistol. So commanded, so done. When Pistol disobeys thee, do this, sweet knight,—fig him like the bragging Spaniard. Thy Pistol will keep the peace till the truce is ended, and his good captain's voice is once more for war.

Fal. Look you, mine ancient, I have not this

day seen Corporal Nym, who of late wears a sour face and claims that I have wronged him in some of his humours, and swears that he neither likes the humour of lying, nor loves the humour of bread and cheese. Prithee, Pistol, when and where didst thou last see the drawling, affected rogue, and in what humour was he then?

Pistol. Sir John, I had speech with that cony-catching rascal last night at Tom Toss-Pot's place near Pie-Corner. He was almost out at heels, as usual, and swore that he must put good angels in his empty pouch, with wit or steel, and said his good humour was to steal at a minim's rest. Convey, the wise it call. Steal! foh! a fico for the phrase! This Mars of malcontents, laying his hand upon his bilbo, said to me in express words: "An I cannot pick a pocket, then slice, I say! *pauca, pauca ;* slice! that's my humour." Let vultures gripe my guts, if I do not think he would, in a flash, slice an off an ear or two, or even a Roman nose, to put a mill-sixpence in his purse, and that his humour hath not cooled. [*Enter Nym.*]

Fal. Look you, Pistol, here comes thy coach-fellow ; thou 'rt t' other of the geminy. Heigh, heigh, the Devil rides upon a fiddlestick ; talk of the Devil and he 'll presently appear ; but let us give the Devil his due. Welcome, Sir Corporal Nym ; thou 'rt a tall fellow and a good soldier as soldiers go in these costermonger times when true valour is turned bear-herd ; but, oho! I see that thou 'rt in so poor a plight as to be almost in a state of mere nature, and must cony-catch, or

14

otherhow shift. Hast thou any money in thy purse?

Nym. Not even a ha'penny, Sir John.

Fal. Hast thou any credit with that inexorable Israelite, Master Abraham Dombledon?

Nym. Jesu! no; not even to the extent of a denier in that hook-nosed devil's book, or with any other clothier that I wot of. By welkin and her star, Sir John, the very rags I wear I filched from the duddery of an old clo' man in Crooked Lane. And this is true: I like not the humour of lying.

Fal. Boy! what money is in my purse? Boy! I say. Where is that whoreson page of mine? Zounds! I 'd quite forgot that yesterday morning I gave him leave of absence till to-day dinner-time. Good Corporal Nym, hast thou a sword?

Nym. Yea, Sir John, I have a sword, a trusty one, and it shall bite on my necessity. That 's my humour.

Fal. Ancient Pistol and Corporal Nym, hark ye both: In the name of Old King Cole, I command you forthwith to take charge of this gang of scurvy, half-clad, unwashed, and unkempt knaves, these hogrubbers, mere serfs, *adscripti glebæ*, who have wilfully and unlawfully left their lord's demesne, and come to London as witnesses for the Crown against Sir John Falstaff. And do ye march them at a double-quick step by way of Saint Albans and Daventry, through Coventry and Sutton Co'fil', thence around by Robin Hood's Barn, thence up hill and down dale, into Gloucestershire, and back home, sweet home, again. Nevermore let them behold the Boar's Head tavern ; nevermore let them in Eastcheap smell hot ribs of beef roasted, or a hot venison pasty, or chew a chewet, or taste pies well baked, or drink small beer, or bottle ale, or the smallest ale, or half-and-half, and much less a good sherris-sack, or sip heeltaps from anybody's *aqua-vitæ* or usquebaugh bottle, or smoke pipes of tobacco in any street, shop, theatre, or church in London town. Nevermore let them hear convivial songs, and the clattering of pewter pots, harp, pipe, and psaltery, or listen to the song of some siren from Billingsgate, chanting in praise .of deceased mackerel, cod, sturgeon, turbot, oysters, lobsters, or good red herring. If Peter Bullcalf, notwithstanding his cold and cough, be found in this city after this day and date, then in the name of Old King Cole, smite him under the fifth rib, or shoot him on the spot. Let a like fate befall Ralph Mouldy, Simon Shadow, Thomas Wart, and Francis Feeble, if they disobey Old King Cole's command, just now proclaimed. If any mother's son of these base Hungarian wights be found, even lurking within the sound of Bow-bells, let his lease of life be at once terminated, let him neither read nor repeat the neck-verse and thereby go hence without day ; but, on the contrary, let his coat-of-arms be blazoned thus :

> Two posts standant,
> One beam crossant,
> One rope pendent,
> With a rogue on the end on 't.

Moreover, mine ancient and my corporal as

ye both are heinously unprovided with horses for yourselves, do ye find a fine horse-thief, one that can steal well, of the age of two and twenty, or thereabouts. As for meat and drink, live off the country, and, in default of the necessaries of life, eat, drink, and be merry—all on my score. Ye see the looped and windowed raggedness of these wretches? The inventory of their shirts shows not one for superfluity. There is in fact such a low ebb of linen with them that there 's but a shirt and a half in all the company. But that 's all one; they 'll find linen enough on every hedge. I regret that the Chief-Justice is not present to say to you as he once said to me : "Well, be honest, be honest; and God bless your expedition"; nor is Sir Hugh Evans, the Welsh parson, here to pronounce a benediction and ask "Got's angels to sprinkle down plessings on all your heads"; but, in their absence, it is enough for me to concur with them, and say, "So mote it be." And now, ancient Pistol, with the aid of Corporal Nym, take command of thy company, and, ere the hands on the dial of St. Michael's church shall point to the prick of five, troop on.

Pistol. I will, good captain. If there be anything in this world better than to be the friend and follower of Sir John Falstaff, I want to see it and be in it.*   Adieu.

---

* Evidences daily multiply that Shakespeare is truly "not of an age, but for all time" in many unlooked-for ways.   In *The Winter's Tale*, Act IV., Scene 4, a servant says to Polixenes : "Master, there is three carters, three shepherds, three neat-

Nym. To troop on thus is the life that I 've long desired. This is my true good humour. 'T is far better for me than to push a costermonger's cart in Whitechapel, swarming with pilfering girls and boys, all progging for fruit, for I 'm no longer Argus-eyed ; 't is even better than petty stealing at a minim's rest. But now, however, I shall thrive ; for, without delay, I'll unbuckle and fling away my hunger-belt, and no longer be off the hooks. Humour me the angels, and let them, by hook or by crook, find their way into my pocket. Farewell, Sir John.

[*Exeunt Pistol, Nym, et al. Enter Page.*]

Fal. Sirrah, you giant—boy !

Page. Sir ?

Fal. Thou 'rt a little yellow curtail dog, long a faithful follower at my heels ; and when we go abroad together, I do walk before thee like a sow that hath overwhelmed all her litter but one, and that one the runt of the lot. By the mass, I cannot discover that thou hast grown a whit in body since the Holy Innocents' day, years ago, when

herds, three swine-herds, that have made themselves all men of hair,[1] they call themselves Saltiers, and they have a dance which the wenches say is a gallimaufry of gambols, because they are not in 't." Here the expression, "in 't," or "in it," is used in its slang sense. In the last line of the second subdivision of *The Passionate Pilgrim*, there seems to be a notable Americanism : " Till my bad angel fire my good one out."

---

[1] *Men of hair :* That is, dressed up in goatskins, to represent *satyrs*, or what the servant blunderingly calls *saltiers*. A dance of satyrs was no unusual entertainment in that day.—ROLFE.

Prince Hal gave thee to me. Then thou wert a pert, abecedarian boy, and such thou art to-day. Thy chin is not yet fledged ; thy voice hath not wholly lost its childish treble ; and, as to thy school-learning, thou 'rt still dawdling over the Christcross-row. After thou hadst been some years in my service, the prince said to Bardolph in thy presence, "And the boy that I gave to Falstaff : he had him from me a Christian, and look, if the fat villain hath not transformed him into an ape," which hard saying cut me to the heart; it did, indeed. God-a-mercy, boy, I do utterly deny that I 've disevangelized thee and turned thee into an anthropoid ape. If Hal put thee into my service for any other reason than to set me off, why then I have no judgment. Thou whoreson mandrake, thou art fitter to be worn in my cap than to wait at my heels. And tell me now, thou naughty varlet, tell me, where hast thou been since yesterday at noontide, when I gave thee leave of absence until to-day dinner-time? I was never manned with an agate till I had thee; and now, unless thou tell the truth, I will inset thee neither in gold nor silver, but in vile apparel, and send thee back again to thy master, now Harry the Fifth, for a crown jewel. The King may keep his own grace, but I can assure him that he 's wholly out of mine since he treated me in such a beastly way and cut my acquaintance on his coronation-day. Boy !

Page. Sir ?

Fal. Thou manikin, give an account of thyself since yesternoon.

Page. All yesterday afternoon, sir, I was playing hockey with some boys in an alley near Cock Lane ; last night, till I heard the chimes at midnight, I was ramping about, here and there, in Eastcheap ; an hour or two of the time I was worming my way in a crowd gathered about a merry-go-round on a vacant lot near Pie-Corner.

Fal. And so thou wert corkscrewing thy way through a crowd last night ! Zounds ! I hope that thou wert not there to filch and to become as familiar with men's pockets as their gloves or their handkerchiefs ? Doth not the Prayer-Book say that 't is thy duty to keep thy hands from picking and stealing ?

Page. By Jeronimy, Sir John, I 'll be sworn upon all the Prayer-Books in England that I 've picked no man's pocket ; I 've filched nothing ; I 'm no pickpurse.

Fal. Thou little rogue, I 'm glad to hear thee say so ; well, be honest, be honest ; and keep good company. 'T is said that a man should be judged by the company he keeps ; and, if this saying be true, so should a boy be judged. There is a thing, my lad, which thou hast often heard of, and it is known to many in our land by the name of pitch : this pitch, as ancient writers do report, doth defile ; so doth villanous company ; company, villanous company, hath been the spoil of many a boy ; therefore pitch not into such company ; don't play pitch, nor in any way defile thyself therewith ; and don't you forget it. And now, sirrah, tell me where thou hast been to-day ?

Page. The most of the time, sir, I 've been play-ing marbles for keeps near Ting-a-ling Cu-shing's laundry in Ram Alley. I took breakfast and dinner at Mother Goosester's short-order house, and paid for both by whistling and making music for her on my mouth-organ. I 've been in several other places. I 've just come from Master Domble-don's shop where I had left your sword and buckler as you bade me some days ago.

Fal. What said Master Dombledon about the satin for my short cloak and my slops ?

Page. He said, sir, you should procure him better assurance than Bardolph : he would not take his bond and yours ; he liked not the security. And he said he 'd consider your sword and buckler as though laid in pawn as part security for the money you 'd so long owed him ; and all at once he grew very mad. His face flushed, and his forehead, clear up to the top of his bald head and clear down to a narrow strip of iron-gray hair which bounds the backside thereof, grew red as blood. He threw aside his work, uncrossed his legs, kicked over his goose, jumped up from his bench, jerked from off a hook near his desk a bunch of old, fly-specked papers, shook the dust thereout, fumbled them over and over, and at last took therefrom a document longer than his yard-stick, which he said was his bill against old Jack Falstaff for clothes which he 'd, from time to time, furnished that senile old liar and swindler since eleven years ago last Michaelmas, and that said bill showed no credits except a few paltry payments hardly worth making a note of. And then he grew madder and madder, and swore terribly, worse than ever I heard any fishwoman in Billingsgate swear. Besides, sir, he called you a measly old malefactor, an incomparable liar, cheat, and dead beat, as full of lies as Egypt was of lice and flies when Pharaoh would n't let the children of Israel go. And he said, sir, that you were covered all over with flies, and were so horribly fly-bitten that,—

Fal. Well, is that all the circumcised old curmudgeon, Master Abraham Dombledon, said to bother me ?

Page. O Lord, sir, no ; I never before heard such strange, abusive, and profane names as he called you.

Fal. Well, sirrah, go on ; tell me what else that parsimonious pricklouse said of me.

Page. He called you, sir, a rascally old repetend ; a least common denominator ; a vulgar fraction of a man reduced to its lowest terms ; a parallelopipedon ; an oblate spheroid ; an asinine asymptote ; an infundibulate icosahedron, whatever these things may be ; and he,—

Fal. Zounds ! old Dombledon must have been a senior wrangler when he was at school, or have taken a mathematical honour in some university or other ; but surely not at Oxford or Cambridge— the Jew, the Ebrew Jew. Boy, say on.

Page. He raved and swore about you, sir, a full hour by St. Michael's clock ; and he said that his daily prayer was that your girdle (for which you 've not paid him) might break and let your guts fall

about your knees.   After he 'd cooled off a little,
he wrote the amount of his account and some other
things on a slip of paper which he handed me, and
told me to give it to you.   I 'm sorry, sir, that I 've
lost the paper ; but I remember that the grand
total of his bill against you, without reckoning any
usury, I think he called it, is £365, twelve shillings,
and fourpence ha'penny, and he said he 'd gladly
take in ready money,—

Fal. Tut, tut, thou tut-nosed boy ; speak not a
word more.   Damn the fourpence ha'penny ; and
let old Dombledon be damned, like the glutton !
pray God his tongue be hotter !   A whoreson
Achitophel ! a rascally yea-forsooth knave ! to bear
a gentleman in hand, and then stand upon security !
The whoreson smooth-pates do now wear nothing
but high shoes, and bunches of keys at their
girdles ; and if a man is through with them in
honest taking up, then they must stand upon
security, or ask payment of an old and mildewed
account.   I had as lief they would put ratsbane in
my mouth as offer to stop it with security, or ask
me to pay old debts, the most of them long since
outlawed.   I looked a' should have sent me two and
twenty yards of satin, as I am a true knight, and
he sends me security.   Well, he may sleep in security ; for he hath the horn of abundance, and the
lightness of his wife shines through it : and yet
cannot he see, though he have his own lanthorn to
light him.   Boy !

Page. Sir ?

Fal. What money is in my purse ?

Page. Seven groats and two pence.

Fal. Give it me, for not a penny have I.

Page. O Lord, sir, I 've lost both purse and money ; I 'm sure your purse was fingered from my pocket last night in the crowd in which I was at Pie-Corner ; I 'm very sorry, Sir John ; and I 'll do my best, by hook or crook, to get seven groats and two pence for you, my good master.

Fal. Aha ! hem, hm, hm ; and so, sirrah, thou hast been in bad company, hast been defiled with pitch, hast fallen among thieves and been spoiled of my purse ! Away, thou longimanous, light-fingered, little rogue, away ; mizzle at once, or thy pocket-picking fingers shall be made acquainted with the pinny-winkles. Aroint thee, ditch-delivered son of a drab.

Page. O Lord, good Sir John,—

Fal. No more prattling ; go, gadfly, go. But, stay a little, boy. Hast thou any money of thy own ?

Page. Not any—not a penny, sir.

Fal. And, as I am a true knight, I 've none to give thee ; and yet thou must live ; London owes thee a living ; surely thou canst niggle along a few days for food and lodging in Eastcheap, or thereabouts. Perchance Mother Goosester will take thee in and thereby entertain a little angel unawares. See the good dame in Ram Alley, and seek her soft side. But first do thou go, wash thy face and hands, and tease thy long, unkempt, flaxen hair with thy fingers, or with a coarse comb, if thou canst find one. Boy !

Page. Sir ?

Fal. What skin disease hast thou ? Hast thou the seven-year itch ? Prithee, tell me.

Page. No, sir, I have not ; I 've never had it. I prithee, good Sir John, why do you thus question me ?

Fal. I 've noted thee at times rubbing thy back against the pillar beside which thou 'rt now standing ; and, seeing that thy long finger-nails are black and very dirty, methought that thou didst scratch thyself for good cause.

Page. The fleas have lately bitten me sorely on the back and bottom of me.

Fal. I see, I see, sirrah ; so thou hast been phlebotomized, as a chirurgeon would say. Go to ; well, I hope 't will do thee good, by letting some bad blood out of thee and making thee a better boy. By the way, in whose dog-kennel dost thou sleep o' nights ?

Page. In nobody's, sir, and I never did.

Fal. Boy !

Page. Sir ?

Fal. Fail not to wash thy face, comb thy hair, and clip thy claws ; and now I give thee leave of absence until to-morrow dinner-time.

Page. Farewell, kind sir.   [*Exit Page.*

And thereupon—according to the manuscript— Sir John soliloquized, substantially as follows :

" I can get no remedy against this consumption of the purse ; borrowing only lingers and lingers it out, but the disease is incurable, unless I make my dwelling-place beside some Pactolian river famous for its golden sands, or turn alchemist and at last discover the philosopher's stone, whereby I can convert the baser metals into gold. Silver and gold may be, indeed, the money of barbarians ; but I 'm barbarian enough to long earnestly to possess bags upon bags of gold, gold, bright and yellow, hard and cold. Even the clinking of silver coins is music in mine ear. Agur prayed, 'Give me neither poverty nor riches.' *Vixi !* Having lived long and seen human life in its various forms, I pray, 'Give me not poverty, but riches.' Timotheus saith, 'The love of money is the root of all evil' ; and now I remember me that when I was a lad at the Yarmouth grammar-school I read something in Virgil to the same effect.* I 've never had a cursed greed for gold ; but poverty irks my very soul ; I would that I could somehow put money in my purse, money enough in my now empty purse. Money is power ; money is character ; money is the sinews of war, and of peace as well. Pounds, shillings, and pence make life worth living. Money well managed deserves, indeed, the apotheosis to which she was raised by her Latin adorers ; she is *Diva Moneta*—a goddess.

"I would that I were King of England and had in mine own proper person the power, by a bull, a rescript, a ukase, or something of that sort, to deprive gold and silver and copper of all use as money, and to cause them to be used simply as commodities. Then, by the Lord, I 'd put in force for

---

* *Quid non mortalia pectora cogis,*
　Auri sacra fames ?　　　　*—Æn.*, III., 56.

this kingdom the Lycurgan law of old Sparta, that
the only metallic money which should be current
in this realm must be made of iron, and that the
pieces should be so big and heavy that to lay up
twenty or thirty pound would require a large closet,
and to remove it, nothing less than a yoke of oxen.
Zounds ! were I king as aforesaid, I 'd put an end
to this farcical trial, revoke Master Robert Shallow's commission as one of my justices of the
peace, give him a non-negotiable warrant on my
exchequer for the ' thousand pound ' I 've so long
owed him, together with good usance thereon, payable in London and in the iron coin current in
Britain ; and, *mehercle !* I 'd hie him home to buy
forty or fifty good yoke of bullocks at Stamford
fair to transport the treasure into Gloucestershire.
Besides, I 'd refit and furbish up the Boar's Head,
pay all tavern-reckonings scored against me, grant
a pension to Bardolph, and allow annuities for life
to Dame Quickly and Doll Tearsheet.   Moreover,
I 'd command the Parliament to provide by statute
for the free and unlimited issue of an irredeemable
paper or parchment currency, not resting on a
specie basis, based upon nothing, redeemable in
nothing, and payable at no time or place, but de-
riving its purchasing and debt-paying power from
the declaratory fiat of the King and the Parliament, and being supposed to have wrapped up in
it as much intrinsic monetary value as if it were
in fact made of silver or gold.   And I 'd also order
my Parliament to enact that whoever, being an
Englishman and within this realm, shall publicly,

by word or deed, deny the virtual transubstantiation of gold and silver into the fiat money aforesaid shall be deemed guilty of a felony, and"   .   .   .

.   .   .   .   *Hic pauca verba*

.   .   .   .   *desunt in MS.*

It seems that Sir John, after the close of his soliloquy, still sat in the dock. The court-room was silent and soon grew darkful. The knight, surcharged with sack and wearied by his extraordinary day's work, fell into a deep sleep, and was presently fetching his breath hard, and snoring with a forty-horse power which shook his chair of state, and even rattled the casements of the two tall windows that overlooked the cemetery. His head sank upon his breast and his snore waxed louder and profounder until the tuneful oratory of his nose resounded throughout the tavern, and caused a clinking of pewter and a tinkling of glasses in the taproom. By and by, a sudden, impetuous, and prolonged blast from his nasal trumpet so affrighted Toby Sneak that he turned deathly pale, forgot to close the cock of the cask from which he 'd just slyly drawn for himself some small beer, let fall the cup, threw up his hands, and wildly exclaimed, " Have mercy, Jesu ! I hear the angel Gabriel blowing his horn; the world 's coming to an end sure. O Lord, have mercy upon me, a miserable sinner." Had Sir John been suffered to sleep on and on without let or hindrance, the aggravated momentum of his snore might before dawn have toppled down the ancient and moss-grown steeple of St. Michael's church and buried

him beneath its ruins. But fortunately about ten
of the clock in the evening, Bardolph, attended by
Snare carrying a lanthorn, entered the court-room,
rushed up to the knight, shook him by the shoulders, and shouted in his ear, "God-a-mercy!
Awake, my Sir John! Arise, thou Jupiter Tonans!"
But the sleeper slept on, snoring defiantly, and
more horribly than before. In this emergency
Bardolph suggested to Snare that he tickle the
knight's nose with spear-grass, but that timid and
retiring officer answered: " If I do so, it may cost
me my life. I 've often heard that he cares not
what mischief he doth, if his weapon be out ; that
he will stab and foin like any devil ; and that when
his blood is up, he 'll spare neither man, woman,
nor child. Indeed, I once heard a woman say that
he 'd stabbed her in her own house, and that most
beastly. I tickle the knight's nose, forsooth ! By
the Lord, I dare not ; and, besides, I 'm not ready
to die just yet." Bardolph replied : " Look you,
Snare ; Sir John hath no sword, is fast asleep in
his chair, and lies as harmless as a new-born babe.
What a coward art thou to funk out in this way ;
and yet some of thy friends call thee a lusty
yeoman." At this juncture Sheriff Fang, who,
along with Grabbe and Ketchum, had quietly
entered the room and witnessed the failure to
awaken Sir John, came forward and boldly said,
" Let me tackle him " ; which he at once proceeded
to do by tweaking the knight's nose, plucking his
gray beard, pulling his ears, slapping his bald
crown, punching his paunch, and so forth. This

petty officer, who bore the sleeper no good-will, would have further assaulted and battered his victim, had not Bardolph bristled up, flourished a stout truncheon, and wrathfully exclaimed : " Let the old man alone. Fang, thou 'rt a sneaking coward to strike a man when he 's down, fast asleep, and utterly defenceless. At thy peril, touch Sir John with force and violence, again. Snare, stand beside me so that the light of thy lanthorn may shine full upon Sir John's face ; watch close and mayhap thou 'lt soon see me work a wonder, almost a miracle, equal to raising one from the dead." Then Bardolph drew from an inside pocket of his jerkin a wickered pint flask, which he uncorked, and, holding it 'twixt his finger and his thumb as though 't were a pouncet-box, he ever and anon gave it to the sleeper's nose and took 't away again. Presently Sir John smiled a smile which widened and lengthened till it o 'erspread and illumined his whole countenance with a kindly light ; and anon he ceased to snore, and whispered coaxingly, " I prithee, some sack, good Francis." " Anon, anon, sir," answered Bardolph in a voice as boyish and Franciscan as he could make it. " Amen," devoutly responded Falstaff, who there- upon opened his optics for a few seconds, rolled them around like a pair of goose-eggs on an axle, and pursed his lips like an infant ready and eager to take its tipple from the nipple of a nursing- bottle. Bardolph instantly put the flask to the open and expectant mouth, and Falstaff fondly seized and sucked it dry without so much as crying

"hem," in his nursing ; and thereupon he closed his
eyes, and fell asleep like an unweaned child that
has just received its nourishment. All efforts to
awaken him having failed, Snare, in a loud and
despondent voice, proposed that he be bolstered
up, made as comfortable as possible, and left alone
in his chair to make a night of it as best he could ;
whereat the sleeper suddenly snorted, and then
murmured in a low, hollow, and sepulchral tone,
" What doth gravity out of his bed at midnight ?
How answer you that ? " Nobody answered these
queries, but all were awed thereby and at once
agreed that a long pull, a strong pull, and a pull all
together, must be made to raise and move Sir John
and put him into bed before midnight. Thereupon, Fang, Snare, Grabbe, and Ketchum jointly
raised and boosted and braced and stayed him
upright at the four cardinal points of his carcass,
while Bardolph held his hand and guided his
hesitating and elephantine steps as he slowly
walked along—Doll Tearsheet heading this group,
swinging Snare's lanthorn, and singing a unique
lullaby song which she 'd long before composed
and often sung with soothing effect to the knight
when he was suffering from an attack of the
megrims. And so they marched Sir John from
the court-room into the street ; thence around the
block in which the Boar's Head was situate ;
thence into the main office of the tavern ; thence
—by permission of Hostess Quickly—up the wide
and winding stairs into the Dolphin-chamber ; and
there—Mistress Doll having first gone out—they

quickly undressed him, and enclothed and sur-
cingled him in an old lady's loose gown, having a
certain motto embroidered on its bosom, and put
into the pocket thereof a pennyworth of sugar-
candy to be used to stop his stertorous breathing—
accoutred as aforesaid, and at dead midnight, they
dumped him into a truckle-bed. All withdrew,
save Bardolph, who volunteered to keep watch and
ward over Sir John until morning. The fat knight
slept soundly in despite of all the fatigues and
perils which he had undergone.

X.

Falstaff Drinks after the Manner of Bacchus.—Bill of Fare for
Breakfast.—Blessings on Dame Quickly and Doll Tearsheet.
Love Grows Cool without Bread and Wine.—Sir John Drops
into Poetry.—"Whoa, Pegasus, Whoa! I Say."—Morals
upon his Predicament in the Dolphin-Chamber.—His
Enemies Gird at Him.—Falling Sickness Befalls Falstaff;
It Befell Julius Cæsar.—A Sudden Death Most Desirable.—
Sir John Has Found the Fountain of Youth and Drinks
Thereat.—Shallow and Silence Fuddled.—Sir John Acts as
a Learned Justicer.—Fears Not a *Præmunire.*

SIR JOHN did not wake until near noon of the
next day; and then, seeing Francis standing on
the threshold of the open chamber-door, and,
though having a pottle-pot in his hands, apparently
hesitating whether to stay or go away, the knight
greeted him thus:

"Zounds, thou naughty coddymoddy, dost thou
not see that I'm abed, and, of course, unwashed,
unkempt, undressed, and altogether unready to be
curiously looked at? Why dost thou thus peer in
upon me in my present negative and unpresentable
state? Henceforth can I never be to thee a hero!
Why art thou here, lad?"

Fran. Anon, anon, sir; good morning, Sir John.
Dame Quickly hath sent your worship a morning's
draught of sack, with her compliments, and she

228

hopes that, hopes that—O Lord, sir, I 've quite forgot the very words of what she did say ; but, anon, anon, sir, 't was something about your health and your sleeping well and having pleasant dreams in her Dolphin-chamber.

The fat knight suddenly jumped, or rather rolled, out of his lowly bed, reared himself upon his hind legs, stood straddling at the round table, and, with his back to the grate where a sea-coal fire had been once on a time, joyously shouted :

" Blessings on good Dame Quickly, so thoughtful of and so kind to me ; and my thanks to thee, Francis ; but tantalize me no longer ; give me the pottle. Marry, and amen, I rejoice to see that 't is not that hateful ' parcel-gilt goblet ' which is sure to give old Jack the heartache whene'er he looks on 't ; but 't is a new and bright two-eared tankard, which mine eyes have never seen before. Boy, do thou reverently set the sacred vessel on the round table, off with its cover, then give me the pottle-pot and see me drink after the manner of Bacchus, and encompass the quart, more or less, of sack therein contained."

Plump Jack seized the tankard, and, holding a handle thereof in each hand, and gazing heaven-ward as if silently breathing a prayer, quickly quaffed off its contents, and, in default of a napkin, wiped his mouth and beslubbered beard on the sleeves of his Mother Hubbard night-gown. And thereupon he sank into an easy and broad-bottomed chair, and looked steadfastly for a little while at a picture, the "Story of the Prodigal," hanging on the wall at the foot of his bed. The high clock, standing like a coffin in a dark corner of the room, struck twelve, and roused him from his reverie. He then inquiringly eyed Francis, who said :

" Anon, anon, sir ; Mistress Doll Tearsheet bade me ask your worship whether you 'd have something to eat as well as to drink ; and she named over many things, more than I could remember ; and so she wrote down their names on a slip of paper which she told me to hand to you. Here 's the paper, Sir John."

Fal. Beshrew my heart, if I 've not lost my spectacles ; read the paper, Francis ; thine eyes are threescore years younger than mine.

Fran. Anon, anon, sir, to wit : A capon ; anchovies ; a dried neat's tongue ; a soused gurnet ; a stock-fish ; a mackerel ; Yarmouth bloaters ; a good dish of prawns ; a conger and fennel ; a choice slice of roasted Manningtree ox with a bit of pudding ; a pigeon ; a short-legged hen ; a joint of mutton ; stewed prunes ; a dish of apple-johns ; pippins ; caraways ; a dish of leather-coats ; eggs and butter ; oysters ; cakes and cheese ; puddings and flap-jacks ; a ha'pennyworth of bread ; sausages and Tewksbury mustard ; pettitoes ; a chewet ; chitterlings, and,—

Fal. Hold, lad, hold ; read no more. So much to eat and not a drop to drink ! Zounds, what does good Doll take me for ? Tell her that my travels thus far along in my life have been mostly betwixt tavern and tavern, and that I can truthfully say *Multum bibi, nunquam pransi.* But, Fran-

cis, stay awhile.   I bethink me of a certain old and
well-known Latin proverb, which I remember me
that I often read in my Priscian when I was a lad
at school.   'T is this : *Sine Cerere et Baccho friget
Venus :* In other words, Love grows cool without
bread and wine ; or, in still other words,

> Without Ceres and Bacchus,
> Venus will not long attack us.

By Minerva—no, no, not by that chilly and chaste
goddess, but by Erato, rather—

> Old Jack's a poet,
> And did n't know it.
> Was he a poet born ?
> Ay, marry, in a horn,
> (*I.e.* in a drinking-horn.)
> His rhymes won't do !
> They will—they have to.
> Then sing, Cockadoodle doo.
> Old Jack will a-wooing go,
> He 'll woo the Muses, io !
> Woo 't woo the Muses ?
> Woo 'em *all* wi' verses ?
> Ha, ha, ha ; te-hee, te-hee ;
> Which one of Nine ? Calliope ?
> Fiddledeedee, 't is n't she.
> Then 't is Terpsichore,
> With flying feet, and kirtle floating free ?
> Hoity-toity ! pish ! tush ! alas ! alack !
> Sir John is a guzzling, not a jumping, Jack.
> Then woo 't woo Euterpe ?
> Well worth wooing is she ;
> But old Jack can't sing a song,
> Nor on the fife prolong
> A tune both sweet and strong.

Woo 't woo—oho,
I know; Clio?
No, not by a jugful,
This Muse is too tristful.
Melpomene, or Urania?
Old Jack wants the bother,
Neither of one nor t' other.
Woo 't woo Polymnia?
Heigh-ho-hum! eh! ah!
And now d' ye see!
Erato and Thalia—they 're the girls for me.
Whither, whither, full of thee,
Bacchus, dost thou hurry me?
Zounds! these verses, rather raucous,
Old Jack will bring to a focus,
And confess 't is the first time
He 's had an incontinence of rhyme,
Or has in any way versified
Since he was larruped—and cried—
As was most meet,
Because his Latin verses were lame in their feet.

Whoa, Pegasus, whoa! I say; let me get down and ease my legs. So, softly and gently,* old Peg, for I feel that galloping apace astride of thee barebacked—being, as I am, almost stark-naked—hath galled me a bit. If I travel but four foot by the squire further o' horseback, and be jolted as I 've just been, I shall break my wind. Whoa! I say; I prithee, fiery Peg, let me get off. I do begin to perceive that I was not born to turn and wind thee, and witch the world with noble horsemanship. I 'm not built that way. But, by the mass, an I had but a belly of any indifferency, I

---

* See Cowper's *John Gilpin's Ride.*—WOPSLE.

were simply the most active fellow in Europe ; my womb, my womb, my womb undoes me.

Sir John paused a little to recover his breath, and, seeing Francis affrighted and standing close to the open door, as if he were about to run away, he gently said :

" Francis, be not afraid at my strange behaviour ; almost unclothed am I, but yet I am in my right mind. Beshrew my heart, if I do thee the least harm. I prithee, lad, stay a little."

Fran. Anon, anon, sir.

Fal. My boy, give Mistress Doll Tearsheet my compliments, and say to her that nothing to eat be sent me, save one half-pennyworth of bread as a set-off to the intolerable deal of sack I 've drank this morning. Zounds ! let the bread, pure and simple, be damned. But, lad, do thou tell dear Doll, the giddy goose, that her honest gander, who has strangely wandered up-stairs and into a lady's chamber, will gladly eat any pretty little tiny kick-shaws *a là* Shallow, which have been prepared by her own fair hands. And now, Francis, wilt thou give me leave awhile ?

Fran. Anon, anon, sir.   [*Exit Francis.*

While washing and dressing in a dreamy and in-consequent way, Sir John mused upon the whimsi-cal situation in which he found himself, and in the light of his variegated, ringstreaked, and speckled career thus far in life, endeavoured to foresee its outcome. At times he thought aloud, the substance of his soliloquy being as follows :

" Old Jack now seems to be, for the time being,

at least, domesticated in Dame Quickly's Dolphin-chamber ; and yet he is surely afloat on a sea of troubles, and far, far from land. Zounds! 't is not a bad omen that he 's in the Dolphin-chamber, a fact which suggests the old story of Arion, a Greek musician, who, when robbed by sailors and thrown into the sea, was carried to the shore by a dolphin which had followed the ship to listen to the music of his lyre. Although the specific gravity of plump Jack is so great that he hath a kind of alacrity in sinking, yet, why may not he be borne to shore somewhere by a life-preserving dolphin, or, what is better, by a mermaid ? But what and where 's the mermaid ? Is 't Dame Quickly, or Mistress Doll Tearsheet ? That is the question. 'T is true that old Jack cannot, like Arion, play upon the lyre ; but they do say that he is an able-bodied liar in and of himself, and that he is the father of liars and lies, an old white-bearded Satan. 'T is also said that he can not only fib, tell white lies, and lie in his teeth, but also lie in his throat, and tell lies as gross, monstrous, and mountain-like as the father that begets them. Well, well, old Jack will help Time to shape this whole matter to the end. In the meanwhile he 'll cling to the Dolphin-chamber as his ark of safety, and thereby scape drowning, a death which he abhors ; for the water so swells a man ! it blows a man up like a bladder. Old Jack fears to have his specific levity increased and to be inflated like a balloon, let go of, and borne far aloft in the devious air. He still wishes to stand upon the solid earth at least a score of years longer, is very loath to leave it, and desires not to go heavenward before his time."

[*Enter Bardolph.*]

Bardolph. Bless you, Sir John.

Fal. And blessings on thee, good Bardolph ; thou 'rt most welcome. Since early yesternight I 've been at times sadly bewildered in my wits. A crock of sack, which I quaffed an hour ago, has not wholly dried the foolish and dull and crudy vapours which environ my brain. I prithee, tell me what, if anything passing strange, befell me last night, and how came I into this chamber ? Tell the truth, Bardolph, and keep nothing back.

Thereupon Bardolph gave Sir John a summary account of the predicament in which he and Snare found him, their efforts to awaken him, and the manner of his transportation into the Dolphin-chamber.

Fal. But, good Bardolph, thou hast not yet said what, in thy opinion, the matter was with me yesternight. Speak out, man.

Bard. Well, Sir John, I 've often heard your friends say that you have a very great brain, in fact, overmuch brains for your body, big and stalwart as 't is for a man of your years. And I 've heard some of your enemies—Sir John, you told me to speak out, I believe ?

Fal. Out with it, Bardolph.

Bard. Well, Sir John, I 've heard some of your enemies say—every man, whether he be great or small, has his enemies, you know—that you have what they call the " big head," and that the large wen on your neck and just behind your left ear and partly hidden by your hair is a necessary addition to your cranium to hold your surplus brains.

Fal. Zounds, Bardolph, mine enemies of all sorts ever did take a pride to gird at me and make me a laughing-stock. Every mother's son of them seems to regard me as a block, a stone, or other senseless thing by the wayside whereat he is privileged to lift up his leg, play the dog with me, and then trot on with impunity. But hast thou ever heard any such pin-headed enemy of mine say that I am a great fool, that my brains are not *bona fide*, and signify no more than the contents of a pompion of monstrous growth ?

Bard. I 've heard it said, Sir John, that there have been great men whose skulls were very small ; and so it would seem that there is more in the quality than in the quantity of the brain. But however that may be, suffer me, Sir John, to pass your question for the present, and to answer in another matter.

Fal. Be it so, Bardolph.

Bard. Well, Sir John, as you 've had much trouble and vexation of spirit of late, and great perturbation of the brain, I am of the opinion that last night you had a touch of apoplexy, or an attack of falling sickness, or heart disease, and that,—

Fal. A touch of apoplexy, a kind of lethargy or sleeping in the blood, a whoreson tingling, a heart failure! fie, fie, fie, Bardolph; 't was nothing of that sort; nor was 't a swooning and a falling down and a foaming at mouth and being speechless—no, no, no. And so thou thinkest that 't was epilepsy, the falling sickness, that befell me?

Bard. Yea, Sir John; for, if 't was not that, what else could it have been?

Fal. Tut, tut, a pin. I 've had several such fits and falls before, and always got the better of 'em. Other great men have had the like. Julius Cæsar, the foremost man in all the world in his time, had, in his last years, such sinking spells and falls, but he regained his feet and thereafter stood like a tower of strength. But, God-a-mercy! there came a day, the Ides of March, when the mightiest Julius, encircled by a coil of conspirators in the senate-house, was mortally stabbed, again and again; and then, looking around and seeing not one friendly face, but only a ring of daggers pointing at him, and saying, according to the legend, *Et tu, Brute!* he drew his gown over his head, gathered the folds about him that he might fall decently, and sank down at the base of Pompey's statue without uttering another word, never to rise again. 'Sblood! from such a falling sickness, let old Jack's litany be, "Good Lord, deliver me." What sayest thou, Bardolph?

Bard. Sir John, did this great Cæsar you 've told me of write a book about a big war he was in somewhere—I mean a Latin book that boys at school have to read, and be flogged if they don't read it right?

Fal. Ay, marry, Bardolph, that he did. He wrote seven books of commentaries on the wars in Gaul, and three books upon the Civil War, containing an account of its causes and history. Ha, ha, ha! thou wert often whipped at the Yarmouth grammar-school because of thy failure to construe Cæsar's *Commentaries* correctly.

Bard. Well, Sir John, that was a long time ago, but I remember it as well as if 't was yesterday. Plague take Cæsar; I 'm glad they killed him; they served him right.

Fal. Zounds! Bardolph, why art thou glad?

Bard. I 'm glad, Sir John, because Cæsar had no business to write such a book as he did to bother boys with, and get them breeched when they could n't translate it. That 's why I 'm glad they killed him.

Fal. I have read in Plutarch that Cæsar, the day before his assassination, supped at the house of Lepidus; and as he was signing some letters, according to his custom, as he reclined at table, there arose a question on the kind of death which was most to be desired. Thereupon he immediately looked up and said, " A sudden one." What sayest thou, Bardolph?

Bard. I agree with Cæsar, Sir John; I think a sudden death is best; but I 'd rather not fall and die as he did. To every man, soon or late, will come a day when he must fall to rise no more. The young man hopes that the dread day is for him far off, and so it may be; but the old man must know that 't is not far off for him. Death is certain to all;

but is 't not for all a leap into the dark? What sayest thou, Sir John?

Fal. Peace, good Bardolph, peace; do not speak to me thus and remind me of mine end. 'T is certain that all shall die. But, as Balaam saith, so say I: " Let me die the death of the righteous, and let my last end be like his." I hope, however, there is no need of my troubling myself yet with thoughts of death. I am not old, but older; I 've found the fountain of youth, and daily do I drink thereat. Have I fallen away vilely during the last score of years? Do I bate? Do I dwindle, peak, and pine? Does my skin hang about me like an old lady's loose gown? Is any part of my anatomy blasted with antiquity? Am I withered like an old apple-john? Am I *sans* teeth? Look you, Bardolph, introspect my mouth, and, by my troth, thou 'lt find therein nature's quota of teeth of the various kinds foreordained, save that they are all double; they 're all there, duly fixed, firm, and sound, save one, to wit, a canine tooth on the left side of my lower jaw, which was knocked out in my youth in a fight at the court-gate at the time I broke Skogan's head. May I not still laugh the arithmetic of Time to scorn? Hath my memory failed? Do I tell the same stories over and over again to the same persons? Hath my eye dimmed, or my natural force abated? In fine, is Sir John Falstaff in his dotage like Justices Shallow and Silence? By the way, Bardolph, what has become of that precious pair of justices who, at high noon yesterday, adjourned until two of the clock in the afternoon, but failed to return, take seats on the bench, and resume the hotch-potch proceedings against me? Also, what has happened to Master Abraham Slender and Sir Hugh Evans, who were likewise absent? Moreover, I did not see thee, Bardolph, lurking in the court-room at any time during the afternoon.

Bard. I was not there at all, Sir John, until last night, when Snare and I found you alone and fast asleep in your arm-chair in the dock near the justices' bench. An hour ago Sheriff Fang told me that early yesterday afternoon Justices Shallow and Silence were attacked with a strange vertigo and a squeamishness of the stomach, and that they were put under the care of Doctor Caius. They are reported to be now doing well, and will, as the doctor thinks, be able to come forth and resume business to-morrow. I am no doctor, Sir John, but, by the mass, I give it as my opinion that they were fap from drinking too much sack at dinner, yesterday. The sheriff also directed me to notify you that the court will meet at ten o'clock to-morrow morning. This I now do, Sir John.

Fal. I pray thee forthwith to tell the sheriff that I 'll be in court to-morrow morning at the hour appointed. And now, Bardolph, wilt thou give me leave awhile?   [*Exit Bardolph.*

Thereupon Sir John soliloquized as follows :

" During the absence of the justices yesterday afternoon, I played the part of a learned justicer *pro tempore*, as though duly commissioned and under the king in some authority ; and, having organized myself into a *quasi* court within a court, I conducted the proceedings to the entire satisfaction of the alleged culprit supposed to be on trial. 'T is true that I sat alone on the bench, and had no sheriff and no clerk ; but methinks I saw at times writing at Sir Hugh's desk, and at other times moving quietly about the court-room, a brisk, inquisitive, and perky young man, who seemed to be closely watching the court proceedings and making notes thereof. I surmise that this reportorial youth who has a most noticeable nose—a nose for news, a nose like a promontory in the geography of his face—is the son of Master George Page of Windsor, to wit, William Page, who, as a former disciple of the clergical Sir Hugh Evans, was compelled to hold up his head, be questioned in his accidence, and be breeched for forgetting how to decline *qui, quæ, quod,* and so forth. This young man was, peradventure, acting as Sir Hugh's deputy, and making memoranda of my sayings and doings. I trust, however, that, in consequence of my conduct yesterday, I have not fallen into the compass of a *præmunire.* But, zounds ! if such a writ be sued out against me, I care not a fico for the punishment consequent upon a conviction thereon ; for I have no lands and tenements, no goods and chattels, to be forfeited to the king, and I have virtually been out of royal Hal's protection ever since his coronation-day."

16

XI.

Peto as a Witness.—Tavern-Reckoning Found in Falstaff's Pocket, Read in Evidence.—His Answer; Declares that Hostess Quickly Gave him a Quittance for All his Debts to Her.—Justice Shallow Refuses to Lend Sir John Forty Pound with which to Buy a Horse.—Did Peto Steal the Seal-Ring of Falstaff's Grandfather?—A New Way to Pay an Old Debt.—The Boar's Head not a Bakery, but a Drinkery.—Peto as a Pickpocket.—Every Man's House is his Castle.—Slender's Opinion of the Law.—The Boar's Head as a "Castle."—Peto's Contempt of Court.—Falstaff Conceals his Contempt for the Court.—Filliping with a Three-Man Beetle.—Sir John Sees a White Pigeon, a Herald of Death.—Charon and the Styx.—Some Sack, Francis.—Charges that Peto Forged the Tavern-Reckoning. —*Hiatus valdè deflendus in MS.*

It seems that the court met at ten of the clock in the morning, according to the notice given by Sheriff Fang to Falstaff. Justice Shallow gazed for a few moments upon Sir John duly seated in the dock, and, after stroking his beard, and uttering several hems and haws, he slowly said : " By my troth, Sir John, what you said yesterday,—no, 't was the day before yesterday and before dinner —what you said, good Sir John, about sack was most excellent, i' faith ; indeed, 't was very singular good ; in faith, 't was well said, Sir John, very well said ; and I, as well as my cousin in commission with me, concur in your opinion of a good sherris-sack ; we do, we do, indeed, we do ; do we not, cousin Silence ? "

Sil. Yea, good cousin, we do. A cup of wine that 's brisk and fine ; be merry, be merry.

Shal. There, there, that will do, cousin. By the mass, did we not drink too much sack at dinner t' other day ?

Sil. Indeed, good cousin, we did to our cost, and for the behoof of Doctor Caius.

Shal. Well, well, this matter is neither here nor there ; by my troth, it hath nothing whatever to do with the case before us. Let me see, let me see ; where were we at ? Sir John, art thou ready and willing to proceed with the case of the Crown against thee ?

Fal. Yea, verily, your worship ; I am always ready, and am even eager to go on with it and to be done with it, whatever the end thereof may be.

Thereupon Peto, who was called and sworn as a witness for the Crown, testified that, before the peep o' day in the morning next after the Gadshill adventure, he discovered the defendant Falstaff fast asleep behind the arras in the Boar's Head tavern, fetching his breath hard, and snorting like a horse ; that, by the command of Prince Hal, he searched the sleeper's pockets and found nothing but papers therein ; and that among them was a certain paper which reads substantially as follows, to wit,—

Fal. Hold, Peto, not a word more just now. May it please your worships : If pocket-picking Peto has in his possession the identical paper which he confesses that he purloined from my pocket at the time and place aforesaid, I have no objection whatever to his producing and reading it as a part and parcel of his testimony ; but, zounds ! I do object to his uttering as evidence merely his recollection of the contents of the original paper, until he has first shown that it 's beyond his reach and control, or that 't is in fact lost or destroyed.

Shal. So, so, so, Peto, what has become of that paper ? Who hath it ? Is 't lost or destroyed ? Let me hear, let me hear.

Peto. Your worship, fearing that I might lose the paper in question, this morning I filed it with Sir Hugh Evans, the clerk of this court.

Fal. I prithee, Sir Hugh, let me see that paper. [*Having inspected it.*] May it please the court : This tavern-reckoning may be read in evidence against me for what 't is worth. I care not.

Shal. Let it be read, let it be read ; read the paper, Sir Hugh.

Sir Hugh. [*Reads.*]

" *Item, A capon*................... .... 2*s.* 2*d.*
Item, Sauce................................. 4*d.*
Item, Sack, two gallons.................... 5*s.* 8*d.*
Item, Anchovies and sack after supper....... 2*s.* 6*d.*
Item, Bread. .... *ob.*"

Shal. Ay, marry, Sir John, how answer you that paper ? Let me hear, let me hear.

Fal. Easily enough, your worship. If the proceedings pending against me are to be metamorphosed and hocus-pocussed into something in the nature of an action for debt brought by the hostess of the Boar's Head against me, why, then, I 'll say just here that when Chief Justice Gascoigne intervened in her action against me to recover a hundred mark, which she hysterically declared that I owed her for board and lodging—declaring, indeed, that I 'd eaten her out of house and home, and put all her substance into this fat belly of mine—his lordship not only took her part, but soundly rated me and ordered me to pay her with sterling money the sum which she claimed that I owed her, and so settle the suit at once. Thereupon Dame Quickly and I talked the whole matter over in a friendly way ; and, as a consequence, she ceased blubbering, washed her face as I bade her, agreed to withdraw her action against me, and, moreover, invited me to sup with her and Doll Tearsheet. After supper the good hostess and I compromised and settled not only her claim for a hundred mark as aforesaid, but also all other demands—including the cost of a dozen superfine, ruffled, and embroidered shirts, made of holland at eight shillings an ell, divers and sundry sums of money which I 'd, from time to time, borrowed of her, and all charges for my diet, lodging, and by-drinkings, which she made upon me to that date, a date long after the time at which Peto confesses that he pilfered from my pocket the tell-tale tavern-reckoning which Sir Hugh hath just read to your worships. As I am a gentleman, I then paid her, all and singular, the debts of every sort which I owed her, and she gave me a quittance in full for everything to that date ;

and thereunto she made her mark, a true cross, which was witnessed and subscribed unto by Doll Tearsheet.

Shal. Ay, marry, Sir John ; let me see, let me see ; where is that quittance ? Was 't duly drawn, executed, and attested ? Prithee, let me see it.

Fal. Your worship, 't is not now in my possession. Methinks 't is in a big bundle of important papers which I sent several years ago for safe-keeping to my brothers and sisters at the old family mansion hard by Yarmouth in Norfolk. If your worship so directs, look you, I 'll forthwith send Bardolph with a letter to be by him carried posthaste to them, directing that they deliver to him the bundle of papers aforenamed that he may bring it hither so that I may find therein the quittance in question for your worship's inspection. I bethink me, however, that I have no horse—ever since I 've grown to be such a horseback-breaker, 't is idle and too costly for me to keep a horse—and as Bardolph is unhorsed, as 't were, I 'll despatch him at once to Smithfield to buy one. But, as he has no money, nor have I, zounds ! I 'm afeard 't will strain my credit to get a horse in that market. Will my old and highly valued friend, Robert Shallow, esquire, lend me forty pound wherewith to buy one ?

Shal. Hem, hm, h-m, h-m-m, h-m-m-m, not a shilling, Sir John, not a penny, not even a farthing. By the mass, if Robert Shallow, esquire, knows himself—and he thinks he does—he 'll not be beguiled of forty pound in this manner. Let not Bardolph go to Smithfield market to buy a horse.

Let the quittance in question go, let it go, even though the result be the utter failure of these proceedings against the defendant. By my troth, the Crown can much better afford to lose the pending case and pay the costs thereof than I can afford to throw away forty pound by lending it to Sir John Falstaff. But let me see, let me see; Sir John, how did you make shift to get the money with which to pay Dame Quickly in full for everything you owed her, and thus get the quittance in question? How answer you that, Sir John?

Fal. 'T is easily answered, your worship. I had a stale demand against the hostess of the Boar's Head for the value of certain property picked from my pockets one night when I fell asleep behind the arras in that famous old mughouse, to wit: three or four bonds of forty pound a-piece, with accrued interest thereon, and a seal-ring of my grandfather's worth forty mark. By the way, I 've sometimes seen a certain man of my acquaintance furtively wearing a ring very like my lost one, which ring was, as I 've before stated, inset with a precious amethyst. And furthermore, I 've noticed that that man was never boozy when he wore the ring aforementioned, no matter how much sack he 'd swallowed, or how heady 't was ; and that when he was in a crapulous condition, no finger or thumb of his the likeness of my grandfather's sealing ring had on. Peto?

Peto. Well, Sir John?

Fal. Peto, confess now : Didst thou not rob me of the ring and the bonds aforesaid at the very time when thou didst pick out of my pocket the tavern-reckoning just read in evidence ?

Peto. 'Sblood ! Sir John,—

Shal. Keep the peace in court ! ho ! silence.

Sil. Here am I, cousin.

Shal. O, ye mistook, cousin Silence. Sheriff Fang, see to 't that order reigns here ; keep Sir John and Peto asunder. So, so, so ; go on, Sir John.

Fal. In our settlement Dame Quickly gave me full credit for the value of the bonds and the ring aforesaid ; and to pay the dregs of my debts to her, I gave her my non-negotiable promissory note —the precise sum for which 't was given I do not now remember—due in a year and a day from its date, with usance, and double usance if not paid at maturity. Bardolph became security on said note.

Shal. So, so, so, Sir John. Still another question : Have you paid and discharged that note?

Fal. Zounds, no ; there is a certain condition therein that hinders and delays the payment thereof ; 't is something like this : 'T is expressly agreed and understood by and between the parties to this instrument in writing that, if from any cause whatever, 't is not convenient for the principal or the surety therein to pay the same when it falls due, neither of said parties is to be teased and worried, harried and hurried, by the holder thereof.

Shal. Let me see,—

Fal. Hence your worship will see at a glance that time—probably a long time, and, mayhap, time without end in the future—is of the very essence of that contract.   And now, your worship, I prithee, let me return to the tavern-reckoning, which is strictly before the court for consideration, and from which we 've strayed a long way.   But, granting that Peto did pick that paper from my pocket at the time and place stated, what does it prove, or even tend to prove?   As evidence of anything charged against me, it amounts to nothing at all— to nothing more than 't would were it a lying epitaph copied from a tombstone in the graveyard of St. Michael's church into which your worships can easily look from the windows hard by your judgment-seat.   This tavern-reckoning—what is it? 'T is a mere memorandum, both headless and tailless ; 't is not headed as an account stated against Sir John Falstaff, or anybody else, as debtor to anybody for so much sack, and so forth, by him had and received, and not duly paid for and liquidated ; and 't is not signed by the hostess of the Boar's Head, as creditor, nor subscribed by any other person as claimant for the sum total due thereon.   Until 't is made definite and certain, it signifies nothing, nothing at all, against Sir John Falstaff.   Is he the only man in London that drinks sack, or eats a capon, or sauce, or anchovies, or bread?   How doth your worship answer that ?

Shal. Bodykins, no, no, no, Sir John ; myriads of men in England drink sack, eat bread, and so forth ; but, so, so, so ; let me see, let me see ; look you, Sir John, there 's a most monstrous deal of sack for but one half-pennyworth of bread set

down in this bill against somebody ; and who can
that somebody be but Sir John Falstaff ? Oho !
Sir John, how answer you that ?

Fal. Easily enough, and without objecting to
such circumstantial stuff as is stated in said bill.
Your hawk-eyed worship will see at a glance that
there are no dates whatever in this bill to show
when the several items thereof were furnished ;
there 's not a *scintilla* of evidence to signify that
the sack and the other items therein were each and
all furnished in a single day ; they might, one and
all, have been supplied during an entire week,
or in a whole month, or even in a year. Two gallons of sack, and also sack after supper—is this an
inordinate, intemperate, and incriminating measure
for a year, or a month, or even a week, for Justice
Robert Shallow, or for Justice Silence, or Master
Slender, or Sir Hugh Evans, or for any other
Christian gentleman ?

Sil. A cup of wine that 's brisk and fine ; be
merry, be merry.

Shal. Peace, good cousin, peace ; chirp not ;
remember that you are not now at an evening
drinking-bout in an arbour in my orchard in
Gloucestershire. Go on, Sir John.

Fal. And now, as to the bit of dry bread which
is put so ignominiously below the sack and so forth,
and at the very foot of the bill : The Boar's Head
never was, and never claimed to be, a mere bakery,
but to be a drinkery, rather. Its reputation rests
little on victual, and mostly on drink. Whoever
would take his ease in this inn is expected to drink

much, and to eat little ; and hence the great in-equality between the amount of bread and the drink, which appears in this bill, may be taken as a type of the character of the entertainment to be looked for in the tavern aforesaid. Moreover, over the door of its dining-chambers are graven in Gothic letters these words—now much obscured by cobwebs and dust and fly-bitten tapestries—to wit: "What ye want in Meat ye 'll have in Drink, who enter here." Now, then, your worship, the name-less somebody against whom this account seems to have been rendered may have regularly bought his bread in Pudding Lane, or at Pie-Corner, for in-stance ; and, if so, why should he buy more than a ha'pennyworth at the Boar's Head ? How answer you that, your worship ?

Shal. Let me see, let me see, Sir John. It doth seem to me that this tavern-bill signifies little or noth-ing, in this case, and that 't is incompetent, irrele-vant, and immaterial as evidence of anything against Sir John Falstaff. What say you, cousin Silence ?

Sil. It so seems to me. It doth, it doth, it doth,—

Shal. There, there, cousin Silence, that will do. Go on, Sir John.

Fal. Zounds ! I see Peto edging his way towards the street door as if to sneak out of and escape from my cross-examination of him.   I ask your worship to order him to remain in the court-room.

Peto. Sir John, you wholly mistake me. I was about to go out a little while merely to stretch my legs, and breathe the fresh air—air that has not been breathed, over and over, and spoken into lying words by one Sir John Falstaff. If I testify further as a witness for the Crown, or be cross-examined by you, I 'm resolved to tell the truth, the whole truth, and nothing but the truth, as my daily practice has always been. I have, indeed, been wedded to truth from my very boyhood up.

Fal. Hem, hm, h-m-m ; Peto ?

Peto. Well?

Fal. How long hast thou been a widower ?

Peto. Old Jack !

Shal. Peace, gentlemen, peace. Peto, stay in court and depart not without leave ; and, bailiffs, Grabbe and Ketchum, see that he doth not go away. Go on, Sir John.

Fal. At the time when and at the place where Peto swears that he took this tavern-reckoning from out my pocket, was he then and there an officer who had a search-warrant, or other legal authority to do this thing ? Your worships, you hear me deny his authority to do this act ; you hear me deny it. If he, without my knowledge and consent, put his hand into my pocket, and ransacked and rummaged it, even though 't was utterly empty, still he stands a felon confessed, and is liable to suffer the pains and penalties which old Father Antic, the Law, has ordained and provided for pickpockets.

Peto. Sir John, I prithee, be not so cocksure in your notions of the law and the facts in this case. While it is true, that I had no written warrant empowering me to go through your pockets, yet I had ample oral authority to do so ; for Prince Hal, who was with me on that occasion, commanded me to search your pockets, and so I did and found therein nothing but papers—the one now before the court being among them. That's the long and the short of this matter, Sir John.

Fal. And tell me now, Peto, tell me, had Prince Hal, then and there, any warrant in due form, authorizing him to ransack and rummage my pockets in the way you did?

Peto. Not that I know of.

Fal. Well, then, Peto, it seems that thou wert but Hal's puppet in this matter. By the mass, the man in the moon, or Beelzebub himself, might as well, and with as much right as the heir-apparent had, have said to thee, "Search his pockets." Prince Hal himself had no right so to do without a proper warrant ; nor did such right inhere in him because of his being then the immediate heir of England. How then could he commission thee to make such inquisition thereinto? Moreover, it hath been decided in England—and 't is the law therein to-day —that the house of every one is to him as his castle and fortress, as well for his defence against injury and violence, as for his repose : In other words, "Every man's house is his castle."* Whoever taketh

---

* William Pitt, first Earl of Chatham, when a member of the House of Commons, opposed with his utmost strength a certain Excise Bill, because it gave the right to search and lay open the private dwelling-house, which every Englishman has been taught to regard as his "castle." There is no report of his speech, but a single passage has come down to us, containing one of the finest bursts of his eloquence : "The poorest man in his cottage may bid defiance to all the forces of the Crown. It may be frail ; its roof may shake ; the wind may

his ease in his inn as a guest therein hath the full benefit of this maxim. Thus saith the law, as we learned it at Clement's Inn, doth it not, Master Robert Shallow ?

Shal. Ay, marry, good Sir John, it doth, it doth, it doth,—

Sil. It doth, it doth, it doth,—

Shal. Peace, cousin Silence, peace. What dost thou know of the law ? Nothing more than my good varlet, Davy, doth. The law, the law, as stated by Sir John—let me see, let me see ; I 've read it somewhere in some old law book ; 't is certain, 't is certain, indeed ; i' faith, I 've read it in the *Mirror of Justices*. I would that I had here from the library in my house, my castle, in Gloucestershire, that ancient book, that I might read, here and there, therein, and be enlightened and guided by the gravity, learning, and wisdom spread upon its pages. Cousin Slender, though thou wast never a student at Clement's Inn, yet thou hast studied at Oxford ; let me see, let me see : What is thy opinion of the law as stated by Sir John Falstaff ? Let me hear, let me hear.

Slen. Ay, your worship—in the county of Gloucester, justice of peace *coram ;* the law ? la ! what do I think of it ? I 've read somewhere of a judge who declared that nothing is law that is not reason; and somebody has said that the law is a sort of

---

blow through it ; the storm may enter it ; but *the King of England cannot enter it !* All his power dares not cross the threshold of that ruined tenement !"—GOODRICH'S *British Eloquence*, p. 65.

hocus-pocus science ; and so I doubt about the law. But, by these gloves, I hope, your worship, I will do as it shall become one that would do reason. If nothing is law that is not reason, then, according to logic as I learned it at Oxford, this proposition may be turned t' other end to, as 't were, so as to read thus : Reason is nothing that is not law. Ay, there 's the point, your worship ; it makes my head swim to reason, and when I do reason, I soon feel as though I 'd just turned a summersault, or was standing on my head. La ! the law may be after all a sort of hocus-pocus science, that smiles in your face while it picks your pocket. All law books are to me books of riddles. 'Od's heart-lings ! I had rather than forty shillings I had about me my *Book of Riddles* that I lent to Alice Shortcake a fortnight afore Michaelmas many years ago ; and la ! I wish I had here my *Book of Songs and Sonnets.* O sweet Anne Page !

Shal. Come, coz ; come, coz ; thy opinion of the law is like thy courtship of sweet Anne Page during thy green and vealy days, a tender, a kind of tender made afar off, made at long range, and coming to naught. Well, well, Sir John, we two must settle and agree upon what the law is, must we not ?

Fal. Ay, marry ; your worship has said well ; we two must declare what the law is. As I 've already said, whoever taketh his ease in his inn as a guest therein hath the full benefit of the maxim that " Every man's house is his castle." So, then, your worship, it follows that Sir John Falstaff, being on the night of the exploit on Gadshill a guest in the Boar's Head tavern, was then and there entitled to the full protection of his " castle " for the time being, even though he was sleeping in his every-day clothes and behind the arras, fetching his breath hard, and, forsooth, snorting like Centaurus himself.

Peto. Rats !

Shal. Order, come to order, Peto. What dost thou mean by this low exclamation ? let me see, by this contempt in the very face and eyes and ears of this court ? Tell me at once.

Peto. What did I say, your worship ? By my troth, I know not. I prithee, tell me.

Shal. Peto, with undue stress of voice, and wholly out of season, you said " Rats ! "

Peto. Great Scott ! your worship ; did I say that ?

Shal. By the mass, Peto, you said so. What did you mean by this vulgar word, which you yelled forth so unseasonably ? How answer you that ?

Peto. Nothing, your worship, nothing that I can now think of more than something like this : Once on a time, and under strange circumstances, I slept, or, rather tried to sleep, behind the arras in the Boar's Head. By the mass, I think it be the most villanous place in all Eastcheap to sleep in ; for 't is a place frightfully infested by rats, mice, fleas, cockroaches, and so forth, especially during the summer season. While Sir John was prosily speaking, I dropped into a doze and dreamed. Methought I was again lying behind the arras in my

" castle " as aforesaid, and that the rats and the mice made such a strife in running round about and over me that I unwittingly cried out " Rats ! " Only this, and nothing more. By my troth, I intended no contempt of this honourable court. Your worship, I prithee, pardon me.

Shal. Hem, h-m, h-m-m ; ay, marry, Peto, it may be so, it may be so ; but mark me, Peto, and mark me well ; don't doze and so dream again.

Fal. Zounds, Peto, thou 'rt twitching thy bristly and grizzly mustachios, and muttering about and sniggering at something. What dost thou mutter, and wherefore dost thou thus laugh? I prithee, tell me.

Peto. I talk to myself for two reasons, to wit, first, because I like to talk to a sensible man, and second, because I like to hear a sensible man talk. And I sometimes snigger at—well—at nothing, at nothing at all, Sir John.

Fal. Didst thou lie behind the arras only and for once only, Peto? Methinks that thou 'rt now lying outside of the arras. But, Lord, Lord, how this world is given to lying ! and, may it please your worships, how subject we old men are to this vice of lying ! "

Here Falstaff paused a moment to regain his wind, and, just as he opened his mouth to utter more to their worships, Justice Shallow cut short his further remarks by vigorously pounding the table in front of him with his gold-headed staff, and angrily exclaiming, " Silence ! silence in court, Sir John " ; which words waked his worship's

snoozing associate, who snorted as though his nose
had been tickled with a straw, and responded in
boyish treble, and as if answering to his name
called at school, "ADSUM." But the senior justice
said :

" Peace, cousin Silence, peace. So, so, so, Sir
John ; let me see, let me see ; what thou hast just
said about lying is neither here nor there ; by my
troth, it hath nothing, it hath nothing at all to do
with the Crown's case against thee ; yea, sir, 't is
impertinent ; 't is even insolent, sir. Didst thou,
sir, intend by thy very last words to show thy contempt for this honourable court, and more especially
for me, one of the king's justices of the peace in
the county of Gloucester—"

Slen. And a gentleman born, who writes himself *armigero*, in any bill, warrant, quittance, or
obligation, *armigero.*

Shal. Ay, that I do, cousin Slender ; and have
done any time these three hundred years. Let me
see, let me see ; so, so, so, Sir John, as I 've said,
if thou didst intend by thy very last words to show
thy contempt for this honourable court, and more
especially for me, by God's liggens, I 'll lay a heavy
fine upon thee, and also send thee to prison wherein thou 'lt abide till thou 'rt fully purged of thy
contempt as aforesaid ; and, peradventure, I 'll
make a Star-Chamber matter of thy behaviour to
this court. If thou wert twenty Sir John Falstaffs,
thou shalt not abuse Robert Shallow, esquire, nor
show contempt for him in his judicial capacity, nor
for his worthy cousin Silence who sits with him.

And then Justice Shallow paused and looked, with eyes severe upon Sir John ; and Silence, gazing reverently upon Shallow sitting by his side, shrilly spoke and piped, " Why, then, say we old men can do somewhat. 'T is so. Is 't not so ? " And thereupon Sir John made a low courtesy to the court, and said : " I show contempt for this court, for your worships ! Zounds, no ! I have all along during this trial done my level best to conceal it. I show contempt for those who are under the king in some authority ! No, no, no, not I. What saith the Holy Scriptures ? ' Honour the king' : ' The powers that be are ordained of God ' : ' Obey them that rule over you,' and the like. Your worships may be quite cocksure that if old Jack Falstaff does not take good heed of and obey these Scriptural injunctions, then is he no true man, no gentleman born, no true knight and loyal subject of the king ; but rather is he a fat-kidneyed rascal whose wit 's as thick as Tewksbury mustard ; and there 's no more conceit in him than is in a mallet. Indeed, in the case supposed, he 'd be little better than one of the wicked. Again, I say that I intended to show no contempt whatever for this honourable court, nor to any member thereof.

Shal. It may be so, it may be as you say, Sir John ; and yet, by my troth, it seems to me that —and, cousin Silence, doth it not so seem to thee—

Sil. Ay, marry, good cousin, it doth, it doth, it doth—

Shal. I prithee, cousin Silence, answer not so soon ; but first hear me through, and then do thou answer. I say, Sir John, that there was at times— let me see—at times a colour of contempt in thy voice and manner, and more especially when thou didst look hard at this court, and, with a villanous trick of thine eye say, " May it please your worships, how subject we old men are to this vice of lying !" The contempt consists not so much in what you said as in the way you said it. Say I well, Sir John ? Have I read you aright ? Let me hear.

Fal. Thou hast said well, Master Robert Shallow; but, as I am a gentleman, and a true knight, thou hast spelt me backward, read me backside before and upside down, and hast wholly misconstrued my thoughts, words, and behaviour. May it please your worships : Fear no colour of contempt in me. When I willfully, purposely, and maliciously show my contempt for this court, or for any member thereof, then may I be at once transformed into a toad, and may the court order Sheriff Fang, assisted by his under-bailiffs, forthwith to squat me on one end of a short see-saw plank, and fillip me with a three-man beetle.* I betray my contempt for this court ! Zounds, if nothing else would prevent me

---

* Steevens says that it is a common sport with the Warwickshire boys to put a toad on one end of a short board placed across a small log, and then to strike the other end with a bat, thus throwing the creature high in the air. This is called *filliping* the toad. A *three-man beetle* is a heavy rammer with three handles used in driving piles, requiring three men to wield it. Such a beetle would evidently be suitable for *filliping* a weight like Falstaff's.—ROLFE.

from so doing, 't would be my respect for the gray hairs of the two venerable justices of the peace now before me ; [and then, as the fat knight glanced closely at the billiard-ball brain-cases of Shallow and Silence, almost innocent of hair of any kind, he added :] the gray hairs of your worships, wherever they may be. Fie ! this is hot weather, gentlemen ; I sweat extraordinarily ; and, alack ! I lack shirts, for I bethink me that of the dozen to my back, once on a time, so generously bought for me by a certain gentlewoman near and dear to me —said shirts having cost five pound apiece, more or less—I have only one for superfluity, and another for use. If I, on such a hot day as this, brandish anything but a bottle of sack, I would that I might never spit white again. Some sack, Francis.

Fran. Anon, anon, sir.

Fal. 'Sblood, I am as melancholy as a gib cat or a lugged bear. [*He drinks.*] I am old, I am old ; I am beginning to feel that I cannot live much longer. When I was a young man I was as vir-tuously given as a gentleman need to be, virtuous enough ; swore little ; diced not above seven times —a week ; paid money that I borrowed—three or four times ; lived well, and in good compass ; but for the greater part of my life I 've lived out of all order, out of all compass. Company, villanous company, as well as sack and sugar, and so forth, hath been the spoil of me. All my life long I 've been unmindful of my P's and Q's.* 'T is time,

---

* In the fifteenth century it was customary for English ale-house keepers to write the scores of their customers on the

't is, indeed, high time, for me to repent, amend my life, consider my latter end, and fit myself—if that be, indeed, possible—for a snug place in old Abraham's bosom, if there be in fact room enough left therein for me. I owe God a death ; my days of grace are gone, and the debt, with compound usance, is to-day overdue, according to the figures written on my bald crown as if 't were a schoolboy's tablet, or a tapster's slate covered o'er with tavern-reckonings. Well, I cannot last ever.

Shal. Certain, 't is certain ; very sure, very sure: death, as the Psalmist saith, is certain to all ; all shall die. Let me see, let me see ; I have lived fourscore years and upward. I prithee, good Sir John, how many years have you lived ? What is your age ? How answer you that ?

But Sir John heeded not Justice Shallow's question ; and, though 't was fretfully repeated, he appeared not to have heard it, and still stood silent and musing. There was that far-away look in his eyes as if he were reviewing the sack-stained cur-

---

wall with a bit of charcoal. The letter P served as an abbreviation for pints and Q for quarts, each being placed at the top of a column, long or short, of figures showing the state of the customer's account. The fact being well known, it became customary for sober friends to withdraw their drinking companions from the taproom by showing them the length of the account, or, in their language, the " state of their P's and Q's." " Mind your P's and Q's " was a common hint to a hard drinker that he was going too far, and the expression easily found favor in other places than taprooms and became accredited as a synonym for " Be on your good behavior."— WOPSLE.

rent of his long life, and anxiously peering into the dim, dark, and shadowy future. He soon attempted to speak, but the words died on his quivering lips. He had seen a herald of death in the guise of a white pigeon * flying against a window hard by the justices' bench, and vainly fluttering her pennons to find some coign of vantage whereon to rest the sole of her foot, but, baffled in so doing, falling plumb down into the cemetery in the rear of St. Michael's church standing just back of the Boar's Head. His face suddenly paled ; his knees smote one against another ; his whole frame trembled as though old man Charon had found him upon the Stygian banks, roughly slapped him on the back, and said : " How now ! old Jack ; you loiter here too long. Judge Rhadamanthus wants you in court over the river. Your name has been duly called, but you 've answered not ; your recognizance has been forfeited, and a writ of *capias* is now out for your body. Go aboard instantly, or I 'll call two or three of my roustabouts who 'll seize you by the scruff of your neck and the slack of your slops, and hustle you into my ferry-boat sooner than you can say ' Jack Falstaff.' All aboard, all of you, and all at once, you greasy knight, you father ruffian, you omnipo-

---

* Among all classes of people in Great Britain there is a widespread belief that the common white pigeon is the herald of death. Thus, a white pigeon alighting on a chimney or flying against a window betokens death to some occupant of that house. On account of this curious belief, the English housewives cannot be persuaded to use pigeon feathers about their beds.—WOPSLE.

tent villain, you old white-bearded Satan." Sir John would, peradventure, have swooned, and dived like a didapper headlong over the railing of the dock whereon he leaned, had not nimble-tongued Francis, who was luckily lurking within range of Falstaff's glaring eyes, affrightedly cried out, "Anon, anon, sir; O Lord, good Sir John, what would you with me? Anon, anon, sir"; which words so revived and resurrected him that he shook and bristled up himself, recovered his equipoise, and hoarsely gasped out, "Some sack, Francis; I prithee, a quart, good Francis." That fleet-footed boy quickly fetched and handed up to the knight a pottle of canaries, which is, as Hostess Quickly once said to Doll Tearsheet, "a marvellous searching wine, and it perfumes the blood ere one can say 'What's this?'" Sir John took a long, strong, gurgling drink from the pottle-pot, wiped his thick white beard on the back of his big fat hand, and at once was himself again. . . . *Hic pauca verba* . . . . *desunt in MS.*

"And now, may it please your worships," resumed Falstaff, "I am not yet done with Peto, who, by the way, seems to be more concerned in this case than the Crown itself is. I am thinking that 't is my duty to charge him with a certain crime, to wit,—"

Shal. Sayest thou so, Sir John? The evidence —what thou hast—let me hear, let me hear.

Fal. Will your worship carefully examine the handwriting of the pretended tavern-reckoning before the court? Prithee, scrutinize the torn and

serrated upper and lower edges of that paper—I
see that your worship has it—and also note the
indented left-hand edge thereof.

Shal. Sir Hugh, I prithee, lend me thy magnifying glass.

Sir Hugh. Here it is, your worship.

Shal. [*After examining the paper.*] Well, Sir
John ?

Fal. Long after midnight of the night during
which, as Peto hath sworn, he filched from my
pocket this tavern-reckoning, I was so overcome
by the fatigues and perils of a certain lark outside
of London, and by the roystering after my return
to the Boar's Head, that I lay down on the bare
floor behind the arras and fell asleep at once.
Near noon I awoke, rubbed my eyes, stretched my
legs, arose, shook myself, and—was dressed. My
sleeping-place was still somewhat dark, but a rent
in the closed window-curtain permitted the sun to
shine through it, and with his rays, to point out
and clothe with all the colours of the rainbow a
mysterious something lying on the floor and beside
the spot where I 'd lain and slept.

Shal. Let me see, let me see ; 't was strange
about those rainbow colours, strange, indeed. The
cause, the cause thereof, Sir John, what was 't ?

Fal. Your worship, the efficient cause of the
phenomenon I witnessed may itself have been the
result of accident or caprice in mending a broken
pane of glass in the arras window so that two panes
inclined and touched their lower edges, whereby
they caught and held between themselves a quar-

ter of a pottle of rain, or thereabouts, which had fallen at cock-crowing ; and, as a consequence, the sun's rays, which shot through the glass and the imprisoned water, were, by some heavenly alchemy, transformed into an iridescent light. I hope that your worship now clearly sees the cause of the rainbow colours in question ?

Shal. Ay, marry, Sir John ; but,—

Fal. Prithee, pardon me, your worship. When we were little and believing boys, did we not sometimes run with utmost speed to catch the end of a rainbow not far away, and to find the pot of gold reported to be buried at its foot ?

Shal. That we did, that we did, that we did ; in faith, Sir John, we did, indeed.

Fal. But, Master Robert Shallow, did we ever clutch the tail-end of any rainbow ? and did any coins from that crock of gold ever jingle in our pockets ? How answer you that, your worship ?

Shal. No, never, no, never ; so, so, then, we 'll not now chase rainbows ; no, no, no ; go on, Sir John.

Fal. The mysterious something which I had thus espied, I picked up and found it to be a little wad of paper, crumpled and rolled into a globular form, and being very like the paper pellets that tricksome boys used to flip slyly hither and thither in the Yarmouth grammar-school. I carefully unrolled this wad, and discovered that 't was composed of three several slips of paper, which seemed to have been warily torn from a large sheet, in the following manner, to wit : One thereof from the top, one thereof from the bottom, and one thereof from the sinistral side, of the sheet of paper aforesaid. The words and figures written on these slips somehow aroused my suspicion of some dirty trick—possibly some crime—either committed or contemplated ; and, thinking that the mystery might be, by and by, cleared up by means of these bits of paper, I 've kept them even unto this day. I may also say that I carried no candle with me when I went behind the arras to rest, and that I lay down and fell asleep in the dark. The next morning I found near the foot of my resting-place a large ivory button, lost from a jerkin, an extinguished rushlight, and, here and there on the floor, drops of tallow and other evidences that somebody carrying a light had hovered around me during the night. I have applied the three paper slips to three edges, respectively, of the tavern-bill before your worships ; and I find that they fit one another exactly, and that the words and figures written on the slips serve as marginal notes, as 't were, to the text of the taverning-reckoning, and illumine what was once dark and mysterious therein. Moreover, the kind of paper, the colour of the ink used, the disguised handwriting, and the water-mark—a fool's cap and bells—are, as I think, one and the same in both. Furthermore, experts who have examined and compared said slips with three or four epistles undoubtedly written by a certain man of whom I 'll only say for the present that letters four do form his surname, give it as their opinion that both were written by one and the same person. At this moment I have in my possession the slips and the epistles aforesaid ; and the experts aforementioned are now within call.   And now,—

Peto. Hold up ! old Jack.   By my troth, I am loath to interrupt thy amusing cock-and-bull story ; but, before any evidence is introduced in the supposed criminal case against me, which thou 'rt cunningly striving to tack to (and thereby hide) the Crown's case against thee, I 'd like to hear what crime I 'm charged with,—what 's the matter with me ?

Shal. So, so, so, Sir John ; Peto's request doth seem to me to be fair and just ; it doth, indeed. Doth it not so seem to thee, cousin Silence ?

Sil. It doth, it doth, it doth,—

Shal. Go on, Sir John.

Fal. Your worship, I am prepared to prove beyond all reasonable doubt that Peto, being instigated so to do by the Devil, and intending thereby to injure my good name and fame for all time to come, did, purposely and unlawfully, willfully and maliciously, concoct, fabricate, and forge the pretended tavern-reckoning which has been so flourished in my face and trumpeted to the world as circumstantial evidence of the strongest kind of my hatred of bread and my love of sack ; and that if Peto did search my pockets and find therein the paper aforesaid as he has sworn that he did, he first put it into my pocket, so that he could pick it thereout, if he did in fact filch it therefrom.

Peto. Your worship, I am not well ; I prithee, let me go to my room and rest awhile.

Fal. Art sick? Art anxious to retire to thy room up the ramshackle back stairs of thy lodging-house in Ram Alley? Zounds ! I 've noticed that when a rat takes poison, he hunts his hole to die in.

Shal. Peace, Sir John, peace ; tease him not. Peto, if thou 'rt sick, though mayest be excused till dinner-time to-morrow—all the while, however, to remain in custody of Grabbe and Ketchum, who will go with thee.

[*Exeunt Peto et al.*

And thereupon .   .   .   .

.   .   .   .

[*Here the MS. abruptly ends.*]

XII.

FALSTAFF'S DEATH.

Nym and Pistol Quarrel.—Bardolph as a Peacemaker.—*Quasi*-Partnership.—Pistol Will a Sutler be.—Sir John Shaked of a "Burning Quotidian Tertian"; Dies and Goes to Arthur's Bosom.—Bardolph, Pistol, and Nym Shog to France.—Bronze Figure of Falstaff at Stratford.—Fate of the Fat Knight's Followers.—Dowden's Critical Comments.

In the first scene of the second act of *King Henry V.*, Lieutenant Bardolph and Corporal Nym meet in a London street, and, after greeting each other, Bardolph asks Nym whether he and Ancient Pistol are friends yet. The corporal, who is as usual ill-humored, answers surlily and vaguely ; and the lieutenant replies by offering to bestow a breakfast to make the two friends, and proposing that they all three become sworn brothers, and then go to France. The corporal returns an irrelevant and repellant answer to this proposal ; and thereupon the lieutenant tells him 't is certain that Pistol is married to Nell Quickly, and remarks that she certainly did Nym wrong, for he was troth-plight to her. The corporal answers that he cannot tell, and that things must be as they may ; and says, in a mysterious way, that " men may sleep, and they may have their throats about them at that time ; and some say knives have edges." As he concludes his inconsequent remarks, Pistol and his wife, formerly Mrs. Quickly, appear on the scene. The dialogue continues :

Bard. Here comes Ancient Pistol and his wife : good corporal, be patient here. How now, mine host Pistol !

The husband instantly flashes fire, and explodes thus :

> Base tike, call'st thou me host ?
> Now, by this hand, I swear, I scorn the term ;
> Nor shall my Nell keep lodgers.

And Mistress Pistol, whose notions of law and morality are somewhat loose and confused, thus goes off :

No, by my troth, not long ; for we cannot lodge and board a dozen or fourteen gentlewomen that live honestly by the prick of their needles, but it will be thought we keep a bawdy-house straight. [*Nym draws his sword.*] O welladay, Lady, if he be not drawn now ! we shall see willful adultery and murder committed.

In spite of Bardolph's request that they keep the peace, Nym growls, " Pish ! " and Pistol howls, " Pish for thee, Iceland dog ! thou prick-ear'd cur of Iceland !" The war of words between these two " braggarts vile " continues but neither hurts the other, belike because Bardolph draws his sword and solemnly affirms that, as he is a soldier, he 'll run him up to the hilts, that strikes the first stroke. It seems that there is a woman in the case, for, in

          Falstaff.

answer to Nym's declaration, that his humour is
to cut Pistol's throat, one time or another, in fair
terms, Pistol defies him, calls him a hound of Crete,
asks, " Think'st thou my spouse to get ? " and declares that he has, and that he will hold, " the
quondam Quickly for the only she." The Boy enters:

Boy. Mine host Pistol, you must come to my master, and
you, hostess ; he is very sick, and would to bed.—Good Bardolph, put thy face between his sheets, and do the office of a
warming-pan.   Faith, he 's very ill.

Bard. Away, you rogue !

Hostess. By my troth, he 'll yield the crow a pudding one
of these days.   The king has killed his heart.   Good husband,
come home presently.   [*Exeunt Hostess and Boy.*

Pistol and Nym continue their quarrel, the latter
demanding eight shillings which he 'd won of the
former at betting, and Pistol retorting, " Base is the
slave that pays."   At last they patch up a peace
between themselves, and enter into a *quasi*-partner-
ship, as follows :

Pistol. A noble shalt thou have, and present pay ;
And liquor likewise will I give to thee,
And friendship shall combine, and brotherhood :
I 'll live by Nym, and Nym shall live by me.
Is not this just ? for I shall sutler be
Unto the camp, and profits will accrue.*

---

* On the 23d of March, 1848, in the United States Senate,
Daniel Webster spoke on the bill for raising a loan of sixteen
millions of dollars for the purpose of carrying on the Mexican
war.   In his speech he said :

" Now, sir, I propose to hold a plain talk to-day ; and I say
that, according to my best judgment, the object of the bill is

And thereupon the hostess returns and says :

As ever you came of women, come in quickly to Sir John.
Ah, poor heart ! he is so shaked of a burning quotidian ter-
tian, that it is most lamentable to behold. Sweet men, come
to him.
Nym. The king hath run bad humours on the knight; that 's
the even of it.
Pistol. Nym, thou hast spoke the right ;
His heart is fracted and corroborate.
Nym. The king is a good king ; but it must be as it may :
he passes some humours and careers.
Pistol. Let us condole the knight ; for lambkins we will
live.

The only authentic account of Falstaff's last
hours and death is contained in the third scene of
the second act of *King Henry V.*, which is laid
in London, and before a tavern—probably the
Boar's Head.

[*Enter Pistol, Hostess, Nym, Bardolph, and Boy.*]
Hostess. Prithee, honey-sweet husband, let me bring thee
to Staines.
Pistol. No ; for my manly heart doth yearn.—

----

patronage, office, the gratification of friends. This very measure for raising ten regiments creates four or five hundred officers ; colonels, subalterns, and not them only, for for all these
I feel some respect, but there are also paymasters, contractors,
persons engaged in the transportation service, commissaries,
even down to sutlers, *et id genus omne*, people who handle the
public money without facing the foe, one and all of whom are
true descendants, or if not, true representatives, of Ancient
Pistol, who said,

> ' I shall sutler be
> Unto the camp, and profits will accrue.' "

Bardolph, be blithe ; Nym, rouse thy vaunting veins :
Boy, bristle thy courage up ; for Falstaff he is dead,
And we must yearn therefore.

Bard. Would I were with him, wheresome'er he is, either in heaven or in hell !

Hostess. Nay, sure, he 's not in hell: he 's in Arthur's bosom, if ever man went to Arthur's bosom.* A' made a finer end, and went away an it had been any christom child ; a' parted even just between twelve and one, even at the turning o' the tide : for after I saw him fumble with the sheets and play with flowers and smile upon his fingers' ends, I knew there was but one way ; for his nose was as sharp as a pen, and a' babbled of green fields. " How now, Sir John ! " quoth I : " What, man ! be o' good cheer." So a' cried out " God, God, God ! " three or four times. Now I, to comfort him, bid him a' should not think of God ; I hoped there was no need to trouble himself with any such thoughts yet. So a' bade me lay more clothes on his feet : I put my hand into the bed and felt them, and they were as cold as any stone ; then I felt to his knees, and they were as cold as any stone, and so upward and upward, and all was as cold as any stone.

Nym. They say he cried out of sack.

Hostess. Ay, that a' did.

Bard. And of women.

Hostess. Nay, that a' did not.

Boy. Yes, that a' did ; and said they were devils incarnate.

Hostess. A' could never abide carnation ; 't was a colour he never liked.

Boy. A' said once, the devil would have him about women.

Hostess. A' did in some sort, indeed, handle women : but then he was rheumatic ; and talked of the whore of Babylon.

Boy. Do you not remember, a' saw a flea stick upon Bardolph's nose, and a' said it was a black soul burning in hell-fire?

---

* Mrs. Quickly is not strong as a Scripturist.—Worsle.

Bard. Well, the fuel is gone that maintained that fire: that 's all the riches I got in his service.

Nym. Shall we shog? the king will be gone from South-ampton.

Pistol. Come, let 's away.—My love, give me thy lips.
Look to my chattels and my movables :
Let senses rule ; the word is '' Pitch and Pay : ''
Trust none ;
For oaths are straws, men's faiths are wafer-cakes,
And hold-fast is the only dog, my duck :
Therefore, *Caveto* be thy counsellor.
Go, clear thy crystals.—Yoke-fellows in arms,
Let us to France ; like horse-leeches, my boys,
To suck, to suck, the very blood to suck !

Boy. And that 's but unwholesome food, they say.

Pistol. Touch her soft mouth, and march.

Bard. Farewell, hostess.   [*Kissing her.*]

Nym. I cannot kiss, that is the humour of it ; but, adieu.

Pistol. Let housewifery appear · keep close, I thee com-mand.   And be thou truly thankful, Nell, that I do not affix to thee a lock-up such as the crusaders were accustomed to apply to their wives to keep them virtuous while they were away at the wars.   *Varium et mutabile semper femina.*

Hostess. Farewell : adieu.   [*Exeunt.*]

Falstaff appears never to have had any horror of being in debt, and to have acted from his youth up as though the world owed him a living which he might, if he pleased, get by hook or by crook.   As at a late stage in his career he declared that he could get no remedy against the consumption of his purse, and pronounced this disease incurable, it may reasonably be presumed that he died intes-tate, and without a penny in his pocket.   'T is not known for certain who took his sword and buckler ; but Bardolph, after so many years of dog-like attachment and faithful service to his master, and so little profit to himself, may have regarded these as his perquisites, and carried them off when he went to France. He certainly needed both sword and shield when, at the siege of Har- fleur, he hallooed to Nym and Pistol, " On, on, on, on, on ! to the breach, to the breach ! "—each of these three swashers, then and there, wishing, as the Boy with them wished, that he were in an ale- house in London, and being willing, as the Boy was, to give all his fame for a pot of ale and safety.

Sir John, though worthy of a column in East- cheap and a monument in Westminster Abbey as well, has no memorial in either place, and sleeps in an unknown grave. Nor has he even a memorial window in the old and always established Church of the Ephesians, in which he was for so many years a burning and a shining light, and the only layman who was ever privileged to sit within its chancel. 'T is, however, some satisfaction to his many friends, all the world over, to know that at one of the four corners of the base of Lord Ronald Gower's statue of Shakespeare, lately erected in the Memorial Gardens at Stratford-upon-Avon, is a bronze effigy of Falstaff—the character figures at the other corners being Hamlet, Lady Macbeth, and Henry V.

Of Falstaff's wild crew, it may be briefly said : Fortune frowned on Bardolph and Nym, " sworn brothers in filching," for both were hanged in France for robbing a church—stealing a *pax*, appraised by Pistol as " of little price " ; and Ancient Pistol, who had " a killing tongue and a quiet sword," was, by Captain Fluellen, a Welsh officer in King Henry's army, at whom he had been galling and gleeking, at last greeted thus : " Got pless you, Aunchient Pistol ! you scurvy, lousy knave, Got pless you !" then soundly cudgelled, compelled to eat a leek because he 'd mocked the custom of Welsh soldiers to wear leeks in their caps on St. David's day, and dismissed with the benediction, " Got b' wi' you, and keep you, and heal your pate." " All hell shall stir for this," said Pistol, but not until Fluellen had departed. Left alone, the knave thus morals upon his predicament and prospects :

> Doth Fortune play the huswife with me now ?
> News have I, that my Nell is dead i' the spital
> Of malady of France ;
> And there my rendezvous is quite cut off.
> Old do I wax ; and from my weary limbs
> Honour is cudgell'd. Well, bawd will I turn,
> And something lean to cutpurse of quick hand.
> To England will I steal, and there I 'll steal :
> And patches will I get unto these cudgell'd scars,
> And swear I got them in the Gallia wars.*

---

* Dr. Johnson remarks here : " The comic scenes of The History of Henry the Fourth and Fifth are now at an end, and all the comic personages are now dismissed. Falstaff and Mrs. Quickly are dead ; Nym and Bardolph are hanged ; Gadshill was lost immediately after the robbery ; Poins and Peto have vanished since, one knows not how ; and Pistol is now beaten into obscurity. I believe every reader regrets their departure."

And so Pistol makes his exit, whither, we know not. After the Gadshill robbery, Gadshill is heard of no more. Whether Peto dies with his boots on, or in his bed, we cannot tell. Poins, the best of the set, vanishes silently, without a word as to his fate.

'T was meet in every way that the fat knight should breathe his last in the inn wherein he had for so many years taken his ease and reigned as its merry monarch. And 't was very meet that the ugsomeness of his death should be somewhat lightened by the lamentably-ludicrous account which Hostess Quickly gives of his passing away from earth.

Dowden, in his *Shakspere—His Mind and Art,* thus comments : " In the relation, by Mrs. Quickly, of the death of Falstaff, pathos and humour have run together and become one. ' A ' made a finer end and went away an it had been any christom child ; a' parted even just between twelve and one, even at the turning o' the tide : for after I saw him fumble with the sheets, and play with flowers and smile upon his fingers' ends, I knew there was but one way ; for his nose was as sharp as a pen, and a' babbled of green fields.' Here the smile and the tear rise at the same instant. Nevertheless, the union of pathos with humour as yet extends only to an incident ; no entire pathetic-humourous character has been created like that of Lear's Fool.

" Pathetically, however, the fat knight disappears, and disappears forever. The Falstaff of

The Merry Wives of Windsor is another person
than the Sir John who is 'in Arthur's bosom,
if ever man went to Arthur's bosom.' The
epilogue to the second part of *Henry IV.*
(whether it was written by Shakspere or not remains doubtful) had promised that 'our humble
author will continue the story with Sir John in it.'
But our humble author decided (with a finer judgment than Cervantes in the case of his hero) that
the public was not to be indulged in laughter for
laughter's sake at the expense of his play. The
tone of the entire play of *Henry V.* would have
been altered if Falstaff had been allowed to appear
in it. During the monarchy of a Henry IV. no
glorious enthusiasm animated England. It was
distracted by civil contention. Mouldy, Shallow,
and Feeble were among the champions of the royal
cause. Patriotism and the national pride of England could not, under the careful policy of a
Bolingbroke, burst forth as one ascending and
universal flame. At such a time our imagination
can loiter among the humours and frolics of a
tavern. When the nation was divided into various
parties, when no interest was absorbing and su-
preme, Sir John might well appear upon his throne
at Eastcheap, monarch by virtue of his wit, and
form with his company of followers a state within
the state. But with the coronation of Henry V.
opens a new period, when a higher interest animates
history, when the national life was unified, and the
glorious struggle with France began. At such a
time private and secondary interests must cease ;

the magnificent swing, the impulse and advance of
the life of England, occupy our whole imagination.
It goes hard with us to part from Falstaff, but, like
the king, part from him we must ; we cannot be
encumbered with that tun of flesh ; Agincourt is
not the battle-field for splendid mendacity. Falstaff, whose principle of life is an attempt to coruscate away the facts of life, and who was so potent
during the Prince's minority, would now necessarily
appear trivial. There is no place for Falstaff any
longer on earth ; he must needs find refuge ' in
Arthur's bosom.' "

XIII.

THE late Llewellyn Jones, for half a century tapster-in-chief of the popular Pig-and-Whistle Inn in the old town of Shrewsbury, was descended from a branch of the multiramified family of Joneses, for ages settled in Caernarvonshire. He was born about three of the clock in the morning of St. David's day, in the picturesque vale of Llanberris, and within reach of the afternoon shadows of the Snowdonian range of mountains. His father, Cadwallader Jones, was, when a young man, admitted to be the champion wrestler and single-stick player in all the country round ; and his mother, Graciosa, *née* Evans, who traced her descent from the clerkly Sir Hugh Evans, was, in her girlhood, best known under the name of the " Llanberris Beauty." Llewellyn inherited from his father a sound body, and from his mother, good looks and a love for books. Little is known of his early life, but it appears that, in his nineteenth year, he was so cruelly crossed in love that he resolved never to fall in

love again ; and, it seems, he kept his resolution—
at least, he never married. In a hot-headed way,
and chiefly to end the heartache, he soon turned
his back upon his birthplace, and left it forever.
For several months he wandered aimlessly and
afoot here and there in Wales and the western
part of England, till near the close of a mid-sum-
mer day, when, weary, hungry, and foot-sore, he
found food and rest at the old Pig-and-Whistle
tavern in Shrewsbury. In that renowned inn he
was destined to take his ease for fifty years and up-
wards. Being a moneyless stranger in that city,
and finding nothing else to do, he accepted employment as an under-skinker in the hostelry in which
he was a guest. Although Llewellyn was then a
big boy, yet he was so prompt with his " anon,
anon, sir," and served so faithfully in his humble
office, that the landlord speedily made him tapster-
in-chief, and paid him wages so liberal as to verify
Falstaff's remark to Bardolph that " a tapster is a
good trade " ; nevertheless, he played no tapster's
tricks, did not " froth and lime," sold sound liquor,
gave fair measure, and remained in office during
the reign of several successive landlords. He soon
forswore thin potations and addicted himself to
sack ; and so it came to pass that some years before
his thirty-fifth birthday, he had lost the lithe and
graceful figure of his early youth, and grown Fal-
staffian in his proportions and carriage of himself.
Also, his clay was like that of his great precursor
and prototype, not a " clay that gets muddy with
drink."

Llewellyn, early in his career, found a hobby-horse, which he rode, day after day, unto the last moment of his life. 'T was Shakespeare. This is how it happened : One dark and gloomy day, a fat and boozy strolling-player chanced to be in the tap-room of the Pig-and-Whistle, and there, before "three or four loggerheads amongst three or four score hogsheads," he personated Falstaff, and re-cited several choice passages from the dramas wherein the fat knight plays his part. The actor was so well pleased by the laughter and applause with which he was greeted that he requested the whole audience to drink with him. This invitation, as well as later ones of a like sort given by him, was, of course, accepted with boisterous alacrity. As he had no money in his purse with which to pay his liquor-bill, he liquidated the score by giving the grumbling tapster a dingy and dog-eared copy of Shakespeare's works. At that time Llewellyn had never looked into the book ; but he soon read *King Henry IV.*, the *Merry Wives of Windsor*, and *King Henry V.*, and knew a new delight. During his leisure hours he eagerly read on and on in Shakespeare, skipping nothing in the plays them-selves, but, for the time being, throwing the notes of all his commentators to the dogs.* Until he had

---

* Dr. Johnson, in his Preface to Shakespeare, says : "Notes are often necessary, but they are necessary evils. Let him that is yet unacquainted with the powers of Shakespeare, and who desires to feel the highest pleasure that the drama can give, read every play from the first scene to the last, with utter negligence of all his commentators. When his fancy is once

read all the plays and poems contained in the volume, he did not trouble himself about the spelling
of the player-poet's surname * ; nor about his ear-

on the wing, let it not stoop at correction or explanation.
When his attention is strongly engaged, let it disdain alike to
turn aside to the name of Theobald and of Pope. Let him
read on, through brightness and obscurity, through integrity
and corruption ; let him preserve his comprehension of the
dialogue and his interest in the fable. And when the pleasures
of novelty have ceased, let him attempt exactness and read
the commentators."

Prof. Corson, in his *Introduction to the Study of Shakespeare*
(p. 10), says : " The fact must not be overlooked, however
ungracious it may be to the patient and laborious delvers in
Shakespearian lore, that much of the study devoted to Shakespeare, in these days, consists largely of a peeping and botaniz-
ing that are really not essential to a full appreciation of his
dramatic power, which is, after all, *the one great thing needful.*
There is reason to believe that there are many mere scholars
at the present day, whose Shakespearian learning, extensive
and thorough as it may be, in respect to editions, and texts,
and readings, and the commentary which, during the last
hundred and fifty years and more, has gathered around Shakespeare, as the desert sands around the Egyptian sphinx, does not
help them much to a higher appreciation of this power ; other
things being equal, they would have quite as much without it.''

* Richard Grant White, in his *Life and Genius of Shakespeare* (p. 6, note), says : '' The manner in which the name is
spelled in the old records varies almost to the extreme capacity
of various letters to produce a sound approximating to that of
the name as we pronounce it. It appears as Chacksper, Shax-
pur, Shaxper, Schaksper, Schackesper, Schakspere, Schake-
speire, Schakespeyr, Shagspere, Saxpere, Shaxpere, Shaxpeare,
Shaxsper, Shaxspere, Shaxespere, Shakspere, Shakspear, Shak-
specre, Schakspear, Shackspeare, Shackespeare, Shackespere,
Shakspeyr, Skaksper, Shakespere, Shakyspere, Shakeseper,
Shakespire, Shakespeire, Shakespear, Shakespeare, Shaka-
speare ; and there are even other varieties of its orthography.

rings * ; nor about the famous mulberry-tree that he planted, and which a reverend iconoclast, a hundred and fifty years afterwards, cut down and destroyed because the frequent incursion, into his garden, of strangers who came to sit beneath " Shakespeare's mulberry " was a troublesome annoyance. Llewellyn did not waste much time in trying to find out what " scamels " are (young scamels which Caliban proposed to get for Trinculo) ; or in trying to discover what Hamlet means by the " dram of eale," or by " Woo 't drink up eisel ? " or what Antigonus means when he says that he would " land-damn " a certain villain. † Nor did he potter over and beat his head against the most disputed passage in Shakespeare, " that runaways' eyes may wink," ‡ in Juliet's soliloquy,

---

But Shakespeare himself, and his careful friend Ben Jonson, when they printed the name, spelled it *Shake-speare*, the hyphen being often used ; and in this form it is found in almost every book of their time in which it appeared. The final *e* is mere superfluity, and might with propriety be dropped ; but then we should also drop it from Greene, Marlowe, Peele, and other names in which it appears. There seems, therefore, to be no good reason for deviating from the orthography to which Shakespeare and his contemporaries gave a kind of formal recognition."

* The immortal Shakespeare is said to have worn earrings ; and Charles I. is reputed to have been the owner of a magnificent pair of pearl earrings, which he bequeathed to his daughter the day before he was executed.—WOPSLE.

† See *The Winter's Tale*, Act II., sc. I.

‡ The condensed summary of the comments upon this great *crux* of Shakespeare's plays fills twenty-eight octavo pages of fine print in Mr. Horace Howard Furness' marvellously learned variorum edition of *Romeo and Juliet.*

where she is longing for the approach of night and her husband, that " Romeo may leap to these arms, untalk'd of and unseen." Having read all the plays, he began to reread them, and to ponder, and compare, and analyze, and seek to fathom—all the while garnering in his retentive memory the poet's best thoughts. Having found his one book—his hobby—he became thenceforth a man of one book, forthwith organized himself into a Shakespeare club of one, and continued to be a true lover of Shakespeare ever after. By and by, he bought other editions of his chosen author—among them a fractional copy of a precious First Folio, and Boydell's Illustrated—and, from time to time, he added to his library the works of several of the best Shakespearian scholars. The staple of his conversation in the taproom often consisted of extracts from his one book. Moreover, he had so saturated himself with Shakespeare that he could talk for days together in the express words and phrases of that immortal dramatist ; and, when well whittled with liquor, he would sometimes wander at night in the streets of Shrewsbury, and soliloquize, hour after hour, by the historic clock that timed the famous fight between Falstaff and Hotspur, and speak all the while as if reading in a book of quotations from Shakespeare alone. And hence it came to pass in after years that many a boor took his pipe from his mouth, and pointing the stem thereof to Llewellyn, remarked with bated breath, " Look 'ee, there goes old Paunchy ; but old as 'e be, and fat as 'e be, and well as 'e loikes 'is liquor, they say 'e knaws all Shagspere by 'art. And they do say 'e 's descended from Sir Jack Falstaff which killed 'Arry 'Otspur 'ereabouts in a big battle a long time ago."

This true lover of Shakespeare became in time so hobbyhorsical that he named the inn wherein he so long dwelt, the Boar's Head tavern ; called the suite of rooms which he occupied the Dolphin-chamber, and the Pomegranate ; drank a toast or two daily in honor of Falstaff ; declared that when Sir John Paunch said to the Prince : "I am not John of Gaunt, your grandfather, but yet no coward, Hal," he spoke the truth; and regarded Sir John as bestriding all other comic characters like a Colossus, while they—petty men and under-lings—walked, as 't were, under his huge legs and peeped about to find themselves dishonourable graves. And he gave it for his opinion, that Sir John Sack-and-Sugar—an old and white-bearded Satan as he was—had, by making millions laugh and not to cry, done more positive good in the world, and deserved better of mankind, than the whole race of military heroes put together. Moreover, he drew up a subscription-paper for the purpose of raising a fund to erect on "that royal field of Shrews-bury" a monument in memory of the fat knight ; and, as the nucleus of such a fund, he subscribed " a thousand pound," and obtained, here and there, a wilderness of shilling, penny, and ha'penny sub-scriptions.

Llewellyn Jones could not last ever. One day his evil genius, in the guise of a bumptious

Yankee book-agent, urged him to buy outright a copy of Mr. Ignatius Donnelly's *The Great Cryptogram.* At first the two talked together amicably, *pro* and *con*, concerning Bacon's cipher in the Shakespeare plays,—one disputant drinking toast after toast, and bumper after bumper, in honor of the statesman-philosopher, and the other doing the like in honor of the player-poet. During their symposium the controversy grew warmer and warmer, until the agent, who was laboring under a certain mental distemperature, known now-a-days as the "Bacon-Shakespeare craze," pot-surely stated that, in the book aforesaid, 't is established, beyond all reasonable doubt—indeed, demonstrated as conclusively as the "Asses' bridge," or any other proposition in Euclid—that that "drunken savage,"* William Shakespeare, who possessed "small Latin and less Greek," did not write, and could not have written, the so-called Shakespeare plays ; that Francis Bacon did write them ; and that William and Francis were secretly in cahoot in this matter, and together shared in the money which was taken in at the gates of the Globe theatre and the Blackfriars. Moreover, he declared that whoever, after carefully reading the ponderous work in question, is not convinced that 't is clearly ciphered out therein that Bacon is the true Shakespeare,† has a congenital incapacity to

---

* As Voltaire regarded him.

† Irving Browne, Esq., in a letter from Europe to the *Albany Law Journal* (Vol. XLIV., p. 126), writes : "Of course, on arriving in England, I steered straight for Stratford. In the evening I took a boat, and the boatman's young

weigh evidence, and is a knotty-pated fool and lunatic knave. Llewellyn serenely answered: " I 'll not say, now the Lord lighten thee ! thou art a

---

daughter rowed me on the Avon till dark, which is here somewhere about ten o'clock. I would willingly have continued all night, to listen to her delicious voice and exquisite enunciation. I am enabled by the courtesy of the verger of the church to present to my Shakespeare-loving readers an authentic version of Mr. Ignatius Donnelly's soliloquy at the tomb of Shakespeare :

> Dismiss your apprehension, pseudo bard,
>   For no one wishes to disturb these stones,
> Nor cares if here or in the outer yard
>   They stow your impudent, deceitful bones.
>
> Your foolish-colored bust upon the wall,
>   With its preposterous expanse of brow,
> Shall rival Humpty Dumpty's famous fall,
>   And cheats no cultured Boston people now.
>
> Steal deer, hold horses, act your third-rate parts,
>   Hoard money, booze, neglect Anne Hathaway,—
> You can't deceive us with your stolen arts ;
>   Like many a worthier dog, you 've had your day.
>
> I have expressed your history in a cypher,
>   I 've done your sum for all ensuing time ;
> I don't know what you longer wish to lie for
>   Beneath these stones or in your doggerel rhyme.
>
> Get up and dust, or plunge into the river,
>   Or walk the chancel with a ghostly squeak—
> You were an ignorant and evil liver,
>   Who could not spell nor write, nor knew much Greek.
>
> Though you enslaved the ages by your spell,
>   And Fame has blown no reputation louder,
> Your cake is dough, for I by sifting well
>   Have quite reduced your dust to Bacon-powder. "

19

great fool, nor that thou art a lunatic lean-witted
fool ; but, between thee and me, this I think, that
when thou 'rt thirsty, a fool would fain have drink."
Thereupon the agent rejoined by plucking Llewellyn by the nose and flirting a heeltap of sack in his
face. Llewellyn instantly snatched up *The Great
Cryptogram*, and, with his utmost strength, hurled
it at the head of his assailant ; then, uttering a
deep moan, and throwing his hands to his head, he
sank into a chair, and in a few moments breathed
his last. He had burst a blood-vessel. The icono-
clastic book, thus used as a projectile, knocked
his adversary prone and senseless ; but it also, to
use the words of Mrs. Quickly, "killed his heart."

Llewellyn Jones died, *sine prole*, as 't is supposed,
but fortunately testate. He left a nuncupative will,
whereby he directed that, after the payment of his funeral expenses and debts, and the distribution of certain articles of personal property among his friends,
the proceeds of the residue of his estate should be
used to aid in erecting a monument to Falstaff, as
near as may be to the spot where, according to
tradition, the fat knight and gunpowder Percy
"fought a long hour by Shrewsbury clock." Among
his papers was found a unique and appropriate de-
sign for such a memorial, and also a sheet of foolscap
written all over with a variety of quotations which
appear to have been collected for the purpose of
selecting therefrom apt ones to be inscribed thereon. Among the quotations are the following :

"I am not John of Gaunt, your grandfather ; but yet no
coward, Hal."

" A plague of all cowards, I say."

" I would to God my name were not so terrible to the enemy as it is."

" I may justly say, with the hook-nosed fellow of Rome, 'I came, saw, and overcame.'"

" The better part of valour is discretion."

" I would 't were bedtime, Hal, and all well."

" I 'll tickle your catastrophe."

" Lord, Lord, how this world is given to lying !"

" Lord, Lord, how subject we old men are to this vice of lying !".

" Shall I not take mine ease in mine inn ?"

" A good sherris-sack ascends me into the brain; dries me there all the foolish and dull and crudy vapours which environ it; makes its apprehensive, quick, forgetive, full of nimble, fiery, and delectable shapes; which, delivered o'er to the voice, the tongue, which is the birth, becomes excellent wit."

" If I had a thousand sons, the first humane principle I would teach them should be, to forswear thin potations and to addict themselves to sack."

" Give me a cup of sack to make my eyes look red, that it may be thought I have wept; for I must speak in passion, and I will do it in King Cambyses' vein."

" *Shallow.* I pray you, go in with me to dinner.

" *Falstaff.* Come, I will go drink with you, but I cannot tarry dinner."

" *Multum bibi, nunquam pransi.*"

" I am not only witty in myself, but the cause that wit is in other men."

" We have heard the chimes at midnight."

" There live not three good men unhanged in England; and one of them is fat and grows old."

" Hal, I prithee, trouble me no more with vanity. I would to God thou and I knew where a commodity of good names were to be bought !"

" Thou hast done much harm upon me, Hal; God forgive thee for it ! Before I knew thee, Hal, I knew nothing; and now am I, if a man should speak truly, little better than one of the wicked."

" Rob me the exchequer."

" I do not like this paying back ; 't is a double labour."

" If I do, fillip me with a three-man beetle."

" *Falstaff.* Master Shallow, I owe you a thousand pound.

" *Shallow.* Yea, marry, Sir John ; which I beseech you to let me have home with me.

" *Falstaff.* That can hardly be, Master Shallow.   Do not you grieve at this."

" An I have not forgotten what the inside of a church is made of, I am a peppercorn, a brewer's horse.   The inside of a church !   Company, villanous company, hath been the spoil of me."

" For my voice, I have lost it with hallooing and singing of anthems."

" Give me a cup of sack, boy."

" If my wind were but long enough to say my prayers, I would repent."

" I think the devil will not have me damned, lest the oil that 's in me should set hell on fire."

" I 'll purge, and leave sack, and live cleanly, as a noble-man should do."

" *Doll.* Thou whoreson little tidy Bartholomew boar-pig, when wilt thou leave fighting and foining, and begin to patch up thine old body for heaven ? "

" *Falstaff.* Peace, good Doll ! do not speak like a death's head ; do not bid me remember mine end.   .   .   .   Kiss me, Doll."

" Some sack, Francis."

" If sack and sugar be a fault, God help the wicked ! "

" Well, I cannot last ever."

" The grave doth gape for thee thrice wider than for other men."

" The king has killed his heart."

" His heart is fracted and corroborate."

" He 's in Arthur's bosom, if ever man went to Arthur's bosom."